RAVES FOR STANLEY HASTINGS AND

BLACKMAIL

"A forever fresh series. . . . An endearing hero. . . . Mr. Hall slyly wins our respect for Stanley's intelligence and perseverance—qualities that give the edge over his bolder and brawnier competition. And the last laugh, too."

—*New York Times Book Review*

✖

"Parnell Hall succeeds in making Stanley Hastings one of a kind. . . . Pleasantly reminiscent of an earlier era, when detectives like Nero Wolfe and Archie Goodwin brought some humor to their chores."

—*Wall Street Journal*

✖

"Charming, chummy, loquacious, self-deprecating."

—*Washington Post Book World*

✖

"[Parnell Hall] is writing some of the funniest mystery novels on the market today. He writes the best, funniest dialogue you will find in any book. The conversations between Stanley and his wife, Alice are hilarious. Alice is the best female significant other in literature today."

—*America Online* "Critics Corner"

✖

"An absolute joy. . . . Every page quivers with comic frustration."

—*Kirkus Reviews*

✖

"The plot ricochets around a large cast of suspects in New York's labyrinthine world of actors, homosexuals, blackmailers, and pornographers."

—*St. Petersburg Times*

more . . .

✖

"Clever dialogue and a Broadway ambience."

—*Hartford Courant*

✖

"This witty mystery . . . shows the hand of a master. The characters are funny, the dialogue sings, and Hall continually confounds the reader's expectations."

—*Toronto Star*

✖

"Hastings is a sheer delight. . . . Hall renders a complicated case in a breezy style that keeps the pages flipping, with enough twists to satisfy any devotee of the devious. . . . Forget your head-banging hot-shots. There's a comfortable Everyman appeal to Stanley Hastings that's hard to resist."

—*Orange County Register*

✖

"Once you make his acquaintance, you'll become addicted to Stanley Hastings. . . . These are exceptionally good mysteries. . . . The plots are interesting, the locales authentic, the dialogue witty, the characters real. They are fast-paced reading. . . . Don't miss them!"

—*Mystery News*

✖

"Highly amusing."

—*Chicago Tribune*

✖

"Stanley Hastings is . . . [an] unusual breed of private eye. He carries the time-honored tradition of the self-deprecating private eye to unheard-of heights, but despite his endless bungling, he manages to get the job done—and then some."

—*Detroit News*

✖

✖

"The spontaneity and wicked honesty of a Nick and Nora Charles. . . . Hall also has an eye for detail, which he uses to bring New York City to life."

—*Raleigh News & Observer*

✖

"Parnell Hall must be a magician. He's managed to create a loser and, in the process, transform him into the hero of a series of whodunits. . . . Hastings deals with his problems with a charming insouciance. . . . In the end, you just know that Stanley is going to emerge a winner." —*San Diego Tribune*

✖

"BLACKMAIL delivers the goods—an intriguing mystery, pleasing characters, gentle humor, and enough suspense to keep one turning the pages. . . . A thoroughly enjoyable farce."

—*Mansfield News Journal* (OH)

✖

"He's a confirmed coward, a relentless kvetch (albeit a painfully funny one), and a magnet for murder. . . . Stanley Hastings is one of the most appealing in a long tradition of sad-sack detectives." —*Booklist*

✖

"A rare and highly readable type of novel. . . . Dramatic and playlike, and the story moves swiftly."

—*Sunday Denver Post*

✖

"A lovable and real hero who has traits anyone can identify with. . . . Look for Stanley Hastings to become a common name in the detective business."

—*South Bend Tribune*

✖

ALSO BY PARNELL HALL

Movie
Actor
Shot
Juror
Client
Strangler
Favor
Murder
Detective

BLACKMAIL

PARNELL HALL

THE MYSTERIOUS PRESS

Published by Warner Books

A Time Warner Company

MYSTERIOUS PRESS EDITION

Cover design by Julia Kushnirsky
Cover illustration by James Steinberg

Mysterious Press books are published by
Warner Books, Inc.
1271 Avenue of the Americas
New York, NY 10020

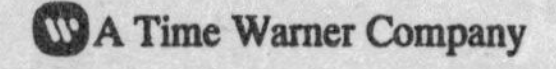

A Time Warner Company

Printed in the United States of America

Originally published in hardcover by The Mysterious Press.
First Printed in Paperback: March, 1995

10 9 8 7 6 5 4 3 2 1

For Jim and Franny

1.

"I'm being blackmailed."

"Oh?"

I think she was the first woman to ever tell me that. No, I take that back. I'm sure she was the first woman to ever tell me that. Which may seem strange, since I'm a private detective, and one might expect a private detective to hear that sort of thing all the time.

Only, I'm not that kind of private detective. Not the kind you see on TV. I chase ambulances for the law firm of Rosenberg and Stone. What that involves is largely interviewing accident victims and photographing cracks in the sidewalk.

It does not involve listening to beautiful women tell how they're being blackmailed.

She certainly was beautiful.

Her name was Marlena Smith. If she was to be believed. I

tended to trust the Marlena and have doubts about the Smith. A deduction which, if I were taking Private Detective 101, would probably not be sufficient in itself to put me in the top ten percent of my class.

We were in my office on West Forty-seventh Street, the one-room, hole-in-the-wall affair with the plaque Stanley Hastings Detective Agency on the door. She'd been waiting for me when I'd stopped by at nine o'clock that morning to pick up my mail. That in itself did not bode well—it occurred to me that the last woman I'd found waiting for me outside my office at nine in the morning had gotten involved in a murder. Compared to which, blackmail was just a walk in the park.

But not for me. I had an appointment this morning in the Bronx with a woman who'd slipped on the newly mopped floor of a McDonald's and broken her hip. With such weighty matters pending, I barely had time for blackmail.

Except she really was gorgeous, this Marlena whatever. And the fastest way to flunk out of Private Detective 101 is to turn down a beautiful woman in distress. At least without hearing her story first.

Which I was fully prepared to do. After all, a woman with a broken hip wasn't going to run away now, was she?

I leaned back in my desk chair, sized Marlena whatever up. She had shoulder-length blond hair, straight and curled under. It framed a perfectly symmetrical face, wide-eyed and innocent as a newborn babe.

Only, newborn babes aren't usually blackmailed.

I used to discourage clients such as Marlena on the grounds that I wasn't a real detective and wasn't competent to help them. I'd recently revised that estimate. It wasn't that I felt any more proficient, it was just that I'd come to the realization that, aside from the detectives on TV, no one else was that hot either.

So, rather than tell Marlena that quite frankly there was probably nothing I could do for her, I cocked my head to one side and gave her a world-weary look, as if for me listening to stories of blackmail demands was about as commonplace as reading the morning paper. "Tell me about it."

She took a breath. I don't know if that was to stall for time or to impress me by inflating an already well-filled sleeveless pullover that did not seem to be concealing a bra.

"That's it," she said. "That's the story. A man is blackmailing me."

"Over what?"

"That's not important. The fact is, he is."

"You have my sympathy."

"I didn't come here for sympathy."

"Very well. My sympathy is withdrawn."

She took another breath. "You're not making this easy."

"I'm sorry, but I'm having a hard time understanding the situation."

"What's to understand? I want you to deal with this blackmailer."

"How am I supposed to deal with him if I don't know what the story is?"

"Don't be silly. The specifics are not important."

"They are to me."

"Why? What are you, some old lady who's afraid she's going to miss all the spicy details?"

"Not at all. But I have no intention of getting involved in *anything* if I don't know what it is. After all, I need some assurance that what I'm doing isn't illegal."

She gave me a look. "Moron. Blackmail *is* illegal."

I looked at her. "Huh?"

"It's illegal to begin with. The legal thing to do is to report it to the police. If I were going to do that, I wouldn't be here. Well, I'm not going to do that. Because I don't want this to come out, I want to hush it up. So you may take it for *granted* what we're doing here is illegal."

I frowned.

"Now," she said. "If you don't want to help me, I'll get out of here and find another private detective who will. One who doesn't have so many scruples. And, believe me, there are such detectives."

I blinked.

Immoral logic always confounds me. So does *moral* logic, for that matter.

So do women.

My wife, Alice, can out-argue me on any subject whatsoever. On any given subject, taking any given side. I haven't got a prayer. If she wants to tell me black is white, I haven't a chance of contradicting her.

And in this case, the position Marlena questionable-last-name-blackmail-victim was arguing was that it was all right for me to allow her to pay me a large amount of money to extricate her from her current problem with a blackmailer.

By a strange coincidence, I happened to need money.

So, what I'm trying to say is, by and large, I would have to concede that at that moment I would probably have served as an excellent textbook example of what was meant by being in no position to argue.

2.

"Should I pay blackmail?"

Richard Rosenberg leaned back in his desk chair, cocked his head at me. "I beg your pardon?"

Richard was one of New York City's top negligence lawyers. He was a little guy but burned up twice the calories of a big guy. The man was in constant motion. And even if he appeared to be at rest, his mind was going a mile a minute. Kind of like a clock with the spring wound too tight—at any moment it might start ringing frantically and hop off the shelf.

Richard Rosenberg had made his reputation by winning a high percentage of negligence cases. Attorneys settled out of court with him because he was so good *in* court. He was a showman, and loved strutting his stuff in front of juries. He was also tireless, and wore other attorneys down through an inexhaustible supply of nervous energy. Opposing counsel tended to avoid him.

So did I, for that matter. Except when I really needed him.

Like now.

"I need legal advice, Richard. I don't know who else to trust."

"Your instinct is right," Richard said. "But your timing is bad. Don't you have a case this morning?"

"Yeah."

"So?"

"I called and said I'd be late."

His eyebrows launched into orbit. "Your told *my* client you'd be late?"

"So she wouldn't worry."

"Worry, hell. Suppose she goes elsewhere?"

"She's got a broken hip. Richard. She's not going anywhere."

"I mean hires another attorney. Suppose she dials L-A-W-Y-E-R-S? Or calls Jacoby & Meyers?"

"She's not gonna do that."

"How do you know?"

"Cause we had a nice talk about how her husband's gonna come down and open the door for me so I can get in. He's expecting me, Richard. But I can't do a good job if I have something else on my mind."

"Oh, sure," Richard said. "How many sign-ups have you done? A thousand? As if you didn't know the drill."

I stood up. "I'm sorry I bothered you. I'll call her back, tell her I'm coming right up."

Richard held up his hand. "Hold on, hold on," he said. "Don't be so damn huffy. I thought we were having a conversation here."

Score one for the private eye. I'd hooked him. I thought I would. Richard might be a stickler for business, but the man loved a mystery. I had a feeling he wouldn't let me out of his office till he found out what the blackmail was all about.

Not that I could really tell him, not knowing that much myself. However, I sat down and gave him Marlena's buildup, just like she'd given it to me.

"So why's she being blackmailed?" Richard said.

"She wouldn't say."

He frowned, shook his head. "No good."

"I know, but there you are. She wants me to pay the guy off."

"Damn."

"Yeah, I know."

"She's offered you money to make a blackmail payment?"

"That's right."

"Without telling you any of the details?"

"You got it."

"How much money are you supposed to pay?"

"She didn't tell me that either."

Richard looked at me. "What *did* she tell you?"

"She's being blackmailed by a man who gives his name as Barry."

"No last name?"

"No."

"Wonderful."

"Yeah, I know."

"You don't know how much you're supposed to pay this guy Barry?"

"No."

"How much is she gonna pay *you*?"

"Is that relevant?"

"*I* think it is."

"Five hundred dollars."

"Five hundred dollars?"

"Yes."

"You're getting five hundred dollars for one day's work?"

"That's right."

"Not to do anything in particular, just to act as a messenger boy?"

"Basically."

"There's nothing tricky involved? No plan to trap this guy, or frighten him off, or put any pressure on him? All you're supposed to do is meet him and pay him off?"

"That's right."

"So why can't she do it herself?"

"I don't know."

Richard frowned, shook his head. "That's the problem. If

the woman is willing to pay a delivery boy five hundred dollars, there's got to be a reason why."

"She doesn't want a delivery boy, she wants a private detective."

"Why?"

"I don't know why."

"Exactly."

It was beginning to piss me off. And it wasn't just that he was belittling my position by persisting in referring to me as a delivery boy. No, it was the fact that he seemed to be expressing the opinion that I should turn down five hundred bucks.

Though he hadn't expressly said so.

"All right, look, Richard," I said. "You know the situation. What would you advise me to do?'

"Blackmail is illegal," Richard said. "As your attorney, I'd advise you to have nothing to do with it."

Damn. Now he *had* expressly said so.

"However," Richard went on, "should you choose to disregard my advice, there are several things you should consider."

Son of a bitch. The sly old dog, while protecting his backside, was with me all the way.

"Really?" I said. "And what might they be?"

"To begin with, you should not think of yourself as a private detective. When I said messenger, I meant messenger. In the context of this job, you are serving in the capacity of a common courier. You are merely delivering one package and picking up another."

"I see."

"Moreover, you take no responsibility for either package. Should either party be dissatisfied with what they receive, that is in no way your fault and should have no effect whatsoever on your payment." He looked at me. "Did you work out a payment schedule, by the way?"

"No, I didn't."

"Well, you should. I would suggest half when she gives you the money, or rather the package you are to deliver, and the other half when you deliver the package you pick up."

"That sounds good."

Richard held up his finger. "And here is where you must be very explicit with this woman. Since you are not being told what it is that you are picking up, you take no responsibility for it whatsoever. So *whatever this man gives you,* when you deliver it to this woman, *your job is done*. And payment is due. It doesn't matter if the woman was expecting treasury bonds and you bring her bubble-gum cards. That is something you should make very clear."

"What if she won't agree to that?"

"Then tell her to go fuck herself. If she can't agree to that, she's totally unreasonable and you should have nothing to do with her. It doesn't matter how much money she's promised you, because if she's like that, you're never gonna see a dime."

I had sat down again. Now I shifted uncomfortably in my chair.

Richard shook his head. "I should charge you for this," he said.

I looked at him in alarm. "Richard, I can't afford you."

"I know that," he said. "I can tell you're not taking this seriously. If you were paying me, you'd do what I said. Free advice isn't worth listening to."

"The advice to turn down five hundred dollars isn't exactly free."

"I'm not advising you to do that. I'm advising you to make sure you get *paid* the five hundred dollars. I'm pointing out that, if the woman won't agree to these terms, there probably wasn't any five hundred dollars to begin with."

"All right," I said. "Well, what else should I do? If I have hypothetically disregarded your advice and taken on this woman's case?"

"First off, I'd be careful not to call it a case. It's a delivery. Aside from that, I'd define everything."

"Such as?"

Richard ticked them off on his fingers. "What you're delivering and what you're picking up. Of course you don't *know* what it is, but that's what has to be defined. That you are picking up sealed envelopes or packages or what have you, the contents unknown.

"Two, who this person is that you're meeting to make this

pickup and delivery. Again, it does not matter as long as it is defined in terms that relieve you of the responsibility of making any verification. If you're told merely to go to a particular place and have a transaction with a man who gives the name of Barry, well, that's fine. But be explicit. Ask, 'How will I know this man Barry?' If she says, 'He'll know you,' you're off the hook. If she says, 'He'll be the man at that address,' you're off the hook. Practically anything she says, you're off the hook. The point is, you have to ask and throw the onus of responsibility back on her."

"Gotcha. Anything else?"

"Spell out the fact that your employment is limited to this pickup and delivery, and terminates immediately upon your delivery of the package to her."

"Isn't that obvious?"

"Not at all. Not unless you spell it out. Suppose she opens the package and says, 'Damn. This isn't everything. Go back. Go back and tell him he didn't give you everything.'"

"What do I say then?"

"If you've been explicit about the fact that your delivery of the package terminates your job, you smile and say, 'Oh? Are you hiring me to do *another* job?'"

"I see."

"Which you are under no obligation to take. Or to do for the same amount. If you want to hold her up for a grand, feel free. If she doesn't want to pay it, feel free to say no."

I frowned. "Suppose she has a good reason."

"Aha!" Richard said. "That's something else again. So far this woman hasn't told you anything. Hasn't seen fit to trust you at all. If she starts giving you *reasons*, wants to explain what's going on, you have a brand-new ball game."

"What do I do then?"

Richard looked at me. "You would have three choices. You could say yes, you could say no, or you could say, 'I'd like to consult my lawyer.'"

"She might not like that."

Richard's eyes widened. "Who gives a flying fuck? I'm not saying you have to do this. I'm giving you options. As you'll recall, my advice as your attorney was to have nothing to do with this whatsoever. Considering you're not paying me for legal advice, and considering I've already given you my legal advice, and considering we're just having a hypothetical conversation here . . ."

Richard broke off and left it dangling, till I felt impelled to ask, "Yes?"

He cocked his head. "Don't you have someone waiting for you in the Bronx?"

3.

It didn't go exactly as planned. Somehow it never does.

"Provisions?" Marlena said. "What do you mean, provisions?"

"Just that. In a deal like this, I have to protect myself."

She shrugged. "If you want to carry a gun, that's up to you. Not that you're going to need it."

"That's not what I meant."

"What *did* you mean?"

"I meant in terms of the deal."

"There's no deal. There's a job. You either want it or you don't."

"But the job has to be defined."

"It's defined. You go meet Barry, pay him off, and bring back the evidence."

"What evidence?"

"That's none of your business."

"Fine. Then I'm not responsible for it."

She looked at me. "What are you talking about? Of course you are."

I shook my head. "If I don't know what it is, I can't vouch for it. I can assure you that I'm giving you what he gives me. But if that isn't what you want, it's not my fault."

"If it isn't what I want, you don't get paid."

"No way. If Barry does the dirty on you, that's not my fault."

"You expect me to pay you for not doing the job?"

"My job is delivering one package and picking up another. If that guy Barry sent you bubble-gum cards, that's not my fault and I still get paid."

She shook her head. "Un-uh. I know what Barry's putting in the envelope. You bring me anything else, it means you pulled a switch."

I stood up. "Then I guess we have no deal."

She looked at me, shook her head. "What a jerk," she said. "Here you are, arguing about things that aren't even important. That are never going to come up."

"If they don't, fine," I said. "Great. But I still have to provide for them *in case* they come up."

"Fine," she said. "You provide for them. Just leave me out of it."

That stopped me dead. I had opened my mouth to say something. I closed it again.

And sat back down.

How the hell did you deal with that? Logic I could deal with. Total illogic had me baffled.

I took a breath. "All right," I said. "Say I deal with it—how will I know this guy Barry?"

"He'll be the guy you deal with."

"Yeah, but how will I know it's him?'

She looked at me as if I were a moron. "If it isn't him, he won't be dealing with you."

"I mean, shouldn't he have some way of proving his identity?"

She stared at me. "You're going to ask a blackmailer for his ID?"

"No, I just meant—"

"That's the stupidest thing I ever heard of. The guy doesn't have to deal with us at all. He doesn't have to keep *us* happy, we have to keep *him* happy. Otherwise he makes good his threats."

"What threats?"

"That's none of your business."

"Right," I said. "My business is picking up a package, the contents of which I cannot check from a man whose identity I can't check, and delivering it to you."

She cocked her head. "You got a problem with that?"

"Only if *you* do."

"What do you mean?"

"Just what I said. If I do that, it should satisfy you."

"It will."

"Right. But what if you rip open this envelope I give you and say, 'Oh, these aren't the papers I want. Go back and tell him he gave you the wrong thing'?"

"I won't say that."

"Fine. But if you do, it's a new job and you'd have to hire me again."

"A new job?"

"Yes. You're hiring me for one pickup and delivery. You want anything else, we're talking more money and a separate job."

"I don't understand. A minute ago you didn't want to take *this* job. Now you want two?"

"I don't *want* two. I'm just saying, if the situation came up—"

"It won't come up."

"Good. I'm just telling you, if it did, you would owe me more money."

"That's silly. Owe you more money for not doing the job right?"

I rubbed my head. "You're missing the point. It's not that you'd owe me more money. If you wanted me to do more work, you'd have to agree to pay me more money. The point is, you would owe me for the job I'd already done."

"For bringing me the wrong stuff?"

I shook my head. "This is getting nowhere. I don't know if

we have a deal at all. If there's any chance we do, it depends on whether you agree to the payment schedule."

"Payment schedule?"

"Yeah," I said. "Obviously, this is a job where we won't have a written contract."

"Of course not."

"That's why we're having problems. Because the contract would spell all these things out. But in the absence of a contract, we have to come to an agreement. Particularly in regard to the payment schedule."

"I don't understand. What do you mean?"

"You're going to give me five hundred dollars for the job, right?"

"Right."

"Okay," I said. "That's the only real stumbling block. If we can work out a satisfactory payment schedule, I'll agree to do the job."

She gave me a look. "Why didn't you say so in the first place?"

"I'm sorry. I was trying to get these matters clarified."

"Clarified?" she said. "You got me so mixed up I don't know *what's* going on. Saying if he does that, if I do that, if you do this. None of that matters. All that matters is, I give you a sealed envelope. You do not open it, you give it to him. He gives you a sealed envelope or package or whatever. And you do not open it, you give it to me. That's the whole deal. All this other stuff is just irrelevant."

"Fine," I said. "As long as you agree to the payment schedule. Here is what I want. I want half—that's two hundred and fifty dollars—when you give me the money, or rather the sealed envelope to go to him. I want the other half payable immediately upon my delivery of the package he gives me. Is that agreed?"

She frowned. "It's fine in theory."

I felt my heart sinking. "What do you mean, in theory?"

"Well," she said. "It's just a little bit complicated."

She opened her purse, took out a wallet.

"Why don't I just give you the whole five hundred now?"

4.

It was a small motel just off the Saw Mill River Parkway. A long, narrow, single-story affair, running parallel to the road. I turned into the driveway, drove right past the office with its Vacancy sign, and pulled into the parking space in front of unit twelve.

It was five minutes to eight by the dashboard clock. I'd been told eight o'clock, but I figured for a blackmailer that was close enough. I turned off the lights, killed the motor, got out, went up to the door, and knocked.

The door was opened by a chunky man with curly red hair and a scowl on his face. "You're early," he said.

"Eight o'clock," I told him.

"Five to."

"Gee, I'm sorry," I said. "You want me to stand out here five minutes, knock again?"

"Don't try to be funny," he said. He jerked his thumb. "Come in."

I figured it was as cordial an invitation as I was likely to get. I pushed by him into the room.

Or started to. He put out his hand, stopped me in mid-stride. Holding me there with one hand, he closed the door behind me with the other, then turned and proceeded to pat me down.

It was early fall, still quite warm, and I was wearing the lightweight suit that I wore for my ambulance-chasing job. I suppose it could have concealed a shoulder holster, though I've never worn one. Barry, if that's what his name was, gave it a check.

When he was satisfied that I was unarmed, he half motioned, half dragged me into the room.

Which was your typical, stark, no-frills motel room. A double bed, a chair, a table, a dresser, and a TV. The bed, though made, was slightly mussed, as if someone had recently been lying on it, sitting on it, or what have you. On the bureau was an ice bucket and a bottle of Scotch. On the table were two empty glasses.

While I was taking all that in, Barry's attention was riveted on me.

"What you gawking at?" he said.

"Nothing. Are you Barry?"

He scowled. "Cut the comedy. You got it or not?"

"That depends."

"Depends on what?"

"On who I'm talking to."

"You're talking to the guy with all the aces in the deck. You're talking to the guy who's calling the shots. You're talking to the guy who's gonna get real pissed off if you don't cut the crap and hand over the money."

"Oh, you know about the money?" I said. "Then I guess you're Barry."

The scowl deepened. "You *guess?* I warned you to stop talkin' cute. You happen to see any *other* guys in the room?"

"No, I assume you're him. Even if you won't say you're him, who am I to argue?"

"Quit yakkin' and give me the dough."

I reached into my inside jacket pocket, pulled out the thick envelope Marlena had given me earlier that evening. I looked at it a moment, then held it out to him.

He snatched it out of my hand, ripped the end off the envelope, turned and dumped the contents out on the bed.

It was a stack of bills, held together by two rubber bands.

Even from where I stood, halfway across the room, I could tell the bill on top was a hundred. Marlena had given me five of them just like it in my office that morning.

Barry grabbed the packet of bills off the bed and riffled through it. He was obviously just checking the denominations on the bills—he couldn't possibly have counted them that fast.

At any rate, he appeared to be satisfied. He was wearing a brown leather coat, and he jammed the wad of bills in a side pocket and zipped it shut.

Then he reached under one of the pillows on the bed and pulled out a large manila envelope.

"Okay," he said. "And here's your pictures."

Oh. What I was buying were pictures. No real surprise, except I wouldn't have known that if Barry hadn't said so. Marlena hadn't wanted me to know. However, if Barry chose to spill the beans, that was hardly my fault.

I held out my hand, but Barry didn't pass the envelope over. Instead he stood there, holding it in one hand and tapping it into the other.

He grinned at me. "Some pictures, huh?"

"I wouldn't know what you're talking about," I told him.

"Yeah, sure," he said.

"I'm just doing my job."

"Oh yeah? Well, so am I. Ain't it a kick?"

I wasn't quite sure what to say to that.

And while I was trying to figure it out, he took the nice nine-by-twelve manila envelope that I had agreed to bring back to Marlena unopened, tore the end off it, and dumped the contents out on the bed.

Oops.

Here was an eventuality not covered by Richard, me, Marlena, or any other living creature on god's green earth. How the hell was I gonna explain this?

The photos had fallen facedown on the bed, so I hadn't actually seen them. It occurred to me I could tell Marlena that. If she happened to believe me, I could sell her some land in Florida while she was in the mood.

I'd just barely had time to think this when Barry rendered the matter academic by picking the photos up, turning them over, and saying, "Here, get a load of this."

I suppose I could have just closed my eyes. But if there's a person alive who would have done that, I'd like to meet him. Anyway, Barry said look and I looked.

The photograph on top was of a man and a woman. They were naked. The woman had the man's penis in her mouth.

All things considered, that was not particularly surprising.

What *was* surprising was the fact that the woman wasn't Marlena.

"That's something, huh?" Barry said, and proceeded to shuffle through the pile of pictures, showing me each one.

There were about a dozen. Each featured the same man and woman, always unclothed. The only difference in the pictures was the location of the man's penis, which, aside from her mouth, showed up in the woman's vagina, anus, and hand.

The woman, an attractive young brunette, seemed to be enjoying all this immensely.

The man didn't look displeased either.

Anyway, the nature of the photos was so distracting, it wasn't until Barry had finished showing them to me that I realized the full extent of the position he had put me in.

How the hell was I going to explain this to Marlena?

There was no time to dwell on this, however. Barry shoved the pictures back in the manila envelope, thrust the envelope at me, and said, "All right, you got what you came for. Now get out of here."

There was nothing else to do. I took the pictures, stumbled out the door. I got in my car, started the motor, turned on the lights, backed out of the space, and pulled out of the lot. I got on the Saw Mill River Parkway, headed home.

I felt like shit.

Marlena hadn't wanted me to know what was in the envelope she gave me, and I knew. She hadn't wanted me to know what was in the envelope I was picking up. I not only knew it was pictures, I'd seen each and every one of them. Well enough to be able to recognize the people in 'em if I ever met 'em again.

So I had a right to feel bad.

I'd just made my first blackmail payment, and it couldn't have gone worse.

5.

"Oh, my god."

Alice was quite right. *My god* described the blackmail photos fairly nicely.

Maybe you're thinking I shouldn't have shown her. Well, maybe not. I don't know what the etiquette is in these things. As I say, I'd never made a blackmail payment before. Maybe showing your wife the blackmail evidence isn't entirely kosher.

If I'd made arrangements to meet Marlena later that night to drop off the goods, that would have been that. I certainly wouldn't have detoured home first to give my wife a peek. But I was meeting Marlena in my office at nine o'clock the next morning per her request. That meant taking the pictures home. And under those circumstances how could I possibly not show my wife?

Alice flipped to another picture. "Oh, my god."

I looked over her shoulder. "Yeah. Athletic, isn't she?"

"That isn't the word for it."

"You getting any ideas from this?"

"You wish."

Alice leafed through another. "Are these porno actors?" she said.

"Of course not."

"How do you know?'

"If they were, why would anyone pay blackmail money for them?"

"Yeah, I suppose. Still . . ."

"Still what?"

"For blackmail photos, these are awfully good."

"None better."

"No. That's not what I mean. I mean the quality. It's not like someone snapped them through a keyhole or something. These are well lit, well focused, well framed. They look almost posed."

I frowned. "Yes, they do."

"So where's the blackmail? These people obviously knew they were being photographed."

"Sometimes people do something, then regret it later."

"True."

"And there's no date on these pictures. What if the woman's a porno actress ten years ago, and she's on the city council?"

"Recognize her face?"

"I don't know. What does it look like?"

"You're awful."

"No, I've never seen either of these people before. I have no idea who they are."

"Me neither. And for that theory to wash—that she was a prominent person embarrassed by something in her past—you'd expect we would. Recognize her, I mean."

"Not necessarily. I know so little about politics, and—"

"And another thing," Alice went on. "Where's the negatives?"

"What negatives?"

"Exactly," Alice said. "There's no negatives. When you buy blackmail photos, don't you always want the negatives?"

"Always? This may surprise you, but I've never bought blackmail photos before."

"Damn it, Stanley."

I sighed. "All right. Yes, of course you want the negatives. I know. The whole thing stinks. It doesn't make any sense. But what can I do? The woman kept me completely in the dark. I wasn't *supposed* to know anything about what was going on. I still wouldn't know, if this guy Barry hadn't forced it on me."

"Why would he do that?" Alice said. "I mean, here's the woman treating you like a total outsider—tell him nothing—and here's the guy treating you like one of the gang—hey, get a load of this."

"That's not so strange."

"Why not?"

"He wouldn't know what she told me. Or how I got involved. I don't have to be a hired messenger boy. I could be her brother or husband or lover, for all he knows."

"Or father."

"Thanks a lot, Alice. Did I mention the woman's age?"

"I think you said young."

"That's a fairly broad range. In her case, *father* would be quite a stretch."

"Fine. Anyway, this guy seemed to think you were the cat's meow who should be told everything."

"Yes, he did."

"Whereas the woman didn't want you to know a thing."

"No, she didn't."

"Hmm," Alice said. "I would think she's gonna be a trifle pissed."

6.

Understatement.

Marlena looked as if she were auditioning for the role of the evil twin sister on a soap opera.

"You *opened* it," she said.

I held up my hand. "No. I did *not* open it. Barry opened it."

"You shouldn't have let him."

"Let? What do you mean, let? He had the envelope. He ripped it open. He didn't tell me he was going to. He didn't ask me if he should. He just did it."

"You should have stopped him."

"How? Shot him dead? You'll pardon me, but you're not being terribly rational."

Her eyes widened. "Oh, really? I'm not being terribly rational. I hired you to do a job. Paid you five hundred dollars. And you didn't do it."

"Yes, I did."

"Oh yeah? Pick up an envelope and bring it here. Unopened. That was the job."

"No."

"No? What do you mean, no?"

"The instruction was *not to open* the envelope. I didn't *open* the envelope. I *received* it opened. A circumstance beyond my control. I'm delivering it in the condition in which I received it."

I was fairly pleased with that statement. I felt Richard Rosenberg might even appreciate it.

Marlena certainly didn't. "What you've done is highly unethical. It violates the confidence of a client."

"No such thing."

"Oh, is that right? Are you telling me you didn't look in that envelope?'

"That's not the point."

"Then you *did?*"

"I had no choice in the matter. Barry showed them to me."

"Barry did?"

"Yeah. And he didn't ask if I wanted to see them, he pulled them out and said, 'Here, look at this.'"

"Sure," Marlena said. "Blame it all on Barry. He's not here to defend himself."

"Defend himself?" I said. "What the hell are you talking about? He's a blackmailer. I'm on *your* side."

"You'd never know it."

"All right," I said. "Fine. I accept your evaluation. I'm totally to blame for everything Barry did."

"I didn't say that," Marlena said.

"Oh yeah? Well, you could have fooled me. Anyway, I did the job for you the best I could. It wasn't much, seeing as how you wouldn't take me into your confidence and tell me anything." I pointed to the envelope. "If you had, I might have been able to do something about this. Because, frankly, these pictures aren't going to help you at all."

She frowned. "What do you mean?"

"You didn't get the negatives."

"Negatives?"

"Yeah. You got your blackmail photos, but you don't have

your negatives. What's to stop Barry from running off a fresh set of prints and doing this whole thing all over again?"

She frowned. Thought a moment. "That's not your problem," she said.

"You're absolutely right. It's not my problem. It's your problem. I just bring it up because, when I do a job, I wanna give service. It's difficult when I'm not being trusted to do it. Nonetheless, for what it's worth, that's my opinion. If I'd been taken in on the play, I would have insisted on getting the negatives as part of the deal."

Marlena gave me such a look. "Gee," she said with scathing sarcasm. "What a shame I didn't have you masterminding this for me."

"You should have had someone," I said. "You might have saved yourself a bit of money."

"What's that supposed to mean?"

"That envelope isn't the only thing Barry tore open. He also opened the one you gave me. I saw the packet of bills that fell out. It was a huge chunk of dough."

"You had no right to see that."

I looked at her. "You'll pardon me, but you realize that sounds a little stupid?"

"You know what I mean."

"I know what you mean. I don't know what your game is. I know that you paid entirely too much money for some very spurious-looking blackmail photos."

She frowned. "Spurious?"

"You confused by the word or the concept? What I mean is, they don't appear genuine. They're posed pictures by willing participants who knew they were being photographed."

"What's that got to do with anything?"

"You tell me."

"I'm not telling you anything. This is none of your business. You had no right to see those photos."

"Yeah, but since I did I can't help commenting on 'em. It's free advice, and you don't have to take it, but I feel obliged to point out what I've observed."

"Thanks for your concern," Marlena said sarcastically.

She was carrying a large, floppy drawstring purse slung

over her shoulder. She flopped it down on my desk, pulled the top open, and stuck the manila envelope in. She pulled the purse shut, slung it over her shoulder, and turned to go.

She turned back in the doorway. "Just remember one thing," she said. "I'm your client. You violate my confidence, I'll sue you for damages and see you lose your license."

Not the most cordial parting remark.

Still, by and large, I think I preferred it to "Have a nice day."

7.

"This makes no sense."

Richard was absolutely right. The whole thing made no sense. Which was one of the reasons I'd stopped by the office to tell him about it. Richard must have been pretty interested in the whole blackmail bit, because he didn't even bother to ask me where I should have been that morning. If he had, the answer was in Queens, signing up a man who fell down in the produce section of a Sloan's, but the subject never came up. Richard just wanted to hear about the payoff.

Until he heard my story. As he listened, his face darkened. When I finished he looked at me a moment or two and said, "Are you putting me on?"

"What?"

"This is a joke, isn't it? Something you dreamed up with the switchboard girls to have a laugh at my expense?"

"Richard."

"Or that homicide cop—what's his name? MacAullif—did you have some bet with him? See if you can tell me this incredible story and get me to bite?"

"Don't be silly."

"Me? Silly? You tell me a story like that and then say, 'Don't be silly'?"

"Richard, I was in here yesterday asking for advice."

"To set up the gag, right? Lay the foundation. So what's the punch line? When you gonna let me in on the bit?"

"There's no bit. I'm giving you the straight stuff. Everything I'm telling you is exactly what happened."

Richard smiled. Shrugged. "I know that. I'm just putting you on. Obviously everything you've told me is true."

"Why obviously?"

"Because if you'd made it up, it would make a lot more sense. Anything this stupid has to be the truth."

"That's not encouraging."

"No, it isn't. The whole thing stinks from the word go."

"It's not that bad, Richard."

"Oh, no? Tell me why it's not that bad."

"So the woman's inept, she didn't think of the negatives. Maybe it's her first blackmail too."

Richard waved his hand. "That's the least of it."

"You mean the fact the pictures were posed?"

"No, I don't mean the pictures themselves. I mean what she did with them."

I frowned. "You mean paying that kind of money for them?"

He grimaced. "No," he said. "No, I'm talking about something she *didn't* do."

"Didn't do?"

"If I understand your story right. It could be you just omitted it."

"Omitted what?"

"All right. You say this Barry showed you the pictures?"

"Yeah, he did. Which is what made the whole trouble."

"Fine. Never mind that. Now, this Marlena—*she* didn't show you the pictures, did she?"

"No." I looked at him. "Is that what she didn't do?"

"You gave her the pictures in the envelope. She started cursing you out for the envelope being opened."

"Right."

"Then you tell me she jammed it in her purse and left?"

"Yeah. So?"

"Did *she* look at the pictures?"

I blinked.

"Well?"

"Son of a bitch."

"She didn't, did she?"

I shook my head.

"Pretty indifferent blackmail victim, wouldn't you think?"

"I sure would. So what does it mean?"

He shrugged. "How should I know?"

"What?"

"I have no idea."

"Oh, come on. You must. You figured it out."

"Figured what out?"

"You knew she hadn't looked at the pictures. You must have some idea why."

"I assure you I don't."

"Then how did you know?"

"Know what?"

"She hadn't looked at them."

"From what you said. From your story."

"How could you possibly have got it from that?"

He looked at me in surprise. "That's what I do. What do you think cross-examination is? I listen to the witness's story, look for holes, then pick 'em apart. The hole in your story was, the way you told it, this woman had never looked at the pictures."

"Yeah, but . . ."

"But what?"

"What if she had and I'd just left it out?"

Richard smiled. "I assure you I would have covered neatly and gone on to something else. You never would have known that was what I was actually getting at. Anyway, it's a moot point, because I was right. She didn't look at the pictures. Which has to be the most telling point yet."

"What does it mean?"

"Well, that, coupled with the fact she's not *in* the pictures, indicates she's not a principal in the blackmail action. Which means she's either an interested party or a paid functionary, not unlike you. The fact that she showed no interest in the blackmail photos, even to the extent of verifying that that's what they indeed were, would tend to indicate that she was a paid functionary, merely following orders."

"Like me."

"Yes. Except, in her case, she would have to have some idea of what was going on."

"Thanks a lot."

Richard raised his eyebrows. "*That* particular observation was not intended to belittle your investigative techniques. I was referring to how much you were told."

"Oh."

Richard frowned and shook his head. "I don't like this at all. Every aspect of this whole affair is entirely unsatisfactory."

"Except for one thing. I got paid up front."

Richard pointed his finger. "And there's another thing. Why the hell would she do that?"

"I have no idea."

"Me either. And it stinks. Not from your point of view—you're happy to get the money. But in terms of making sense. Who the hell pays for something like this in advance? For something this speculative. There's no guarantee you're going to pull it off. It's gotta be COD."

"Yeah. So why did she do it?"

"I don't know. It's like not looking at the pictures. It's another indication she wasn't that concerned with the outcome."

"Okay," I said. "That may well be. But the fact is, I'm happy I got paid. Now, considering I did the job and got my money, am I in any trouble? Is there anything I gotta worry about? Legally, I mean."

"Probably not," Richard said. "If all the interested parties were to come forward and accuse you of compounding a felony and conspiring to conceal a crime—to wit, blackmail—well, that might be somewhat embarrassing. But, barring that, I would say you were in the clear."

"So at this point, I really have nothing to worry about?"

"I didn't say that."

"Why not? I thought you just said I was in the clear."

"I think you are. It's just that everything you told me indicates just one thing."

"What's that?"

"It isn't over yet."

8.

My beeper went off later that afternoon while I was out on a case. No, not the case in Queens. That's a common misassumption people get from TV—that the private detective is always working on *the case*, like he's got nothing else to do and if someone hires him he immediately drops everything and starts working just for them. In practice, I handle three to four cases a day and sometimes more. In this particular instance, after talking to Richard, I'd done the case in Queens, another in Jersey City, and a third in the Bronx. When the beep came through I was in Brooklyn, Bed Stuy to be exact, contemplating a third-floor walkup in remarkably poor repair, and speculating on whether the two rather tough-looking black men hanging out on the front steps would help me, hassle me, mug me, or kill me if I attempted to enter the building.

My beeper postponed the moment of truth. When it went

off the two black men looked at me in surprise. In their neighborhood, anyone with a beeper was selling drugs.

Except me. Sorry, guys, I am no pusher. The beep would be either Wendy or Janet, one of Richard's switchboard girls—who happened to have identical voices so you could never tell which one of them you were dealing with—beeping me to give me a case. Which was likely to be for tomorrow, since it was now four-thirty. Unless it was an emergency case, which was rare.

It was neither. When I called in, it turned out Wendy/Janet had beeped me to give me a message to call Marlena.

"She was most insistent," Wendy/Janet said. "She said it was urgent and she had to see you right away."

Wendy or Janet, whichever one of them it was, was laying it on thick, in a voice that implied in no uncertain terms that she suspected some hanky-panky going on here.

I refused to play along, just copied down the phone number and broke the connection. I fished a quarter out of my pocket, dropped it in, and called Marlena.

She answered on the first ring. Small miracle there. Aside from a voice, Wendy and Janet shared an uncanny inaccuracy. Getting a phone number right was indeed a noteworthy occasion.

"Marlena?" I said.

"Yes."

"Stanley Hastings."

"Oh, thank god."

"What's the matter?"

"What you said."

"What do you mean?"

"I was a fool. Blind. Irrational."

"Oh?"

"I'm sorry. I should have listened."

"That's very gratifying. What should you have listened to?"

"You. You were absolutely right."

"About what?"

"Barry, of course."

"What about him?"

"I'm sorry. I'm not telling this well."

"You're not telling it at all. Calm down and start over."

"Right. Right. I'm sorry." There was a pause, then, "It's about the negatives."

"Oh?"

"Yes. Just like you said. He called me up. Arrogant. Taunting. He has the negatives. He has more prints. Do I want them?"

"Do you?"

A pause, then, "What are you talking about? Of course I want them."

"Oh?"

"Why do you say that?"

"Since you're not in the pictures, I wondered why you cared."

"Please. That's not important. The fact is, you've gotta help me."

"That remains to be seen."

"What?"

"I did a job for you. It's done. We have no business relationship anymore."

"Don't be like that."

"I'm not being anything. I'm just telling you how it is."

"Well, I wanna hire you again."

"That may or may not be possible."

"Don't be silly. I'm in trouble. I need help. We can work something out."

"We can try."

"Fine. We'll try. You gotta come meet me."

"When?"

"Now."

"I'm in Brooklyn."

"How long will it take you to get here?"

"Where's here?"

"Manhattan."

"That's rather vague."

"Downtown. The Village."

"A couple of hours."

"A couple of hours?"

"I got a case first."

"*Now?* You got a case *now?*"

Yeah, I did. Which meant walking past two guys who looked like they'd like to rip my arms and legs off in order to steal my camera, beeper, wallet, or whatever, or just for the hell of it.

On the other hand, it's amazing how one's perceptions are colored by events. When I got off the phone with Marlena, I dropped another quarter in the phone and called up the client just to verify the address, since, as I say, Wendy/Janet are not always accurate. But when I did, not only was the address correct, but the client told me his brother and cousin were sitting on the front steps and could let me in.

Sure enough, that's who the two guys hanging out proved to be, and in no time at all I had signed up my fourth case of the day and was tooling back to Manhattan to keep a rendezvous with the fair Marlena.

Which was not entirely kosher. It was, in fact, the very thing Richard had warned me about. Specifically, he had told me if something like this happened, to call him first.

Only, Richard always left the office by four, so by the time I got the phone call from Marlena, he was long gone. And his home number was unlisted and I didn't have it, so there was no way I could get in touch with him. That may seem strange for a lawyer, but Richard wasn't a criminal lawyer, he was a negligence lawyer, and accident victims weren't going to be calling up at three in the morning wanting to be bailed out of the hospital.

Anyway, there was no way I could reach him, so I had to make the decision myself. Which was not that hard. After all, I hadn't agreed to do anything except meet her. And it was either that or turn her down. In agreeing to the meeting, all I'd really decided was to postpone the decision.

Or so I told myself as I sailed over the Brooklyn Bridge, curved around the southern tip of Manhattan and headed up West Street. I went crosstown on Fourteenth, then back down Seventh Avenue to Sheridan Square.

She was right where she'd said she'd be, on the corner in front of United Cigar. I pulled into the curb, leaned over and opened the passenger door. She jumped in, slammed and locked the door, then turned to me breathlessly.

"Drive," she said.

That was a little much.

"Hey," I said. "What's the big deal?"

"Damn it, don't talk. Just drive."

I gave her a look, but pulled out from the curb and headed on down Seventh Avenue.

"All right, what's the deal?" I said. "Are you being blackmailed, or threatened, or what?"

"You don't understand."

"I certainly don't. I'm not sure I want to. You wanna tell me why all the cloak-and-dagger stuff?"

"I don't know if I'm being watched."

"By whom?"

"I don't know."

I let that sit there, continued to drive. Seventh Avenue turned into Varick. I kept on going downtown.

"Where are you going?" she said.

"I have no idea," I said. "You told me to drive. You wanna name a destination, I'll head for it."

"No. Just drive. I'll tell you when to turn."

"Nice of you."

"Damn it," she said. "Don't tease me. I'm scared."

"So I gathered. You realize I have no idea why."

"I told you. It's Barry. He has more pictures. And the negatives."

"I understand. But why does that pose a physical threat?"

"It doesn't, but . . . I don't know. I'm just scared."

"How's Canal seem?"' I said.

"What? Oh yeah. Fine."

I hung a left on Canal, headed for Chinatown.

"All right, look," I said. "You wanna tell me what you want?"

The big floppy purse was on her lap. She reached in and pulled out a sealed envelope. A fat one.

"I want you to take this and give it to Barry."

"In return for?"

She looked at me. "What do you think? The negatives and the prints."

"Well, that's a bit of a switch."

"Why?"

"Before, I was buying a sealed envelope. No questions

asked. Now I'm buying negatives and prints. Am I supposed to verify the fact that what I'm buying *are* the negatives and prints? I mean, if Barry *doesn't* open the envelope this time, should *I* open it?"

It was hard to watch her closely and drive down Canal at the same time, but I think her eyes faltered some at that. But I could have just imagined it, 'cause I happened to be negotiating a yellow light.

"Barry will show you the negatives," she said.

"What if he doesn't?"

"Why do you ask, what if he doesn't? He *will*."

"I haven't agreed to do this yet," I said.

"What are you talking about? Of course you're going to do this."

"I never said so. We're just talking here."

"Why wouldn't you do it? It's exactly the same thing."

"No, it isn't," I said. "Which is exactly the point I'm making. You hired me before as a delivery boy. Deliver one package and pick up another. I didn't even know what they were. Now I do know, and it's very specific—negatives and prints. Now, does that become *my* responsibility, or am I still just a delivery boy, bringing you back whatever this creep chooses to give?"

"You're responsible for the negatives and prints. Because that's what he'll give you."

I sighed.

I pulled the car over to the curb and stopped.

"What are you doing?" she said.

"I'm stopping the car."

"Why?"

"Because I am a free and independent human being. And that is what I choose to do."

"I don't understand."

"Me neither. I am wondering if *you* are a free and independent human being, doing what you choose to do."

"I'm being blackmailed."

"Aside from that." I shrugged. "I know that sounds stupid, but try the concept. You'll pardon me, but you sounded like you were parroting instructions someone had given you. If this is the case, we have little to discuss, and I would like to talk to that person. Because I am not prepared to proceed the way things are. I am asking for specific instructions to govern certain eventualities. If these things can't be discussed, that ends my involvement in this affair."

She put her hands on my shoulders. "No, no. I'm sorry. We can get by this. What was your question again?"

"If Barry doesn't show me the negatives and the pictures, do I open the envelope myself to verify that's what they are?"

She took a breath, exhaled, seemed to be making up her mind. "Yeah," she said. "Do that."

"And if the negatives aren't in the package, I don't hand over the money?"

"They will be," she said. When I looked at her, she added hastily, "But if they aren't, of course not. Then you wouldn't pay."

"I see," I said. "So, I'm right."

"About what?"

"About this being an entirely different transaction. I'm no longer just a messenger. I'm being employed to take charge and deal with the situation."

She frowned. "I suppose so. What's the difference?"

"The difference," I said, "is that the added responsibility would of course command more money."

She'd had trouble with what I'd been saying before, but she had no trouble with that.

"Of course," she said.

And she pulled open the top of her drawstring purse, took out her wallet, and calmly counted out ten one-hundred-dollar bills.

9.

I know I shouldn't have done it. But as I said, I couldn't reach Richard. And you have no idea how big that stack of hundred-dollar bills looked to a family man trying to support a wife and kid in New York City.

And, what the hell. Richard's advice had been to make the first blackmail payment. Well, not really. Actually, his advice had been not to make the first blackmail payment. Once I'd chosen to do so anyway, his opinion was that I probably wouldn't get into any trouble doing it.

And this was really just the same thing. Even though it wasn't. Not with me empowered to insist on the negatives. Though that probably wouldn't matter, since Barry'd probably show them to me anyway. After all, he'd showed me the pictures the first time.

And he wasn't supposed to.

That was the unsettling thought. He'd shown me the pictures when he wasn't supposed to. So what would he do when he was supposed to? Show them to me because he *liked* showing them to me? Or not show them to me, because he liked being contrary?

Why was I indulging in such profitless, idle speculation? Perhaps because I had nothing better to do. Because tonight Barry didn't happen to be in unit twelve of the motel, the nice, convenient motel just off the Saw Mill River Parkway. The one that was a piece of cake to get to and that I felt comfortable with and that I wished I was driving to right now. But no, that would have been entirely too easy.

So what was I doing instead? Hanging out on a street corner next to a pay phone waiting for it to ring.

Did you ever do that? Probably not, unless you're a pimp or a dope peddler or a member of some other profession who naturally uses a pay phone in the normal course of your business. But in case you don't happen to fall into that category, let me tell you it's no fun.

What made it worse was the pay phone didn't happen to be anywhere near Canal Street, which was where Marlena and I were when I agreed to do it. Or anywhere near Sheridan Square, which was where I dropped her off again. No, the pay phone happened to be way the fuck uptown, right by the George Washington Bridge. Well, not by the bridge exactly, that would have made it in the water, but on Broadway in front of the bus terminal. Which is right where the bridge comes out, which is probably why the bus terminal is there.

Why *I* was there was beyond me. Now don't get me wrong—from *my* point of view, I was there for the stack of hundred-dollar bills Marlena had counted out. I meant from Barry's point of view. Why of all places did he have to send me there?

But he had, and he'd been very specific. Marlena had given me not only the location of the phone booth but the phone number as well, so I could double-check that I was at the right phone. Which I had and I was, so there I was, standing on the corner like an asshole, waiting for the damn thing to ring.

Which, Marlena had told me, might take some time. She had been instructed to have her representative there by eight o'clock. She didn't necessarily mean the phone would *ring* by eight o'clock—I was to be there between the hours of eight and ten. That seemed pretty damned excessive to me, but then I guess blackmailers have never been noted for their consideration. All I know is, I got there at a quarter to eight, and no matter what I'd been told, I *expected* the phone to ring at eight o'clock, and when it didn't, I was pissed.

I was also somewhat hassled. See, by virtue of being right outside a bus station, this particular phone happened to be rather popular. Since I had to keep the line free for an incoming call, I was forced to stand there holding the receiver and surreptitiously pressing down the metal lever that hangs up the phone, and pretending to talk.

This did not fool one little old lady with a suitcase almost as big as she was who wanted to call a cab. She was most insistent, and I might have had to give in to her if a vacant taxi hadn't happened to drive by and I wasn't able to hail it for her. With a great feeling of relief, I helped her load her suitcase into the back of the cab.

Just in time to see the meter maid coming down the block toward my car. I was at a meter, my time had just run out, and I was suddenly thrust onto the horns of a dilemma—I had to either risk losing my precious phone or concede a parking ticket of at least twenty-five dollars.

Not that tough a choice. I had already been paid for making the blackmail payment, and I was not on an expense account.

I ran down the block, screaming and waving my arms.

The meter maid, a plump, black woman, laughed and said, "All right, all right. Put your quarter in."

And the phone rang.

If the meter maid thought I was funny before, she had to love me now, because I flipped her the quarter and then did a pretty fair impression of a cartoon character whose legs start going faster and faster before he takes off and starts running. I raced to the phone booth, scooped up the phone on the fourth ring.

It was Barry.

"Hi, champ," he said. "Pretty slow picking up the phone. What's the matter, you got something better to do?"

"Cut the shit, Barry. What's the deal?"

"Hear you like the pictures."

"I love 'em. Why?"

"I understand you like 'em so much you'd like to buy some more."

"Actually, Barry, I was thinking about the negatives."

"Me too. Good thinking. I can tell you're a class act. It's a pleasure doing business with you."

"Cut the shit. What do you want?'

"I want the envelope you have in your jacket pocket. The one Marlena gave you. The one with all the money in it. The one you're supposed to give me."

"Then why aren't you here? Why are we just talking on the phone?"

"Well, that's a problem."

"What's a problem?"

"Well, you may find this hard to believe, but I don't trust you."

"Aw, Barry."

"Hey, don't take it personally. I'm sure you're a perfectly nice guy. But you can't be too careful. Now, I'll tell you what I'd like. You got your car there?"

"Yeah."

"Good. Then you'll have no problem getting around."

"Around where?"

"I dunno. How does Queens sound?"

"I was just there this morning."

"Were you? Then this will be a breeze. Northern Boulevard and 193rd Street. Northeast corner. One hour."

"You'll be there?"

"No. *You'll* be there."

"What is this, another pay phone?"

"You're a very smart man."

"What if it isn't working?"

"Good point. If the phone is broken or has not rung by ten o'clock, you wash it out and you're back here by eleven."

"Back here?"

"To this phone. The one that *is* working."

"Oh, great."

"You got that?"

"Yeah, sure. Look, couldn't we just *pretend* the phone in Queens doesn't work and we're back here at this one?"

"Sorry, that would be highly irregular," Barry said, and hung up.

I got in my car, took the bridge over to the Bronx, took the Major Deegan to the Triboro and over into Queens. I don't know how long Barry had counted on it taking me, but I was on the designated street corner inside of half an hour. In other words, by nine o'clock.

So I'm standing on another street corner staring at another pay phone that didn't necessarily have to ring until ten.

Some days you get lucky. The call came through at nine-fifteen.

"Gee, champ," Barry said. "You made good time."

"Pretty good," I said. "I've been hanging out here for almost twenty minutes."

"Well, aren't *you* the early bird," Barry said. "The early bird catches the pornographic prints. Not to mention the negatives."

"Right," I said. "Now, you wanna tell me where we're supposed to meet?"

"Obviously not, or we wouldn't be doing this."

"Doing what?" I said. "Just what the hell is it that we're doing?"

"Actually, I'm just making phone calls and you're driving around like a lunatic."

I took a breath, said nothing.

"Losing your sense of humor?" Barry said.

"It's your show. I'm just waiting to see what happens next."

"Fair enough. Actually, I think you've been a good boy and you deserve a break. So I'll tell you what I'm going to do."

"What's that."

"I'm gonna send you some place you know."

"And where might that be?"

"You know that motel just off the Saw Mill River Parkway?"

I think I paused a moment before I said, "I believe I do."

"Fine. Try unit twelve," he said, and hung up the phone.

I was pissed driving out there. It was like I was being blackmailed by contestants on the "Amateur Hour." First Barry runs me all over creation for no earthly reason, and then he sends me back to the place we met before.

Rendering the runaround useless. I mean, what was the point of me going to Queens and back if I was going to wind up at the same motel? What was the point of me going *anywhere* if I was going to wind up at the same motel? The point of the runaround had to be to keep me from knowing where the actual meeting and transfer would take place. So I couldn't set Barry up by bringing the cops into the deal. So what does he do? He *tells* me where it's gonna take place. What was to stop me from hanging up the phone on him, dropping in a quarter, and calling the cops?

Well, he could have been watching. There was always that possibility. He could have been pulling this runaround from Queens, inside some diner that overlooked the corner with the pay phone. He could have been in there all night making the calls, waiting to see just what I did after he told me to go to the motel. And if I had picked up the phone and made another call after I had hung up on him, he could simply have not shown up and then contacted Marlena and said, "Hey, what's with the double cross?"

But I hadn't done that. I had hung up the phone, hopped in my car, and headed back over the Triboro Bridge. By all counts, I was playing it on the level. So if Barry was playing it on the level, it should go off without a hitch.

At least, that's what I told myself as I turned into the entrance of the motel.

There was no car in front of unit twelve. Of course there hadn't been the first time, but as I pulled in it seemed to me the unit looked dark.

I walked up and knocked on the door.

There was no answer.

I leaned my head closer, listened for sounds from within.

There were none.

I knocked again, listened.

Nothing.

I tried the doorknob.

It was locked.

That was a relief.

I didn't like this at all.

That's when I saw the paper. It was folded up small and wedged in the crack in the door.

I pulled it out, unfolded it.

On it was written *89 Prince—2A*.

Oh, boy.

That had to be an address on Prince Street.

Back to Manhattan.

It was a drag, yeah, but in a way it was almost reassuring. Because, as I said, meeting at the motel just didn't make any sense. But it turned out the motel wasn't the final destination. Just another stop in the runaround.

I wondered what 89 Prince was.

It had to be the next stop. Not necessarily the last, certainly the next.

Still, having been told to show up at the motel, I was loath to leave it. And even though I knew he wouldn't show, I couldn't help hanging out and waiting for Barry, at least for a while.

Which was about ten minutes by my dashboard clock. Then I started the motor, pulled out, and headed back to Manhattan.

As I paid a buck and a quarter upon leaving the Bronx, it occurred to me the tolls on this thing were beginning to add up. I'd had that bridge twice, the Triboro twice at two-fifty a throw. Not to mention the gas. Thank god I'd avoided the parking ticket.

I took the West Side Highway downtown and got off at Canal Street. That figured. The address I was going to was only blocks from where I'd been with Marlena earlier that afternoon. Oh, well, sometimes it's necessary to go a long distance out of the way in order to come back a short distance correctly. Edward Albee. *Zoo Story.*

I wonder if he ever paid blackmail?

I turned onto Prince Street, located 89, pulled in to the curb and parked. It was an old factory building that had been converted into lofts on a block of such structures.

The downstairs door was unlocked. I pushed it open and went in. Facing me was a long staircase and a door with a regular lock and a police lock. The door had no number on it, but as I was looking for 2A, this couldn't possibly be it.

I went on up the stairs. At the top was a landing with two doors in front of it. One was labeled 2A, the other 2B.

What could be easier?

I took a breath, walked up to 2A and knocked.

I think I would have been surprised if there had been an answer. When there wasn't, I took it as a matter of course.

I also began looking for a folded-up piece of paper, the next clue in the treasure hunt. But there was nothing stuck in the cracks of this door.

I tried the knob, again expecting nothing.

And it turned and clicked open.

What?

Not possible.

This door had a regular lock and a big police lock, just like the door downstairs. And none of those locks were engaged? It didn't add up.

And then suddenly it did.

The runaround, the treasure hunt, the blackmail, the whole bit.

That's when I knew I didn't want to open that door. Because I knew what was on the other side. Barry would be lying there dead.

It was too perfect. I mean, here I am, running around, getting involved with this guy Barry. I meet him once, pay him off. End up having the whole business with him on the phone, running around all over the place. Then I'm sent from Queens back to the motel. Where I find the note sending me here. Two long trips back and forth. And what happens in the meantime? Whoever's pulling this off kills Barry and drops his body at the address he's left for me to find.

And there I am.

Perfect patsy.

Perfect frame.

So I didn't want to open that door.

But I had to. There was no help for it. Given the situation, it was something I simply had to do.

So I did. I took a breath, gritted my teeth, turned the knob, and opened the door. Knowing full well that when I looked, Barry would be lying there dead.

He wasn't.

Marlena was.

10.

The thing about the law of averages is, it never works. Oh, it works in terms of the lottery—you'll never win that. But in terms of anything practical, the law of averages simply hasn't got a chance.

Yeah, I know. I'm babbling. Finding a dead body will do that to you.

So will the presence of Sergeant Thurman.

Which is what that whole law-of-averages thing is about. I don't know how many homicide cops there are in Manhattan, but there's gotta be a lot. So what were the odds of me coming up with Sergeant Thurman for the third time running? Well, maybe not as long as the odds of Sergeant Thurman solving a case.

Yeah, I know. It's a horrible cliché. The obtuse, dense, plodding, and unimaginative policeman, who couldn't do anything if it weren't for the help of the hotshot P.I. on the case. But don't blame me for that. In my experience with the police, I'd found it to be the exact opposite—most homicide cops were ten times more equipped, resourceful, and capable than me.

And then there was Sergeant Thurman. A bull of a man, whose crewcut, broken nose, and guttural speech made him look and sound like a college football coach. One with a team record of 0 and 13.

Dumb as he was, Sergeant Thurman remembered me. I don't think he appreciated the mathematical significance of us hooking up for the third time together, and I doubt if his vocabulary included the term déjà vu, but it still penetrated his consciousness that this had happened before.

At least I gathered that from what he said when he first saw me. He stopped, scowled, and said, "You."

A tough P.I. is supposed to joke in the face of adversity. I'm not tough, but I try to pretend. So I didn't let on that the sight of his face was like a kick in the stomach. I just smiled and said, "Gee, this must be my lucky day."

"What the hell are you doing here?"

"I'm the one who called the cops."

"Oh, shit. No."

"Yes."

"You found the body?"

"Yes."

"Did you kill her?"

"No."

"Are you sure? You wouldn't wanna confess now and save me a lot of grief?"

"Sorry, sergeant. I didn't do this one."

"Any idea who did?"

"None at all."

We were standing just inside the door to the loft. Sergeant Thurman looked past me to where Marlena's body was lying on the floor. "Who's the stiff?"

Marlena's floppy purse was lying next to the body. I pointed to it.

"She may have ID in her purse."

"You didn't look?"

"Of course not. I saw she was dead and called the cops."

"From here?"

"Don't be silly. From a pay phone on the corner."

"This corner?"

"Actually, I had to walk a few blocks."

"You leave the door unlocked?"

"I didn't touch a thing. Everything is just as I found it."

"So while you were calling the cops, anyone could have come in or out, or even made their escape?"

I shrugged. "I suppose. You wanna beat me up now, or after you investigate?"

Sergeant Thurman glared at me, deciding whether or not to punch me in the nose. Instead, he said simply, "Finding you here has not made my day."

No kidding. It hadn't made mine either. It was, in fact, a disaster of epic proportions.

Fortunately, with the crime scene to contend with, Sergeant Thurman couldn't spend all his time with me. He bellowed to one of the beat cops and assigned him to take me off in the corner and ride herd over me and make sure I didn't touch anything.

Which I had no intention of doing. I read murder mysteries and I'm not entirely stupid. Scattering my fingerprints over the crime scene would not be a particularly swift move. I stood in the corner of the loft and watched the cops go about their business.

Marlena had apparently been shot in the head. I say *apparently* in the same way newspapers use the word *alleged* to refer to some suspect the police have apprehended with the murder weapon in his possession and boasting moronically about how cool he was for doing the victim in. Marlena was lying in a pool of blood that had come from a wound in the back of her head. A pistol that smelled as if it had recently been discharged lay next to the body. That was the evidence on which I based my opinion that she had been shot. However, considering my accuracy in these matters, I use the word *apparently* just in case she happened to actually have been poisoned and I was just too dumb to see it.

As I watched, one of the detectives from the crime-scene unit picked up the supposed murder weapon with the tip of his pen, dropped it in a plastic evidence envelope, and wrote his name on it.

Sergeant Thurman, perhaps taking his cue from me, bent down and examined the purse lying next to the body. He reached in, pulled out a wallet, snapped it open.

The detective who had just bagged the gun gave him a funny look. I figured Thurman's handling of the evidence wasn't entirely kosher, but the guy didn't dare call him on it. When Thurman finished with the purse, the detective surrounded it, almost protectively, and began bagging the stuff.

Other detectives were searching the loft, which was not that big, by the way, it being 2A and there being two lofts per floor. Nor was it that furnished; that is to say, not at all. It was your basic bare loft—high ceiling, exposed pipes, plumbing fixtures at one end. Pretty much empty, with the exception of one corpse.

The medical examiner arrived about then. A white-haired, bespectacled man who to the best of my knowledge I had never seen before. He conferred briefly with Sergeant Thurman, then bent to examine the body.

After a few moments he looked up and nodded.

I don't know what that meant, but it meant something to Thurman, because he turned his attention back to me. Which wasn't really that surprising. This being a vacant loft, there wasn't that much else to concern him.

Thurman strode over, inserted himself between the cop and me, and jerked his thumb over his shoulder, inviting the cop to scram. The cop gave him a bit of a look in doing so, and it occurred to me Thurman must be deeply admired on the force.

Left alone with me, Sergeant Thurman jerked his thumb again, this time at the body. "Doctor says she's just dead."

I nodded. "That figures. If he'd said she was alive, I'd have been totally shocked."

Thurman scowled. "You know what I mean. *Just* dead. Like in *real recent.*"

I nodded. "Again, I'm not terribly surprised."

"Oh?" Thurman said. "What time was it when you found the body?"

"Approximately ten-forty-five."

His eyes narrowed. "Approximately?"

"I'm not wearing a watch. It was ten-forty-two by the dashboard clock when I parked my car outside. It took a couple of minutes for me to get inside, go upstairs, knock on the door, and get no answer."

"Then you tried the door?"

"Yeah."

"Why?"

I shrugged. "Force of habit. Because it's there. I turned it, it opened."

"And went in?"

"No. I could see she was dead from the door. I closed it and ran to call the cops."

"You didn't go in and look for a phone?"

"No. I don't think there is one, but if there had been I wouldn't have used it."

"But there wasn't a phone on the corner and you had to go several blocks?"

"Not several. Two. One down and one over."

"You called the cops by when?"

"I don't know."

"Yeah, well, we will. There'll be a record of the call."

"Good."

Thurman grunted. He jerked his thumb again. "Cops say they got here ten-fifty-seven."

"That sounds about right."

"And found you back upstairs here."

"Yeah, but outside the door."

"But you'd *been* inside."

"No, I'd opened the door. Small difference."

"Uh-huh," Thurman said. If he'd believed me, you wouldn't have known it. "Anyway," he said. "The woman on the floor. The dead woman. What's her name?"

"You look in her purse?"

"You know I did. You were watching me."

"So?"

Thurman's eyes narrowed. "Let's not have any trouble here. You're the civilian. I'm the cop. I ask the questions. And the question is, what is the name of the woman on the floor?"

"No," I said. "What is the name of the man on second base."

He stared at me. "What?"

"Exactly."

He frowned. "*Who* is on second base?"

"No," I said. "Who is on *first* base."

"What?"

"No, what is on *second* base."

"I don't know," Thurman cried in exasperation.

I pointed. "Third base."

Thurman finally got it. His eyes blazed. "Shut the fuck up!" he growled.

"He's the manager," I muttered.

Yeah, I know I shouldn't have done it. It was a murder case, it was serious and all that. But the thing is, when you're totally fucked, you got nothing left to lose.

And I was now dorked beyond all recognition. I had been, from the moment Sergeant Thurman asked me her name. It was a question I could not answer, only evade. But sooner or later, even Sergeant Thurman was going to pin me down.

And he did. By a great effort he managed to restrain himself from hauling off and decking me. Instead, he summoned all his mental capacities and managed to ask the question right.

"Listen, fuck-up," he said. "I'm asking you one question, I want a straight answer and I want no shit. Did you ever see the dead woman before?"

Damn. That was the one question I could not answer. I mean, it was a murder and I wasn't involved in the murder. I could happily tell him anything he wanted to know about that. And as a citizen it was my right and my duty to do so.

Except for the blackmail. That's a crime. A felony. And anyone who participates in it is guilty at the very least of being an accessory. Of aiding and abetting in the commission of a felony.

Of course, being guilty of that, I had a right not to incriminate myself. In point of fact, it was Sergeant Thurman's duty to so inform me. Not that I expected him to do so. The point is, I had a constitutional right not to tell him a goddamn thing. And in light of the fact that I'd been paying off blackmail, I was sure that was exactly what Richard would advise me to do.

I looked at Sergeant Thurman standing there glowering at me, waiting for me to answer. And I have to tell you, I did not expect him to take it well.

I took a breath. "I'm sorry," I said. "I can't tell you that."

11.

He beat the shit out of me.

I'd heard the expression before, but this was my first first-hand experience with it. And I don't just mean by a police officer. This was the first time I'd been beaten up by *anyone* in the practice of my profession. Of course, as I say, my profession mainly involves cracks in the sidewalk, and who is apt to get too upset about that? But still.

At any rate, it was a first. And what a first. Though only an amateur myself, I would have to rate Sergeant Thurman as a pro. He was brutal, thorough, and painful. And, as I was to discover later, he didn't leave a mark.

Of course, Sergeant Thurman was probably a few years older than me, which meant he began practicing his chosen profession in the days before Miranda, in the golden days of the third degree and the rubber hose. I'm sure Thurman was a master of the latter. At any rate, he did a perfectly adequate job with his bare fists.

I can't say that I really blamed him. Well, I did, but intellectually speaking, you know. First off, I'd asked for it with the Abbott and Costello routine. And then by refusing to answer his questions. That was my right, but still.

The thing was, I knew Sergeant Thurman's point of view. I knew that, in his eyes, he wasn't a bad cop. That he didn't see anything wrong with using me as a punching bag. The good guys and the bad guys, that was how Sergeant Thurman saw it. The cops were the good guys, the crooks were the bad guys, and there was no in-between. And if I didn't want to help the good guys, then I was on the side of the bad guys, and I deserved what I got. And so did anybody else who wanted to help people break the law.

You think I thought all that as I was getting pummeled? Not hardly. I doped my feelings out later on. At the time, all I did was try ineffectively to cover up.

When I refused to answer Sergeant Thurman's question, he turned to one of the cops on the scene and said, "See I'm not disturbed." Then he grabbed me by the scruff of the neck, yanked me out the door, hustled me down the stairs, and dragged me around to the back alley.

Had there been an innocent bystander with a video camera in that back alley, we would have made the network news. And I betcha Sergeant Thurman would have made the LAPD look tame.

I didn't see the first blow coming. But I sure felt it land. Moments later I was puking my guts out behind a dumpster. Before I was even halfway finished I was straightened up and busted in the gut again.

After that, I could not clock the punches. But all were to the body, all were hard. There was another punch to the stomach that made me gag and vomit again, and yet another that I think made me pass out. It's hard to tell when you're having so much fun. The next thing I remember clearly was sitting in the back of a police car, all alone, staring at the bars in front and wondering if the doors were locked.

They were.

Sometime after that, I had no idea how long, Sergeant

Thurman came and climbed into the front seat. When he turned around to look at me, I was suddenly glad those bars were there.

"How's your memory?" he said.

"I remember being hit in the stomach."

"You wanna remember it again? Just keep makin' wise answers like that."

I did not *really* want to remember it again. I said nothing.

"Listen, asshole," Thurman said. "I got a dead woman here. You know something and I want it. So give."

"I want to talk to my lawyer," I said.

"Fine," Thurman said. "Let's see if he's in the back alley."

"You gonna beat me up again?"

"Again? Hey, I never laid a hand on you."

"Sure."

"Swear to god. I treat my suspects right."

"Suspect?"

"You got it, asshole. Any witness who don't talk is a suspect. That happens to be you. You're on my suspect list. You're on my shit list. You're slightly lower than garbage. You wanna get off, you drop the lawyer crap and loosen your jaw."

"I know my rights. I wanna talk to my lawyer."

Sergeant Thurman just sat there long enough for me to wonder if we were going in the alley again. Then he said with what for him had to be a rare display of patience, "You know who talks to their lawyers? Criminals. When you arrest 'em, they get their phone call, they call their lawyers. Witnesses, they don't call their lawyers, they tell what they know.

"Now, you say you got a right to call your lawyer? Well, sure you do. But not yet. Not if we're just talkin' here. Not unless I suspect you of something—I'm gonna arrest you—then you got a right to a lawyer.

"But the way things stand, what you're saying just don't make no sense."

"Right. Beaten senseless. Can I quote you on that?"

Thurman stuck out his jaw. "You can see a fuckin' demonstration. Now, I'm not gonna ask you again. You gonna talk or not?"

"I wanna call my lawyer."

"Fine. Like I said, you can only do that if you're under arrest. So, fuck you, you're under arrest."

"What's the charge?"

"Who gives a shit?"

Sergeant Thurman jerked the door open, got out, and went back inside. He came back minutes later with the two uniformed cops who had been the first to answer my call. I was not in good shape to judge, having just survived a severe beating, but it occurred to me they didn't look too happy.

Sergeant Thurman gave them some final instructions, went back inside. The cops got in the car and pulled out.

"Where we going?" I said.

The plumper cop, who was driving, said nothing, but the taller, thinner of the two turned around in his seat. "We're going downtown," he said. "You're bein' booked."

"Oh?" I said. "What's the charge?"

He muttered something unintelligible.

"What's that?" I said.

The plumper cop half turned around in his seat. "Drunk and disorderly," he said.

My mouth dropped open. "What the hell?"

The taller cop shrugged. "Orders is orders."

"I demand a breathalizer test."

"Sorry. We don't do that."

"What the hell—"

The taller cop held up his hand. "Listen. Take it easy. I understand you wanna call your lawyer. When we book you, that's your chance."

Fat chance.

I didn't have Richard's home number. When I called the office number, I got a service saying to leave a message and Richard would get back to me. I said it was an emergency and asked when Richard would get that message. And the nice woman on the line told me she was not at liberty to say.

Great.

That made two of us who weren't at liberty.

12.

They threw me in the drunk tank. A popular scene in TV shows, books, and movies. Only they never do it justice. In TV shows, books, and movies, it's always exciting and often humorous.

Tell me about it.

To begin with, it stank of vomit. I know that's a given, but even so. A description can't really suffice. You have to imagine the stench of large numbers of people vomiting again and again, building up over a very long period of time. The stale odor of old vomit mingling with the sharp, pungent odor of the new.

In a way, I was lucky I'd thrown up myself. I had my own nauseating breath to filter the atmosphere through.

But Jesus Christ.

It was a large room. Or cell. Or tank. Or whatever the hell you wanted to call it. The floor was stone. And wet. Wet with vomit, and wet with water sprayed on periodically with hoses to wash the worst of the vomit away. Not that that did any good. Probably merely served to freshen it up by keeping it moist.

In the cell were maybe twenty bunk beds. Rickety steel-framed affairs, with paper-thin, rotting mattresses. All were occupied, so there was no chance of my choosing one. Not that I would have. For any number of reasons.

Aside from the forty men in the bunks, there were another forty or fifty doing without. Some of these were actually—gag—sleeping on the floor. Others were standing along the side with their arms through the bars, as if for support. A few were conversing, if that's what you could call it, in a loud, obnoxious, slurred manner that left no doubt as to why *they'd* been interred. But most of the occupants of the pen were in no shape to do anything.

Which was fortunate. Because the one thing I was most afraid they would do was me.

I must admit I am a paranoid schizophrenic by nature. But I have to think that even if I'd been a brave man I would have been scared.

Raped in jail. That was the phrase that kept going through my head. Raped in jail.

A frighteningly real possibility.

I tried to tell myself this was just paranoia, but I couldn't make myself believe it. *Why me,* I asked myself. *There's almost a hundred people in this tank, why would they pick on me?*

Unfortunately, I had the answer: because I was probably the youngest, whitest, healthiest person there.

Is that racist? I don't know, but it happened to be a fact. The majority of the occupants of the drunk tank were minorities, mostly black and Hispanic. A larger number were old, and an even larger number were sickly, or at least appeared so as a result of either drugs or alcohol. By drunk-tank standards, a healthy, clean-shaven man in his forties was positively nubile.

I stayed off to one side near the bars and prayed they would not come.

They came.

First off was a skinny Hispanic who might have been anywhere from forty to sixty. He boasted a scraggly two-day growth, a missing front tooth, and breath that would have felled a bull elephant. Which was saying something, considering it had to penetrate the vomit stench to even be noticed.

He came over, leaned in conspiratorially, and said, "What you in for?"

I paused a second or two, trying not to breathe, then said, "Drunk and disorderly."

He stood there, looking at me. His eyes blinked twice. They traveled over my body, looking me up and down. I felt like meat.

"Same as me," he muttered.

That concept seemed to overwhelm him, and he wandered off.

I understood his confusion. He was dressed in close to rags and looked as if he'd been on a seven-day binge. I was, of course, still wearing my suit and tie. It occurred to me Sergeant Thurman was going to have a hard time making drunk and disorderly stick if this guy couldn't even buy it.

Next up I almost pissed in my pants. For a lot of reasons. For one thing, I really needed to go. There was a single seatless toilet in the far corner of the cell. But the one thing I knew for sure was that no matter how great the urge, there was no way I was whipping my dick out in front of these guys. But I certainly had the need.

I also had the impetus. It arrived in the form of a two-hundred-and-fifty-pound skinhead black man who looked like he could have played linebacker for the New York Giants. At least in soberer days. Now he looked lucky to be able to walk.

But walk he did, or at least stumble, far enough to reach where I was standing by the side of the cell. He lurched up, grabbed a bar for support, hung on, and leaned up close to me.

"Well, ain't you cute," he said.

Not exactly what I wanted to hear.

My heart started palpitating, and I wondered if I was about to have an anxiety attack. If not a heart attack.

Good god.

See what I mean? In a book, movie, or TV show, the hero would have some snappy comeback, joking bravely in the face of fear.

Well, sorry. I have to admit that at that moment my wits had left me, and I couldn't think of a single thing to say.

Instead, I weighed my chances. If the guy got hold of me, I was lost. If not, he was very drunk or stoned or whatever, and I could probably outrun him.

But I didn't want to run. Not there. In the drunk tank. Tripping through the vomit. With nowhere to go but round and around.

And that wasn't the half of it. I didn't want to run because I didn't want the others to see me run. Because to even the most drug- or alcohol-deadened mind, that would make me the *quarry*. The *hunted*. The *object of pursuit*. Not a role I particularly coveted. Not a part I wanted to play.

But I couldn't just stand there and let him grab me.

So what the hell could I do?

That decision was made for me when the gentleman in question suddenly belched, doubled over, and vomited at my feet.

I moved away, but it didn't look like flight. Arnold Schwarzenegger would have moved.

That was the last I saw of that particular chap. After recovering from his fit of indigestion he seemed to have forgotten all about me. Or so I concluded from my observation point, way on the other side of the cell.

No one bothered me for a while after that. I wondered if it was a result of the incident. If somehow I'd gotten a reputation. If people who hadn't really been watching had come to the conclusion that *I* had made the guy throw up. Slugged him in the stomach, perhaps.

At any rate, after that I was pretty much left alone. Pretty much. It was still a perfectly nerve-wracking experience. But after a while I got into a kind of a rhythm. A kind of turn, move away, tiptoe through the vomit, and reach another isolated spot to stand a while alone.

Never, of course, making eye contact. Not that tough for a New Yorker, already well disciplined in the art.

And so it went.

All fucking night long.

For of course I could not stop. Could not rest. Ever.

And so I played my game of paranoid, no-peek, hide-and-go-seek freeze tag keep away, from the time they threw me in the drunk tank right up until Richard showed up to bail me out at nine-thirty the next morning.

13.

"It's not that bad," Richard said.

I gave him a look. "That's easy for you to say. You didn't spend the night in the drunk tank. You don't smell like vomit."

Richard crinkled his nose, peered at me from behind his desk. "A valid point. I wonder if you should be sitting in that chair."

"Damn it, Richard."

He held up his hand. "Sorry. But you *do* need to get cleaned up. If I'm to work out any sort of deal."

"Do you think you can?"

"Oh, absolutely. That's why I say it doesn't sound that bad."

"Great,"' I said. "Listen, Richard. I've had no sleep. I spent the whole night absolutely terrified some huge drunk with AIDS would cornhole me. Largely because I don't have your unlisted number."

Richard shook his head. "The service should have called."

"Don't tell me. Tell them. Anyway, I'm too stressed out to appreciate subtleties. Just tell me straight out what you mean."

"Okay," Richard said. "What I mean is, from what you say, there's no real reason for anyone to assume you did this. The murder, I mean."

"This Sergeant Thurman's a moron. He won't *need* a reason."

Richard waved it away. "Fuck him. Who cares what he thinks. I'll deal with the A.D.A."

"How?"

"Like I said, make a deal. I'll get you immunity and you'll talk."

"Will he go for that?"

"He should. That's the nice thing about your story. As far as the cops are concerned, you've got a lot of information. About this guy Barry. About the porno prints. They'll eat that up. Plus, it's all a great reason why you had nothing to do with the killing."

"Why is that?"

"Because you're the dumb-ass messenger boy, of course. You're not important."

"Thanks a lot."

"Don't get huffy. I'm on your side. Anyway, that's why your story is nice. The only problem with it is, you gotta admit to a few counts of blackmail."

"Oh, come on."

He shrugged. "Hey, you're an accessory. But actually that's a big advantage. If you were innocent of the blackmail, it would be tough to prove. But what the hell. You're guilty. Which is real nice. I don't have to prove your innocence, just exonerate your guilt. Which is a snap. I get you immunity on the blackmail in exchange for your cooperation on the murder."

"Will they go for that?"

"They should, if I lay it out right."

"Yeah, but how? The guy's not going to know what my story is till I tell it. And I'm not going to tell it till I get the immunity. It's a chicken-and-the-egg situation."

"Or an after-you-Alphonse. But that's no problem. I am quite well versed at stating hypothetical situations.

"Then, of course, we have the benefit of this shit-head sergeant who threw you in the drunk tank."

"What about him?"

"He's a wonderful bargaining chip. We have a false arrest and unlawful imprisonment to trade against the blackmail counts. You should come out of this smelling like a rose."

"'Tis a consummation devoutly to be wished. Richard?"

"Yeah?"

"What about the murder?"

"What *about* it?"

"Someone killed her."

"I know."

"Yeah, but who?"

He shrugged. "That's not my job. Even if it were, my choices for speculation would be somewhat limited. Assuming it wasn't you, Barry and the couple in the pictures are the only people we know who are involved."

"Yeah, I know."

"Fine. So don't worry your head about it. Right now, let's us just clean up the details."

"Such as?"

"Let's start with the money."

Of course I'd had the blackmail money on me when I'd been arrested. It had been taken from me, along with my wallet, car keys, pocket change, belt, and beeper when I'd been booked. Everything else had been returned to me when I'd been released. But the envelope had been held for evidence.

"What about the money?" I said.

"First off, do you have any idea how much it was?"

"Probably five thousand dollars."

"Why do you say that?"

"Because that's what it was the first time."

"How do you know?"

"I told you. I saw it. Barry tore the envelope open, dumped it out on the bed. It was a stack of hundred-dollar bills, and from the size of it, it appeared to be fifty of 'em."

"And the envelope the cops have?"

"Same thing."

"Did you open it?"

"No, I didn't. But from the feel of it, that's what it is."

"So the cops are holding an envelope with five grand?"

"That's right."

Richard nodded. "Good. Then our position is, we want the money."

I looked at him. "What?"

"Well, why not? They're not entitled to it. That money was in your possession."

"Yeah, but . . ."

"But what?"

"It was given to me to pay blackmail."

"Pish tush. By a woman who's dead. What are you going to do, give it back to her?"

"No, but . . ."

"But what?"

"I'm wondering about the legality of the situation."

"Don't do that. I'm the lawyer. That's my job."

"Yeah, I know. But . . ."

"You worry too much. This is a minor matter. A detail to be straightened out. But if there's five grand kicking around, who should have it, us or the cops? Anyway, don't let it worry you. Let it worry me.

"Okay," Richard said. "I think the situation is quite clear. Our position is, they have our money and we want it back."

"Fine."

"So why don't you go home, get cleaned up. Meanwhile I'll line up this A.D.A. and we'll play 'Let's Make a Deal.'"

14.

A.D.A. Henry Frost looked like a chubby baby. A chubby baby with horn-rimmed glasses. They adorned a pudgy, round face, topped by thinning wisps of cornsilk hair, and they appeared totally out of place, as if some preadolescent had tried on his father's glasses in an attempt to make himself look older. A wholly unsuccessful attempt, by the way. A.D.A. Frost looked positively immature.

Which I found strangely disconcerting. Maybe it was just that it was later that same afternoon and I still hadn't had any sleep. Or maybe it was just that I was still shaken by the trauma of the drunk tank. Or maybe it was just that as I sink deeper and deeper into the sludge of my forties, the people around me seem younger and younger. But for whatever reason, it was a sobering thought that my fate rested in the hands of this child. And I must say, I found the prospect of being grilled by him positively weird.

Grilled. Maybe that was it. I expected to be grilled, even though by rights I shouldn't be. First off, Richard was there to protect me. Second off, he had made his deal. So I was free to say anything I wanted. I just didn't want. Because, even with immunity, confessing to something is just no fun.

A.D.A. Frost adjusted his glasses, nodded to the stenographer, and said, "Very well, let's begin."

Before he could ask his first question, Richard jumped in. "Yes, let's. Let the record show that I am Richard Rosenberg, and that I am present as attorney for Stanley Hastings. Let the record further show that my client, Stanley Hastings, has been granted immunity for any crime other than murder that may be revealed during the course of this questioning. That under those circumstances, I am prepared to waive his constitutional right against self-incrimination."

"Fine," Frost said. "Now, if we may get on with it." He turned to me. "What is your name?"

"Stanley Hastings."

"What is your occupation?"

"I'm a private detective."

"Are you acquainted with a woman by the name of Patricia Connely?"

I frowned. "Who?"

"Patricia Connely. Do you know a woman named Patricia Connely?"

"No, I do not."

A.D.A. Frost scowled. "Just a damn moment," he said. "What the hell's going on here?"

What was going on, of course, was that Marlena hadn't given me her right name. She was not Marlena at all, but some woman named Patricia Connely. Which of course I didn't know. On the other hand, since I'd refused to talk to the police, they didn't know I knew her as Marlena. Hence the total mix-up.

"Well, that's a fine state of affairs," A.D.A. Frost said. He looked very much like a sulky child. "So what have I got to do now, drag you down to identify the body?"

"Oh, come on," Richard said impatiently. "He's *seen* the body. All you have to do is refer to the body he found last night at the address on Prince Street. That's the body in question, he saw it, let's not waste each other's time."

"Right," Frost said. "Referring to last night, October 12. Did you have occasion to go to apartment 2A at 89 Prince Street?"

"Yes, I did."

"What, if anything, did you find there?"

"I found the body of a woman lying on the floor."

"Was she alive?"

"She was dead."

"What did you do?"

"I left and called the cops."

"Why did you leave?"

"I didn't want to touch anything in that apartment. I didn't want to use that phone. Actually, I don't think there *was* a phone in the apartment, but I didn't find that out till later. But if there had been, I wouldn't have used it. Anyway, I went out, found a pay phone, and called the cops."

"Okay. We'll come back to that. Referring to the woman you found in the apartment—had you ever seen her before?"

"Yes, I had."

"When and where was that?"

"Actually, the first time was two days before in my office, about nine o'clock in the morning."

"The woman met you there?"

"Yes, she did."

"You'd never seen her before that?"

"No, I had not."

"Did she have an appointment with you?"

"No, she did not."

"She just showed up?"

"That's right."

"She didn't call first?"

"No, she did not."

"Just came and knocked on your door?"

"Actually, she was waiting outside my door when I showed up at the office."

"And where is this?"

I gave him my address on West Forty-seventh Street.

"What name did this woman give you at the time?"

"Marlena."

"No last name?"

"Smith."

"She referred to herself as Marlena Smith?"

"That's right."

"Did she ever refer to herself as Patricia Connely?"

"No, she did not."

"Had you ever heard that name before?"

"Not before we began this discussion."

"Did you have any reason to believe Marlena Smith was not this woman's name?"

"No real reason. Except for Smith being a common alias."

"I see. And what did this woman ask you to do?"

"She asked me to deliver a package to a man named Barry and to pick up another package in return."

Richard cleared his throat. "I think I should step in here. We want to be absolutely clear and correct about this. What the woman stated at this time was that she was being blackmailed. What she asked my client to do was to take an envelope containing blackmail money and pay it to the blackmailer, in exchange for another envelope containing the evidence." He looked at me. "Isn't that substantially correct?"

I gulped. "Yes, it is."

"Fine," Richard said. "Proceed."

Frost seemed perfectly happy with that answer. "And you did that?" he asked.

"Yes, I did."

"What did you do, exactly?"

"I went to the appointed place. Which was a motel on the Saw Mill River Parkway. I don't recall the name, offhand, but I could find it all right. I went there. Unit twelve. And met this man Barry."

"Can you describe him?"

"Yes. He was somewhere in his late twenties, early thirties. About six feet, stocky, with red hair."

"Long or short?"

"Medium length. Curly."

"Freckles?"

I frowned. "He had a ruddy complexion. I'm not sure if it was freckles."

"Glasses? Mustache? Beard? Sideburns?"

"No. Clean shaven. No glasses."

"How was he dressed?"

I tried to think, but my mind was mush. "Slacks and a sleeveless shirt. Light blue. Leather jacket."

"Yes?"

"Yes, what?"

"Can you give us any more than that?"

"Not at the moment."

"Will you cooperate with the police sketch artist?"

I looked at Richard.

"Yes, he will," Richard said.

"Fine. Then let's move on. What happened when you met this man Barry?"

I described the scene in the motel, including Barry ripping the envelope open and dumping the money out on the bed and then showing me the blackmail pictures.

Frost seemed quite interested in them. "Had you seen the people in the pictures before?"

"No, I hadn't."

"You have no idea who they were?"

"No, I don't."

"But the woman in the pictures was not Patricia Connely, the woman who came to your office and gave the name Marlena Smith, the woman you later found dead?"

"Absolutely not."

"You say these were eight-by-ten, color glossy photos?"

"That's right."

"And in your opinion, they were posed?"

"That's right."

At least he didn't shake his head and tell me that didn't make any sense.

"And all this was on the day before you found the body?"

"That's right."

"And did you deliver these photos to the woman?"

"Yes, I did."

"When?"

"The next morning."

"And what did she have to say about it?"

"She was upset that the envelope was opened."

"Besides that. Did she make any comment about the pictures? Anything that would indicate who they were?"

"No, she did not."

"You didn't discuss the pictures with her?"

"Not as such."

"What does that mean?"

"Well, I brought up the fact that she only bought the pictures and not the negatives."

"What did she say to that?"

"That I was to mind my own business."

"She wasn't concerned that she hadn't gotten the negatives?"

"No."

"What happened then?"

"She took the pictures and left."

"And was that the last time you saw her before you found her dead?"

"Not at all. I saw her later that day." I jerked my thumb at Richard. "She called his office, asked them to beep me."

"Beep you?"

"Page me. On my beeper. They beeped me, I called in, and they told me she called."

"And left you a number to call her?"

"That's right."

"Did you call her there?"

"Yes, I did."

"And got her?"

"Yes."

"You have that number?"

"It would be in my notebook. You want me to look it up?"

"Please."

I fished my notebook out of my jacket pocket, located the page, and read the phone number into the record.

"So what did she want you to do?" Frost said.

"I was in Brooklyn, she was in Manhattan. She wanted me to drive in and meet her."

"Did you?"

"Yes, I did."

"Where?"

"Sheridan Square. On the corner by the cigar stand."

"You met her there?"

"Yes."

"At what time?"

"It was late afternoon. I spoke to her on the phone around four-thirty. Then I had to call on a client. By the time I got finished, I got back to Manhattan somewhere between six and six-thirty."

"You met her then?"

"Yes, I did."

"And what did she want?"

"The negatives. Now she wanted the negatives."

Frost frowned. "She told you she wanted to buy the negatives?"

"That's right."

"From this guy Barry?"

"Yes."

"She sent you back to the motel?"

"No."

I told him about the runaround Barry had given me on the phone. He seemed to find that quite interesting.

"Are you certain of the identity of the man you were talking to on the phone?"

"No, I'm not certain," I said. "In the first place, I have no idea who this Barry was—I only met him once. I assumed I was talking to the same person on the phone, and he certainly sounded like him. And he identified himself as him. But whether he actually was, I couldn't swear to it."

"But it was this voice that eventually sent you back to the motel. You found a note on the door of unit twelve with the address of the loft on Prince Street?"

"That's right."

A.D.A. Frost reached into his briefcase, pulled out a plastic evidence bag, and slid it across the table toward me.

"Is this the note you're referring to?"

I looked. It was indeed the piece of paper I'd found in the crack of the motel door. I'd completely forgotten about it, but it had been in my jacket pocket. The cops had taken it last night when they'd booked me and never given it back.

"Yes, that appears to be it," I said.

"You went to this address, walked in, and found the woman dead?"

"That's right."

"How did you get in?"

"The door was open."

"Are you referring to the downstairs door or the upstairs door?"

"Both were open. Or, rather, both were unlocked."

"And you went in and found the body?"

"Yes, I did."

"And then proceeded to call the police?"

"That's right."

Richard held up his hand. "I'd like to interject something here. If we could go off record for a moment."

Frost motioned to the stenographer. "Don't take this." Then to Richard, "Yes? What is it?"

"Before you ask any more questions pertaining to the finding of the body and the arrival of the cops, I'd like to make sure everything is entirely kosher here."

Frost frowned. "What do you mean?"

"Well, I notice you just presented my client with a piece of paper with an address written on it. I believe you stated that it is a piece of paper that was taken from his person."

"That's right."

"Well, I was not aware that that had happened. That the paper had been taken from his person and was being held in evidence."

"You have a problem with that?"

"I have no problem with that. I concede that the paper may be held in evidence. After all, it has no intrinsic value *other* than as a piece of evidence.

"However, this is not necessarily true in every case, and I would like to bring the matter up now."

"What matter?"

"I believe my client was in possession of an envelope, which was taken from him at the time of his arrest and has not been returned."

"I see. Would you be referring to the envelope your client has already testified the decedent gave him on the night of the murder? The envelope he was supposed to turn over to this gentleman named Barry?"

"That is correct."

"I'm not certain I follow this. Exactly what is your contention?"

"My contention is that the envelope was taken from the person of my client. As such, it must be considered my client's property. And he is entitled to it.

"Now, insomuch as it may be considered evidence, it may be opened, inventoried, and processed as such. And it is conceivable you could wish to cross-examine my client on it and even ask him to produce it in court.

"However, if, unlike the address you produced of the loft on Prince Street, the contents of this envelope should turn out to have some intrinsic value, it belongs to my client and it should be returned to him."

Frost's smile was somewhat smug. "That is your present contention?"

"It is."

He reached into his briefcase once again, removed a second plastic evidence bag. Inside was a fat envelope which had been slit open.

"Is this the envelope you are referring to?"

Richard looked at me. "Stanley?"

I shrugged. "I don't know. The envelope I had was sealed. This one appears to be opened."

"It was opened to examine the contents," Frost said. "However, I assure you it is the envelope that was taken from your possession."

I looked at Richard.

He said, "On your assurance that it is the same envelope, my client, without identifying it as such, states that it certainly appears to be."

"Fine," Frost said. "And your contention is that it should be returned to your client on the basis of the fact that its contents are valuable?"

"That is correct."

Frost opened the plastic evidence bag and took out the envelope. He turned the envelope upside down and dumped the contents out on the table, just as Barry had done on the motel-room bed.

I looked at it and gasped.

It was a thick packet, held together with rubber bands.

It consisted of pieces of newsprint, cut in the shape of dollar bills.

15.

I gawked at the table.

"That can't be right."'

"Stanley!"

I looked up to find Richard holding up his hand.

"Thank you," Richard said. "We may be off the record, but there is no reason for you to make a statement at this time. A.D.A. Frost has assured us this is the envelope you had in your possession. He stated that it was sealed when it was taken from you and then cut open. Under the circumstances, it would be highly inadvisable to make any statements concerning the envelope.

"Now, then, I suggest we go back *on* record and clear these matters up."

"Suits me," Frost said.

"Before we do," Richard said, "I would like to point a few things out. The contents of this envelope caught my client by surprise. As you observed. This happened while we were off the record. When we go back on record you are going to present my client with this evidence again. It will naturally *not* catch him off guard. However, you just saw what happened here. And since we're just talking off the record and it binds you in no legal way, I ask you to consider the fact that my client's astonishment at the contents of this envelope appeared genuine to me, and I'm sure it appeared genuine to you. In light of that, I would be *extremely* unhappy if a transcript of my client's statement was used at any later date to show that he did *not* appear surprised by the contents of this envelope—if it was used either explicitly or implicitly to imply that this was due to the fact that he himself had placed that newsprint in there."

"I assure you that is not my intention," Frost said.

"I'm glad to hear it. Because I would consider such action tantamount to breaking our agreement. And then other matters might come out."

Frost's eyes narrowed. "Such as?"

"Police brutality. False arrest."

"You waived those rights."

"Not in exchange for testimony," Richard said. "You and I would never be a party to that. My client is testifying in exchange for immunity. In the matter of the blackmail. We happen to have waived our right to sue, as a show of good faith. It was an oral stipulation, naturally, but I have no intention of reneging on it.

"However, the stipulation was only not to sue. It was not a gag order. If my client wants to tell what happened, he may."

Frost's eyes blazed. "That's dirty pool."

Richard matched his tone. "Is it?" He pointed his finger at me. "This man asked to call his lawyer before he talked. In return for this, he was savagely beaten and thrown in the drunk tank. I would say that went somewhere beyond Miranda/Escobedo. The ways things stand, Sergeant Thurman will not be charged and the police department will not be sued. But we expect some consideration at this point, and I should say we richly deserve it."

A.D.A. Frost had regained his composure. He smiled slightly. "I don't see what we're arguing about. You stated you would be very upset if I implied your client put those papers in that envelope. I assured you I had no intention of doing so. At which point, you got very upset anyway. Perhaps just to show me what would happen. At any rate, this is not the time for threats, promises, or what have you. I suggest we move on."

"Yes, let's," Richard said testily.

"Fine," Frost said. He sat back in his chair and folded his hands. He still looked like a baby wearing glasses, but his smile was rather smug. "However," he said, "I can quite understand an attorney being upset to learn his client didn't have five thousand dollars he thought he had."

That may have been the first time I've ever seen Richard at a loss for a comeback.

16.

Richard seemed perfectly satisfied. "Hey," he said. "Could be worse."

We were sitting in a small sandwich shop near the courthouse after our session with A.D.A. Frost. I was chugging down coffee and trying to keep my eyes open. Not that I was falling asleep. With everything that had just happened, my mind was going a mile a minute. But my eyes kept closing. It was as if my body was smart enough to know what my mind refused to grasp.

"Oh yeah?" I said. "Perhaps you could explain that to me. From where I sit it looks like a fucking disaster."

"Well, thanks a lot," Richard said. "Next time square your own blackmail rap."

"Yeah, I know. I'm sorry. It's just everything else."

"Right. What have you done for me lately?"

"Richard—"

He put up his hand. "Hey, I quite understand. Losing five grand's a bit of a kick in the ass."

"It's not that."

"Well, what is it? You want to sue that bastard Thurman? I can understand that, but it was simply not to be. You may feel like shit, but you don't have a mark on you. So it's your word against his. That false-arrest bit—so the guy made a mistake. We'd have to prove malice."

"You think there wasn't malice?"

"Hey, I know it and you know it. It's another thing to prove it."

"I know that, Richard. That isn't it."

"Then what's your problem?"

"My client's dead."

"That's hardly your fault."

"That's not the point."

"What's the point?"

"That five thousand dollars."

"So it *is* that."

"Yes and no."

Richard sighed. "You're too fucking complicated, you know it?" He leaned back in his chair, took a sip of coffee. "Do you understand what I just did for you? The cops had you dead to rights on blackmail. Two counts. They also had you as chief suspect in a murder." He put up his hand. "Now, granted, that's just because they didn't have any other suspects. But still. All in all, it was not an enviable position for a young gentleman to find himself in.

"Now, bear in mind I'm a negligence lawyer. This is not my field of expertise. But what do I do? I waltz into the courthouse and parlay all that into total immunity. Well, not on the murder, but no one seriously thinks you did it. It's a home run all the way around. And if that five grand had existed, you can bet your ass we'd have wound up with that too. It's the only thing I couldn't swing, and only because it wasn't fucking there.

"And then I ask you if that's what's bothering you and you say yes and no."

"I'm not upset we didn't get the money. Hell, getting the

money was your idea. I wouldn't have even thought of it. I'm upset that it was paper."

"Me too," Richard said. "But that's not what you mean, is it? No, you want to know who put the newsprint in the envelope and why it happened."

"Don't you?"

"No. If I thought the cops did it, and I thought I had a chance of proving it, then sure. There's nothing I'd like better than to make them cough it up. But I can't see that happening."

"You really think they did it?"

Richard shrugged. "This Sergeant Thurman does not strike me as an entirely honest cop. But he wasn't there when you were booked, was he?"

"No."

"Right. But there's nothing to stop him from showing up later. Identifying himself as the officer in charge of the case and asking to look at your personal possessions."

"Could you prove that?"

Richard held up his hand, fluttered it back and forth. "Iffy thing. The cop in charge is probably in his hip pocket. I'm not saying he'd lie for him, but he probably wouldn't volunteer anything. Which means you wouldn't get an answer till you got him in court. And even if you did, it's an iffy thing. Whether the cops did it, I mean."

"And if they didn't?"

"Your client handed you a packet of paper."

"That's what I can't understand."

"Do you have to?"

I sighed, nodded. "Yeah. I do."

Richard nodded. "See? That's the difference. I don't." He took a sip of coffee, cocked his head. "On the other hand, I'm only human."

I looked at him. "What does that mean?"

He smiled. "If you happen to find out, let me know."

17.

I didn't expect Sergeant MacAullif to be too pleased to see me. Last case we worked on together, he'd come close to beating me up. I'd spoken to him once since then. The only thing that had kept him from beating me up on that occasion was the fact we happened to be talking on the phone.

MacAullif was reading some report or other when I came in. I'm sure he was aware of my presence, though he took no notice of it and went on reading. After what seemed an interminable amount of time, he lowered the paper and looked up.

"You got a lot of nerve," he said.

"I beg your pardon?"

"Coming in here."

"I need to talk."

"You always need to talk. You're un-fucking-real."

"There's no reason to be hostile."

"No, of course not. You come in here to shit on a fellow officer. I should just sit back and applaud."

"What makes you say that?"

"I'm not dumb. You think I'm not up on the Patricia Connely homicide?"

"I'm glad to hear it. That's what I'd like to talk about."

"I bet you would. You should talk to Sergeant Thurman. It's his case."

"Last time I talked to him, I wound up in the drunk tank."

"Yeah, I heard about that."

"So?"

"So, it's embarrassing."

"Oh, really?"

"Yeah. Damn good idea. Wish I'd thought of it."

"MacAullif—"

"Imagine letting Sergeant Thurman steal a march on me like that."

"Very funny."

"And such a neat, effective idea. I bet you can't even prove false arrest, can you?"

"I've already waived it."

"You have? Son of a bitch. That makes it look like one hell of a dandy move now, don't it?"

"Yes and no. It got me out of two counts of blackmail. If Thurman hadn't jumped the gun, he might have nailed me on those."

"You got immunity?"

"You bet your ass I did."

"Then you *are* lucky. A smart cop would have nailed you to the wall."

"You sound like you're up on the case."

"Of course I'm up on the case. I saw you were involved, I said, holy shit, I'd better protect myself."

"Then you know why I'm here."

"Sure. You're a meddling, pain-in-the-ass son of a bitch can't leave well enough alone."

"I mean aside from that."

MacAullif squinted up at me. "You know, you look terrible. You been to sleep yet?"

"Not so's you could notice."

"Why don't you go home, get some sleep? Your brain's foggy, you're not thinkin' straight. Not that you ever did, but still. When you wake up, maybe you see things a little clearer. Maybe get a little smarter. Like, maybe you'll realize talking to me ain't such a great idea."

"Just who should I be talking to?"

"What A.D.A. caught this case?"

"Guy named Frost."

"Oh. Baby-Face."

"Oh? You know him?"

"Not personally."

"I see," I said. "You just know him from the guys making jokes."

MacAullif nodded. "Hmm. Maybe you're not too tired after all. Anyway, what's wrong with talkin' to him? Aside from the fact you might slip up and offer him a pacifier or something."

"I couldn't take this up with him."

"Why not?"

"It's rather delicate. That's why I'm asking you."

"Well, ain't this my lucky day. What's so fuckin' delicate?"

"How much do you really know about this case? I mean, you didn't know Frost was A.D.A."

"No. I just know you stumbled on a body and clammed up on Thurman, who threw you in the drunk tank."

"What about the blackmail?"

"What about it?"

"When I said I traded away two counts of blackmail, you said I was lucky, a smart cop would have nailed me on it."

"So?"

"So what do you know about the blackmail?"

"Nothing. I was just yankin' your chain."

I exhaled. "MacAullif."

"Hey, you're the one come chargin' in here giving me a hard time. You don't expect me to fight back?"

"Then you *don't* know about the blackmail. Right. Of course you don't. Because Frost didn't know till Richard made the deal. Well, that's the setup. The dead woman had hired me to pay blackmail. I was following telephone instructions from the blackmailer when I stumbled on the body."

MacAullif made a face. "Do I really need to know this?"

"Frost does, so you'll be hearing it anyway. What's the big deal?"

"Frost's an A.D.A. who grants immunity. Me, I'm a cop. I feel funny listening to a guy talking about paying blackmail."

"You rather I call it something else? How about a rent payment? The woman hired me to pay her rent and—"

"Fuck you."

"Anyway, I made one payment, bought the lady a nice set of dirty pictures."

"Of her?"

"No. Two other people I never saw before, but looked like porno actors."

"So?"

"So second verse same as the first, except now I'm getting the negatives."

"You didn't get 'em the first time?"

"Don't start with me. I was making a pickup and delivery, no questions asked, and no one was letting me call the shots. Anyway, the second time the guy I'm meeting is running me all over town before he's willing to hook up and make the switch. And the last place I wind up there's a corpse."

"Gee, what rough luck. A nice, legitimate private detective engaged in the perfectly respectable art of making blackmail payments and something like that happens. It's enough to make you cry."

"Here's the point. When I found the body I had the money on me. For the payoff. In a sealed envelope. When they booked me and threw me in the drunk tank, that envelope was taken from me along with everything else."

"So?"

"When I was released, they hung onto the envelope."

"Naturally. What's your point?"

"Frost produced it this afternoon. Only, when he did, it had been slit open."

"And?"

"Instead of the five grand I expected to find in it, it was stuffed with newsprint."

"No shit?"

"None. Which makes no sense at all."

"Why not?"

"I knew this woman. I talked to her. There's no way she throws me to the sharks with a packet of newsprint. I mean, why? What the hell could she possibly hope to gain?"

"I have no idea."

"Me either. So what if she didn't?"

MacAullif's eyes got hard. "What are you saying?"

"I'm talking about Sergeant Thurman. You once told me he's not the best of all possible cops. I wanna know, straight out. Would he take the money?"

"Not on your fucking life," MacAullif said. "Jesus, don't you learn anything? Don't you remember what I told you? Thurman's not the smartest cop in the world, but he's straight. At least he thinks he is. He might rough you up and throw you in the drunk tank, but bag five grand? No way. Sergeant Thurman don't *bag* five grand. Sergeant Thurman *busts* a cop who bags five grand."

MacAullif came around his desk, stood there towering over me. "You got that?"

"That seems rather clear. But in that case, where did the five grand go?"

"How the fuck should I know?"

He glared at me a moment, then turned around, walked back, and flopped himself down in his desk chair. He ran his hand over his head. "Boy, you're a pain in the ass," he said.

He opened his desk drawer, reached in, pulled out a cigar, and began to unwrap it.

I had him.

MacAullif's doctor had made him give up cigars. He'd quit smoking them, but he still played with them from time to time when he was thinking things out.

He took the cigar, rolled it between his hands, frowned. "Don't think I don't see your problem. Your client's dead and the cash disappeared. I put myself in your shoes, and I can understand your bein' unhappy." He leveled the cigar at me as if it were a gun. "Only, I wouldn't *put* myself in your shoes. Because to do that's condoning blackmail, and I don't condone blackmail. You got it?"

"I got it the first time."

He shook his head. "No. The first time was when this broad asked you to do it. You didn't get it then. If you had, we wouldn't be here."

"If you just want to lecture me—"

"Oh, right," MacAullif said. "Like *I* started this. Like *I'm* in *your* office giving *you* a hard time." He drummed the cigar on his desk. "Where was I? I dunno. Doesn't matter. Oh yeah. The money. You were askin' me what happened to the money. And I was gettin' pissed off at you askin'.

"All right. No. I'm not sayin' it's impossible a cop took it. But if so, it wasn't Thurman. If it wasn't Thurman, it isn't likely, so I don't think it happened at all."

He shrugged. "This Baby-Face Frost—like I say, I don't know him. Did he say *he* opened the envelope?"

I frowned. "I don't think so. I think he just said it was opened."

"Yeah. Well, like I say, I don't know him. But then I can't imagine a young A.D.A. riskin' his position for a measly five grand."

"We're in a recession."

"Tell me about it. But even so."

"What are you trying to say?"

"I think you should consider the possibility your client gave you a load of newsprint."

"That makes no sense."

"Maybe from your point of view. But you met the woman. I didn't. She got nice tits?"

"What's that got to do with it?"

"Colors the perception. See, I got no preconception whatsoever. Just think of her as the woman who gave you the envelope, a factor in the equation. You see her as this person you met and it fucks up your head."

"That's not true."

"Fine. I don't really want to debate it. Anyway, I got no problem with the idea she's the one pulled the number on you."

"You got no problem with that?"

"None at all."

"What about the fact it doesn't make any sense?"

"How do you know it doesn't? Try this. The woman wants the photos. Or the negatives. Or whatever. The guy's askin' five grand. Only, she ain't got five grand. So she takes a shot. She gives you a sealed envelope full of shit, hopes the guy won't notice till you made the switch, and you're outta there. Then if the guy ain't happy, she's got the pictures and the negatives, so there's nothing much he can do about it."

I shook my head. "Doesn't fly."

"Why not?"

"The first payoff was exactly the same thing. She gives me a fat envelope to buy the pix. Only, that envelope actually had five grand."

"Right. Which cleaned her out. Which is why she's broke now. Which is why she does the dirty."

"You don't understand. The reason I know there was five grand in there is, when I gave the guy the envelope, the first thing he does is rips it open, dumps the cash out on the bed."

"So?"

"So I told her that. So she knows he's gonna do that. *Before* he gives me the pix. So there isn't a prayer that could work."

MacAullif stuck his cigar in his mouth, waggled it back and forth. "So maybe she's setting you up."

"Huh?"

"Maybe it's a setup. Maybe she *knows* the guy will rip open the envelope. And she sends you there with it anyway. Maybe she's setting you up."

"Why? A woman I never met before?"

MacAullif took the cigar out of his mouth, held it up. "Aha. Not quite true."

I frowned. "What do you mean?"

"You met her *the day before*. You did a job for her. You paid blackmail money. You bought dirty pictures. You'd done the job, now she's through with you, she wants to get rid of you, so she sets you up."

"With the same fucking blackmailer? Tell me how that makes any sense."

"I don't *know* how it makes any sense. Because I don't

know what the facts are. But even without knowing anything, it makes more sense than a leopard changing his spots. Like Sergeant Thurman suddenly grabs five grand out of evidence."

"I get the point."

"Do you? Good. Now, why don't you go home, get some sleep, maybe you'll start thinking straight. Jesus. Come in here, ask me if a cop'll take five grand. Some would, sure. But not Thurman. But let me tell you something. You start makin' noises like he would, you're gonna piss him off.

"Which would not be wise. He's still the officer in charge of the case. And it would seem you're in pretty deep."

"Not anymore. I got immunity."

"On the blackmail, yeah. But you gotta remember, you're dealing with Thurman."

I frowned. "What do you mean by that?"

"Like I say, you're in pretty deep." He shrugged. "I don't suppose you happened to get immunity on the murder."

18.

I slept for sixteen hours. From five o'clock that afternoon till nine the next morning. It was a bit of a shock when I woke up and realized I'd done it. Nine o'clock? That didn't compute. I'm up at seven o'clock every morning to run Tommie over to the East Side Day School before heading out to work. Today Alice had taken him herself and let me sleep. I recalled that was her announced plan last night—or rather yesterday afternoon—before I passed out. Still, the actuality was a shock. Nine o'clock. How could it be nine o'clock? I ought to be at work.

On the end table, next to the clock radio whose digital readout by now actually said 9:06, was a handwritten note: *Take the day off.* I recalled this was also part of Alice's master plan. I would sleep late, she would run Tommie to school, then take the car to New Jersey, shopping. She would be free to take the car because I would not be working.

That was not *my* plan, that was Alice's. I had had no sleep, been beaten up and thrown in the drunk tank. After all that I still might have been able to deal with Sergeant Thurman, but I was no match for Alice. If she thought I was taking the day off, I was taking the day off.

Besides, running off to New Jersey with my car was a hell of a persuasive argument.

I stumbled out of bed, staggered into the kitchen, where Alice had left coffee in the percolator and another note. This one said, *Slow down. You're not working.*

I smiled. Alice's argument yesterday had been that I had just made fifteen hundred dollars in two days and I could damn well take the day off. Well, I sure as hell wasn't chasing around the five boroughs signing up accident victims via subway. I poured myself a cup of coffee, dialed Rosenberg and Stone.

Wendy/Janet was surprised to hear from me. She'd already gotten the message on the answering machine that I wasn't working today. I hadn't left one, of course—that was Alice.

There's no fighting Alice. I said I was just making sure she got the message and hung up the phone.

So what the hell was I gonna do today?

I had no idea, but I figured the decision could wait till I had coffee and read the paper. I sat down at the kitchen table where Alice had left the *Times* and the *Post*.

I wasn't surprised the *Times* hadn't covered the murder of Patricia Connely, but I expected to read all about it in the *Post*. After all, wasn't this the sort of thing the tabloid news thrives on—an attractive woman brutally slain? But I couldn't find a thing.

I wondered if the cops were sitting on the story. Or at least the blackmail angle, which would have really made it newsworthy. And if they were, I wondered if it had anything to do with the missing five grand.

Of course, it was none of my business. That was what Richard, MacAullif, and Alice had taken great pains to impress on me. It was out of my hands and there was nothing I could do. Alice's argument had been particularly strong, and her logic particularly forceful.

I knew why. Underlying all of Alice's judgment was a desire to keep me from having to deal with a moronic, brutal cop who hated my guts and who at the very least was apt to maim me and jail me, if not frame me or kill me. Which certainly made sense.

Or did it?

After all, Sergeant Thurman's only beef with me was that I wouldn't talk. Well, now I'd talked. Not to him, but to A.D.A. Frost. Still, Thurman would be privy to the information. And I was now free to discuss it.

I wondered if Sergeant Thurman might like to do that.

19.

“You got a lot of fuckin’ balls.”

I flipped open the front of my suit jacket, pretended to peer down the front of my pants.

Thurman’s scowl lines deepened. “Listen, asshole,” he said. “You’re probably too dumb to see it, but I got a short fuse on this one. You got about ten seconds to talk or you’re flyin’ out that door on your ear.”

“That’s a bad line to take,” I said. “If anyone’s got a beef, it’s me.”

“The hell!”

“I’m the guy got beat up, spent the night in the drunk tank.” I put up my hand. “And never mind the denials. It’s just you and me talking here. And I’m not wearing a wire. You wanna check?”

“I don’t give a fuck *what* you’re wearin’. You can wear a fuckin’ ballet outfit for all I care.”

"Fine," I said. "Anyway, now you know why I wouldn't talk. I had a perfectly good reason."

"Oh, sure," Thurman said. "'Cause you're guilty of blackmail. Just a nice, honest, upstanding citizen, exercising his constitutional rights. Makes me fucking sick."

"I take it you've been over my statement?"

"Good guess."

"So whaddya think?"

"I think it's a fucking crime you got immunity."

"Aside from that."

"I think you better get the fuck out of my office."

I took a breath. "Look. You were pissed off I wouldn't answer your questions. Now you're pissed off that I got immunity. The way things stood, I couldn't talk till I got it. Now I got it, now we can talk."

"Christ, you got a lot of balls. And don't look in your fuckin' pants again. What makes you think I got anything to say to you?"

"You were so hot to ask me questions, I thought I'd give you another chance."

"I got your signed statement now. That's all I need. Unless you were holding something back. Is that what you're trying to tell me? That you were holding something back?"

"Not at all."

"Then we got nothin' to talk about."

"Except . . ."

"Except what?"

"You got a case that doesn't make sense."

"It makes a lot more sense now. I mean, now I got your story. It's a blackmail. Things happen in a blackmail. Blackmail scheme, something's *apt* to go wrong. A lot of times, blackmail leads to murder."

"Yes," I said. I added gently, "But it is not the wicked blackmailer who lies dead, it is the lady."

Thurman frowned. "Huh?" he said. "What the fuck was that?"

That happened to be a line Hercule Poirot said in Agatha Christie's *Evil Under the Sun.* But I thought that explanation might be somewhat lost on Sergeant Thurman.

"Yeah, blackmail leads to murder," I said. "But isn't it always the blackmailer who gets killed? Right? The victim kills the blackmailer to shut him up. Or to avoid paying. At least that makes sense. But why would the blackmailer kill the victim?"

To my surprise, Sergeant Thurman had an answer. "What if he's double-crossed?"

"What?"

"What do you think the guy is, honorable? He's a blackmailer, so all he's gonna do is blackmail? No, he's a schmuck. That's why he's doing it in the first place. You do what he says, you pay him off, you make out fine. You cross him, it's another matter. You piss him off, he does one of two things. He makes good on his threat—smears you with the evidence you were trying to buy. Or he kills you."

"Yeah, but . . ."

"But what?"

"What good does that do?"

"It sends a nice little message to anyone else the guy may happen to be blackmailing that they'd damn well better pay up."

"Yeah. Maybe. But . . ."

"But what?"

"She didn't double-cross him. She was paying off."

"Oh yeah?" Thurman said. "What about the wad of newspaper you were carrying around instead of bills? It looked to me like she meant to double-cross him just fine."

Now that was mighty interesting. First off, it confirmed the fact that Sergeant Thurman knew about the bogus money. Which I could assume, since he was familiar with the rest of my statement. Second off, taken at face value, it would tend to indicate Sergeant Thurman wasn't the one who had made the switch. But most interesting about Sergeant Thurman's deduction was that he had made it. Frankly, I wouldn't have thought him capable of it.

Not that there weren't a lot of things wrong with it. Like the fact that it was totally ass-backwards and didn't add up.

"There's a small problem there," I said.

"Oh? Like what?"

"You're saying the guy kills her for double-crossing him by giving him bogus cash."

"Right."

"Except I got the bogus cash."

"Yeah? So?"

"So how does he know that? I haven't given it to him yet. It's in my pocket in a sealed envelope. It was still there when I found the body. She's already dead and I've still got the envelope and he hasn't seen it yet, so how does he know?"

Thurman shrugged. "How should I know? But say he does."

I sighed. That was the problem with dealing with Thurman. Logic wasn't going to get you anywhere.

"Yeah, but how?" I said. "The whole thing's gotta make sense. How does any of that make sense?"

"Who gives a shit?" Thurman said. "When I get the guy, I'll find out how. But the way I see it, the guy's got you out there running around with the cash. Meanwhile he and the babe hook up. How, I don't know, but most likely she isn't planning on seeing him, since she thinks you are. So he surprises her. Says, 'Hey, babe, I think you're doin' the dirty on me. You got your boyfriend runnin' around out there, but just between you and me, I don't think he's got shit. So I've decided on a little insurance. You're gonna be with me when he makes the payoff. And if it don't go smooth as silk, it's your ass.' And the broad panics and says, 'Hey, wait a minute. We can work this out.' And he wants to know what the hell there is to work out. And she panics because when you show up she's in deep shit, and to try to head that off and get out of it, she finally confesses to him there ain't gonna *be* no cash when you show up. Only it don't get her out of it, it gets her into it, 'cause when he hears that he blows her fuckin' head off.

"Now, how's about that?"

I would have loved to have pointed out a flaw in the reasoning. But on the spot, standing there gawking at Sergeant Thurman, I have to confess, I couldn't think of a thing.

Which shouldn't have been that surprising. I mean, yeah, Thurman was dumb. But even a stupid person has *some* reason for his opinions. After all, the guy was in charge of the case. He couldn't have no theory at all. So why should it be such a shock when he did?

I guess it was just that I didn't think him capable of any theory more complicated than the private eye found the body, so the private eye must have done it.

Maybe that was it.

Maybe I was just shocked to find he suspected someone other than me.

"So you think this guy Barry might be it?" I said.

"I'd certainly like to talk to him." Thurman cocked his head. "It's a little hard with the description we got to go with."

I winced. After I'd given A.D.A. Frost my statement I'd put in an hour with a police sketch artist, trying to come up with a likeness of Barry. The end result resembled him somewhat, but probably no more so than it did Woody Allen, Bo Jackson, or Connie Chung.

"Maybe so," I said. "But if you start digging around in her background, you're bound to come up with him. So whaddya got so far?"

Sergeant Thurman frowned. "Excuse me?"

"On the dead woman. Patricia Connely. What have you got on her? Let's see if it has any connection to this guy Barry."

"Are you kidding me?"

"No. I know you're looking for this guy Barry, I thought maybe I could help."

"Well, ain't that sweet. Why you so eager to help me?"

"I'd like the matter cleared up."

"Oh, you would? What, are you related to the commissioner? 'Cause he'd like it cleared up too. Maybe the two's of you should get together. See what else you can come up with."

"Yeah, great," I said. "So, you wanna see if there's any way we can connect these two up?"

Sergeant Thurman cocked his head. "You're askin' me if I'd like your help?"

"No, not really. I—"

"You're offering to help me solve this crime?"

"No, I'm just—"

"You're down here in my office with more balls than you find on the average guy, and you'd like me to tell you what I know—and let me be sure I got this right—so that you can tell me what it all means?"

"Oh, now look."

Sergeant Thurman pointed his finger. "Get the f*uck* out of my office. Get the *fuck* out of my life. And get the *fuck* out of this case. You got no business messin' around in this. I catch you messin' around in this, you know what it's gonna make me think? It's gonna make me think you're more mixed up in this than I think you are. So maybe I don't have to find this Barry creep after all. Maybe I got my killer right here."

On second thought, maybe Sergeant Thurman really *didn't* want to talk to me.

20.

There's more than one way to skin a cat.

Now there's a phrase. Aside from delighting cat lovers everywhere, just what the hell does it mean?

I know what it's *supposed* to mean—that there's more than one way to do something. But where did skinning cats come into it? Who the hell ever skinned a cat, and for what reason? It's not like you were going to make something out of it. I mean, I could see someone getting pissed off at a cat yowling all night, and going out and wringing its neck. But skinning it? That seems a little much.

Now please don't write in. This is not an attack on cats, just on our language. And I didn't make the damn phrase up. It just occurred to me when I bumped into the Sergeant Thurman stone wall. That there was more than one way to skin a cat.

Which makes about as much sense to me as the cat's pajamas. But that's another story. Unless the pajamas were made to dress up a skinned cat.

Anyway, if Sergeant Thurman wasn't going to talk, I had to try something else. I just had to figure out what.

I was on my way down into the subway station when I got my first clue. It came in the form of a *New York Post* headline staring up at me from a paper in a trash can. The headline was "Guilty!" I'd seen the headline in the *Post* this morning and that wasn't it. I wondered who'd been found guilty that was so important the *Post* had gotten out an extra with a new headline.

They hadn't. And when I realized, it explained a lot. It was yesterday's paper. I hadn't seen it because I'd been in the drunk tank, which had knocked me twenty-four hours into the future. Which is why the Patricia Connely murder hadn't been in today's paper. It was yesterday's news.

"Actress Slain" was the headline on page nine. That stirred memories. I hadn't known Patricia Connely was an actress, but if so, she was the second one I'd known who'd been murdered. I pushed the thought from my mind, read the story.

It was sketchy at best. A Patricia Connely had been found shot in a loft in SoHo. There was no evidence of robbery or rape, and the police had no suspects or motive. The article gave her address on East Ninety-first Street and said she was survived by her husband, Bradley. It occurred to me if he actually happened to live at that address, it would be the cat's meow.

He did.

The address turned out to be a high rise between Park and Lex, and when I asked for Mr. Connely, the doorman nodded, picked up the house phone, and buzzed upstairs.

"And who shall I say is calling?" he asked.

"Stanley Hastings."

He listened a moment, said, "Yes, a Mr. Stanley Hastings to see you." After another moment he looked at me and said, "And what is this with regard to, sir?"

"It's about his wife."

The doorman gave me a reproachful look—if I was a plainclothes cop, I should have said so. If not, I shouldn't be there. However, he relayed the message and got the approval to send me up.

"Sixteen D," he said, pointing in the direction of the elevator.

I went up to the sixteenth floor, located apartment D, and rang the bell.

I was in for a bit of a shock. The door was opened by a young man with long blond hair. That in itself wasn't strange. What was strange was the uncanny resemblance. You know how some people get to resemble their dogs? Well, Mr. and Mrs. Connely had gotten to resemble each other. His long blond hair curled under, and his thin, sensitive face made him look very much like his wife.

"Mr. Connely?" I said.

"Yes?"

"I'm Stanley Hastings."

"I'm sorry, but I don't place the name."

"Surely the police must have mentioned me. I'm the man your wife hired." I paused a moment. "And the one who found her."

"Oh," he said. He looked at me as if seeing me for the first time. "Oh. Of course. Please. Come on in."

He ushered me into the living room, asked me to sit down. The room was furnished in what I guess would be described as starkly modern—chrome and leather furniture, Plexiglas coffee table. I looked around for his favorite chair, couldn't spot it, decided to wait for him to sit. He did, on the couch, and I took a chair opposite.

"Now," he said, "you're not with the police?"

"No."

"No, of course not," he said. "Forgive me if my thoughts are scattered. It's all such a shock."

"I understand."

"Do you?" he said. It wasn't sarcastic, but it wasn't a question either. Even rhetorical. Just sort of musing aloud. Then he looked up at me, and his eyes were wide. "I'm trying to understand, that's the thing. It's all sort of overwhelming. I'm trying to understand, but it doesn't seem to make any sense."

I caught myself on the brink of saying "I know" again. If he wanted to talk, I should let him talk.

When I didn't answer, he looked up at me. "Maybe you can help me," he said.

"How?"

"I don't know. But you were there. You talked to her. This whole wild scheme." He ran his hand over his head. "I'm saying it badly. See, I'm the husband. The police told me what happened. But maybe they didn't tell me all, you know? Because I'm the husband. So they try to shade the truth. Make it less awful." His lip quivered. "Less awful. How could it be worse than she's dead?"

I am not good with grieving kin. I'm not sure who I am good with, but a grieving spouse has to be way down on the list. I wished the hell I was somewhere else.

As if sensing that, he pulled himself together. "I'm sorry. I was trying to tell you how you could help."

"Yes?" I said.

"Like I said, the police may not have told me everything. But you were there, so you know. So you can fill me in."

I didn't like it. I felt like I was finking on my client to her husband. I know she was dead, but even so.

"Didn't you know about it?" I asked him.

He shook his head. "Not a damn thing."

I took a breath. "Okay," I said "Tell me what the police told you. I'll see if they left anything out."

I could tell that didn't suit him. He wanted me talking, not him. I could see him trying to think of a way of insisting. Either he couldn't come up with one or decided it was easier to give in.

"Okay," he said. "What I know is sketchy at best. My wife hired you to pay off a blackmailer. Why, I couldn't imagine. Her life is beyond reproach. She's never done anything to warrant blackmail. The whole idea is just absurd." He paused, took a breath. "But as I understand it, the pictures you bought had nothing to do with her. They were of someone else."

And not you, either, was the thought that flashed to mind. Not that I'd ever thought they would be. On the other hand, there was no reason to assume they wouldn't.

"That's true," I said.

He shook his head. "Then the whole thing makes no sense. No sense at all. But that doesn't matter, does it? Because we have to carry on as if it did."

"Exactly," I said. "That's the whole problem."

"Okay, then where was I? Oh yes. The pictures. She hired you to get the pictures. From a sleazeball named Barry."

"That's right," I said. "And I assume the police have looked."

He looked at me. "I beg your pardon?"

"For the pictures. I gave your wife the pictures. I'd assume the police made some effort to find them."

He nodded. "They were here, yes. Searched the place from top to bottom." He shook his head. "Didn't find a thing."

"Is there any other place your wife might have kept them?"

"Exactly what they asked. But no, there isn't."

"So she must have given them to someone."

"Of course. Whoever she was getting them for. Who would most likely be one of the people in the pictures." He looked at me. "The police gave me a description. I assume that was based on your account. It was sketchy at best. I wonder if you could do any better."

Oh boy. My only real impression of those people was that they appeared to be porn actors. Which was a description I wasn't eager to give, in case they turned out to be friends of his.

I said, "There isn't a prayer I could describe those people well enough for you to recognize them. If there was some individual feature or mark, something distinctive. But there wasn't. It really could have been anyone."

That didn't sound too convincing to me, but he didn't press it.

"All right," he said, "but what about the guy—this Barry—what was he like?"

"Overbearing. Obnoxious. What you would expect of a blackmailer."

"What did he look like?"

I had a wild impulse to say, "Connie Chung with red hair." I can't help it. As a frustrated writer, images flash on me, usually comic ones. And often at inappropriate times. This was sure one of them. I had to tell myself, it's his wife, for Christ's sake. Even so, I think the corners of my mouth quivered.

"He was big, stocky, maybe six foot, with curly red hair. Clean shaven, no glasses, no scars, no other identifying features. He had a sardonic sense of humor, seemed to enjoy pushing me around."

"In what way?"

I tried to think. "Well," I said, "maybe this is colored by my perception. But I'd been told not to open the envelope—the one with the pictures in it. He ripped it open, made a point of showing the pictures to me. Seemed to get a kick out of doing it."

Connely nodded. "I see. Did *he* know who the people in the pictures were?"

"If so, he didn't let on." I frowned. "That sounds wrong. I mean, it wasn't like he was trying to hide anything either. What I mean is, nothing he said would tend to indicate one way or the other. See what I mean?"

"I think so. Though it's not particularly helpful."

"No, it isn't."

"Now, as I understand it, she paid you money. Is that right?"

"Yes. She did."

"How much?"

"Five hundred dollars the first time, a thousand the second."

"Fifteen hundred in all?"

"That's right."

"Plus the money you paid him?"

"Yes."

"And how much was that?"

"I don't know for sure. My best guess is five thousand dollars."

"Based on what?"

"What I saw. This guy Barry ripped the envelope open, dumped the money on the bed. I saw bills held together with a rubber band. The denomination I saw was a hundred. If the packet was fifty, that's five grand."

Connely shook his head. "That's what doesn't make any sense."

"What do you mean?"

"Patricia and I have a joint account." He blinked. Gulped slightly. "*Had* a joint account. Both checking and savings. But just the two accounts. That was all. And I've been to the bank. Along with the cops. And the bank confirms—she didn't take out any of that money. None of it. From either account. There are no unusual cash withdrawals."

"I see," I said.

"So everything points to the fact that she was doing this for someone else."

"Right," I said. "And you have no idea who?"

"None at all. There's no one she's that close to, who's that great a friend, that she would take such a risk."

I didn't comment, but I took that remark with a grain of salt. An actress in New York City just might get involved with some other actor her husband didn't know about.

"The paper said she was an actress," I said. "Is that right?"

"Aspiring actress," Connely said. He smiled sadly. "I wonder how they missed that word. Yes, we're both actors. Would-be actors. Aspiring."

"Was there anyone she was working with—who might have gotten in trouble?"

He shook his head. "But she wasn't, you see. She did a showcase two years ago. And we've both done summer stock."

"Recently? Do you make the rounds?"

"We audition, yes. And we know people in the business. But no one this applies to."

"How can you be sure?"

"If my wife had been seeing someone, I would know. I don't mean like that—another man. I mean if she were handling a blackmail payoff for someone. She'd have to meet them, discuss it, get money from them, give them the pictures. See what I mean? And I wasn't aware anything like that was going on."

"Do you work?" I said. "I beg your pardon. Outside the home, I mean. Aside from the acting."

He shook his head. "I'm an investment broker," he said.

"But not on Wall Street. I have my own office here. No need to go out, with computers, modems, fax machines. I can handle everything from here quite nicely."

"Then didn't your wife ever go to auditions without you?"

"Oh, of course," he said. "You're saying she must have had the opportunity to meet someone. Well, that goes without saying. It happened, so she did. What's strange is the fact that I had no inkling of it. That's why it's all such a shock."

"I understand."

Damn. I said it again. Fortunately, this time he took no notice.

"Now then," he said. "As I understand it, the second time you went out, you were to get the negatives?"

"That's right."

"Patricia gave you an envelope to make the payoff?"

Shit. I wondered if the police had told him about the phony money.

"That's right," I said.

It turned out they had.

"Now, this envelope had nothing in it? No money, I mean. Just paper."

"Newsprint," I said. "Strips cut from newspapers."

He ran his hand over his head, then shook it slowly. "That's the other thing. She wouldn't do that. Patricia. She was the kindest person in the world. If she knows what's in it, there's no way she gives you that envelope."

"Maybe she didn't know."

He nodded. "That's the only way I can see it. And if that's true, it's just too cruel. It's like she died for something she didn't know."

"I beg your pardon. I'm not sure I follow that."

"If that's why she was killed."

"I wouldn't think so," I said. "That envelope was in my possession. Unopened. How could the killer know what was in it?"

Connely considered that. "You're right," he said. "I'm upset. I'm not thinking clearly. There's no theory accounts for that."

I didn't point out a sergeant named Thurman had come up with one. In the first place, it was so convoluted I didn't feel like explaining it. In the second place, I was glad to see someone agreeing with *my* opinion.

"Right," I said. "I think we have to conclude these are ruthless people, and the killing would have occurred whether the money was phony, genuine, or what."

Connely sighed heavily. "Then we're right back where we started."

I had a feeling I knew where that was, but I waited for him to say it.

He did.

"The whole thing makes no sense."

21.

"He did it."

"I don't think so."

I could understand Alice's opinion though. It was actually the same as MacAullif's—that, in a homicide, the most likely person was usually the spouse.

But not in this case. There were just too many other things going on.

"Why do you say that?" Alice persisted. "Because you like him?"

"That's got nothing to do with it," I said.

I was sure it didn't. In fact, I hadn't even considered the question, whether I liked Bradley Connely. I *felt sorry* for him, sure. But like him?

Well, maybe. I suppose I appreciated the fact that when he found out I wasn't from the police, he didn't throw me out on my ear. And it didn't hurt that he was willing to treat me as an equal and discuss the crime. But I assure you, none of that made me grateful enough to exonerate him from murder if the clues happened to point his way. If they did, I'd be perfectly happy. The fact is, they didn't.

"Alice, I don't know if I like the guy or not. It's just, logically, I don't think he did it."

"Uh-huh," Alice said.

She was only half listening. It was later that night, and she was in our bedroom watching her favorite soap opera. She'd missed it earlier in the day by taking the car to New Jersey. But through the miracle of VCRs and video tape, we were able to have the same parade of plastic people grace our TV set at nine o'clock at night. And they say there's no such thing as progress.

The soap-opera dialogue was getting on my nerves. So was Alice's insistence that Bradley Connely must be guilty. The combination of the two made me reckless, drove me to do something I should never do.

Argue with my wife.

"She was mixed up in a blackmail plot, Alice," I said. "There were thousands of dollars involved. The police have been over her books. And his. The money didn't come from their accounts. It's not just some husband-wife tiff."

"I didn't say it was simple," Alice said. "It could be quite complicated."

"Such as?"

"There could be another woman involved."

I jerked my thumb at the screen. "Like one of your soap-opera plots?"

"Why not?"

"Indeed. Why not?" I said. "So there's another woman involved. Maybe the woman in the photographs. Having an affair with her husband. Who's being blackmailed. So kind, broad-minded, understanding Patricia Connely does them both a favor by trying to get the pictures back."

"There's no reason to be sarcastic," Alice said.

"I'm sorry. I just haven't been having an easy time."

"Whose fault is that?"

"Hey."

Alice pressed a button on the remote control. On the television, two soap stars froze inches away from an embrace.

"I thought we'd been over all this," Alice said. "Your part in the case is over. Richard got you immunity and got you out of it. There's no reason for you to do anything else."

"I have an obligation—"

"No, you don't. What, an obligation to a dead woman? To do what? Get those pictures back? Getting those pictures was your job, you didn't get them, so you didn't do it?"

"Well, there's that."

"No, there isn't. She gave you play money. So there was no way you could have done the job, even if things had worked out."

I said nothing, which is usually my only defense in arguing with Alice.

Tonight it wasn't working. "You know why you're doing this?" Alice persisted. "You know why you won't let go?"

"No, why?"

"That cop. That Sergeant Thurman."

"You mean he's so dumb I figure he can't solve it himself?"

"No," Alice said scornfully. "Come on. That's no motive."

"Motive?"

"Yeah. For why you're doing what you're doing. Everyone has a motive. You just have to look for it. And a motive isn't intellectual. It's instinctual. It's basic."

"Have you been watching PBS again?"

Alice ignored that, bored in. "So you know what your motive is?"

I sighed. "No. What?"

"Revenge."

"Huh?"

"That's all. Revenge. Simple. Basic. The cop beat you up and threw you in the drunk tank. You're angry and you want revenge."

"Oh, come on."

"Don't be so defensive. There's nothing wrong with that. It's perfectly natural. What's *un*natural is not being able to admit it. So look what you do. This afternoon you go down to the guy's office to try to discuss the case. Just as if nothing had happened. Well, that's bullshit. Because something *did* happen. You're mad as hell at this guy. But you're down there in his office, pretending to be something you're not. Pretending you'd like to help him with the case. But you'd really like to stick a knife in his back. Show him up and let everybody see what a stupid, brutal bully he is."

I ran my hand over my head. "Good god."

"There's nothing wrong with feeling like that," Alice said. "You shouldn't repress it. If that's how you're feeling, admit that's how you're feeling. Then you'll feel better."

Oh boy. I didn't need to hear that. As I say, it's hard enough to argue with Alice anyway. But on top of that, to get an amateur psychiatric opinion of my behavior was a little much.

Particularly when there might be a grain of truth in it. A small one, but enough to make the whole thing distressing.

I don't know what I would have said just then, but I was saved from having to by the VCR snapping off. It does that if you freeze the picture for too long, shuts off automatically so as not to burn the video tape. Of course, when that happened the regular TV channel came on. It was a sitcom, and it was loud as hell. That's because the video tape doesn't play as loud as the regular TV, so Alice had the volume way up. After the silence of the frozen soap opera, the roar of canned laughter from the sitcom was really jarring.

Alice hit the play button on the remote control, starting the VCR again. After a moment's delay, and a whir from the VCR, the soap-opera stars finally embraced and kissed.

Alice let it play. Praise the lord. The soap stars finished kissing and resumed talking. I wondered for the hundredth time who writes this garbage, and for the thousandth time wished I did.

While Alice sat up watching the soap, I lay in bed and reassessed the day in light of what she'd just said. Was I doing all this for revenge? I sure hoped not. What a petty, unflattering motive that would be.

But why *was* I doing it? What did I hope to accomplish? Particularly if neither Sergeant Thurman nor MacAullif were going to cooperate. There was so much information I didn't have access to.

The gun, for instance. Surely by now the police had traced the gun. Knew where it came from. Knew if there were any fingerprints on it. Even knew for Christ's sake if it had actually fired the fatal shot.

Little things like that.

So what the hell was the point of me trying to compete with them? Unless, as Alice said, it was to take revenge against Sergeant Thurman. Because I certainly had no standing in the case.

Though I sure wanted some. It occurred to me that the whole time I'd been talking to Bradley Connely I'd been keenly aware of the fact that here was an interested party with enough money to hire me to investigate, if he saw fit. The fact that he hadn't had been a disappointment. And not just for the money. It would have been nice to have had official standing in the case. Only, now I wondered if part of the *reason* having official standing in the case would have felt nice was because it would have given me a motive *other* than taking revenge against Sergeant Thurman.

Boy, can Alice fuck up my head.

As I lay there in bed and the soap opera droned on, it occurred to me that Alice was usually right, and much as I hated to admit it, she was probably right in this case. And the best thing I could do for myself and Alice and Sergeant Thurman and Sergeant MacAullif and Baby-Face Frost and Bradley Connely and his dear departed wife and all concerned would be to butt out and go about my business. After all, I hadn't worked for Rosenberg and Stone today, and if I didn't work for Rosenberg and Stone tomorrow there would be no money coming in. I should call up first thing in the morning and tell Wendy/Janet I was on the beeper and I needed a case. Yeah, that was what I ought to do.

I looked over at Alice, wondering if I should inform her of my decision. Though to do so now would look too much like I'd been beaten into it.

A commercial came on and Alice picked up the remote control and fast-forwarded through it. It occurred to me that I wished there were parts of life you could fast-forward through. My drunk-tank experience, for instance.

As I watched the images dance across the screen, my eyes suddenly widened.

"Stop!" I cried.

Alice looked at me in surprise. "What?" she said.

To do so, she had taken her finger off the fast-forward button, and now the tape was playing at normal speed. It was a commercial for Double-Mint Gum, complete with singsong jingle.

"Back it up," I said.

Alice stared at me. "What?"

"Back it up."

Alice pressed the rewind button. The tape lurched, and the images on the screen marched backwards.

"Stop," I yelled again.

Alice released the button, let the tape play. She squinted at me sideways, puzzled that I would be so interested in a soap-opera commercial. It didn't help that it turned out to be for a hemorrhoid preparation.

"Freeze that," I said.

Alice pressed the button, froze the picture.

As she looked at the screen, her frown disappeared and her eyebrows raised.

I nodded. "It's him," I said.

I'm not great at faces. Alice is always pointing to people on TV or in the movies and saying, "Do you know who that is?" and I never do.

But in this case I did. There was no doubt about it.

The face on TV, with the curly red hair and the deep frown lines, supposedly brought on by his painful itch, was none other than your friendly neighborhood blackmailer, Barry.

22.

It wasn't easy.

I couldn't begin to tell you how many phone calls it actually took. All I know is it included calling the station, taking a wrong turn with the soap-opera production company, getting steered to the network to talk to an executive responsible for selling commercial time, then back to the station again to talk to the executive there in charge of selling local commercial time.

Next, a word from our sponsor. Who wasn't *that* disappointed to find I wasn't interested in buying suppositories, and who eventually steered me to the Madison Avenue agency that had produced the spot.

After that I only had to go through three or four people before locating the one who actually had the information. And only three or four more before obtaining clearance for that individual to release it.

But the end result was by eleven-thirty the next morning I had a name and address, all without leaving my apartment.

The name wasn't Barry. It was Cliff McFadgen. I figured the McFadgen might well be genuine, but had doubts about the Cliff, which sounded like a stage name. Not that it mattered—as far as I was concerned the guy was Barry, the guy was a blackmailer, and the guy was in deep shit.

I suppose I should have just called up Sergeant Thurman and dumped this in his lap. But I could think of a lot of reasons why I didn't want to do that. And if revenge was one of them, so be it. If I'm going to get revenge, I might as well make a good job of it.

I suppose I could have called up MacAullif. But after the coolness of our last meeting, I wasn't sure how he'd take it. Actually, I figured he'd just refer me to Sergeant Thurman.

On the other hand, I could have called Richard and told him what I intended to do. Or at the very least, I could have waited till Alice got home and told her where I was going.

But the thing is, I never really stopped to think. I was a bloodhound on the scent, and the minute I got the name, I was out the door like a shot.

The address was an apartment house on West Seventy-fourth between Amsterdam and Columbus. I drove down, got a parking meter on Broadway, and walked on over.

It was a brownstone, which figured. The apartment was 3A, which was apt to be a studio on the third floor.

I went up the front steps into the small foyer and checked the mailboxes. Sure enough, 3A was Cliff McFadgen.

There was a buzzer, of course, with a call box. But it occurred to me I wasn't really set with a snappy response when Cliff called down, "Who is it?" I wasn't sure just what I could say that would get me in the door. Open Sesame? Probably not.

The door in question had a spring lock that looked formidable, but was actually somewhat exposed. When I examined it, I found a sizable crack between the door and the frame.

The lock itself I was sure I could never deal with, but the gizmo attached to it, the thing that sticks into the door, whatever the hell they call it, the thing detectives on TV always "loided" with a credit card, looked vulnerable as hell. If I'd tried that, I'm sure that part of the card with my name on it would have snapped off and gotten stuck in there, qualifying me for the Asshole Detective of the Year award. But there was another way. The gap between the door and the frame was so wide I was able to slide my house key into it, gouge it into the metal gizmo, and slide it back.

And the door opened.

I can't tell you what a thrill that was. After all my years as a private detective, after all the cases I've handled, this was my first picked lock.

Considering that, I count it to my credit I didn't stand around admiring it. Instead I slipped right inside and closed the door. There was a door to my right marked 1A and a stairway to my left. I took the stairs up one flight to a hallway with two doors, the nearest marked 2B, and went up another flight that ended near a door marked 3A.

There was a peephole in the door, of course. I wondered what Barry or Cliff McFadgen or whatever the hell he wanted to call himself would do when he saw me through it. I considered knocking on the door and standing off to one side so he wouldn't see anything when he looked through. But would he open the door under those circumstances? Would anyone? No, I was perfectly content to let him get the shock of his life looking out and seeing me standing there.

Except for two things. One, I wouldn't be able to see his face when he did, and somehow I really wanted to. And two, if he was a killer, what if he started shooting through the door?

I told myself that was silly. The blackmailer doesn't kill the blackmail victim. The guy got mixed up in something that got out of hand, and it's backfiring in his face. The poor guy probably needs help. He'll probably be glad I found him.

Yeah, sure.

Maybe I should just call the cops.

That thought was the impetus I needed. I sure wasn't calling Sergeant Thurman. I took a deep breath, banged on the door.

No answer. Wouldn't you know it. I pick my first lock,

then go through all that mental anguish, and the guy isn't even home.

I banged again with no hope. This had to be a studio apartment. There was no way the guy couldn't hear the door. He simply wasn't there.

I would have liked to have gotten in, searched the place. Optimally, turned up the missing blackmail photos and clinched the case. But the police lock on the door looked prohibitive. And in this case, there was no space between the door and the jamb. Still, I tested the bolt by jiggling the knob.

And the door clicked open.

Uh-oh.

This was not in the normal course of events. This did not compute. I don't give a damn what the situation was, there was no way that door should be open.

But since it was, I couldn't pass it up. I had to take a shot. Much as I hated to. Getting caught in that apartment would be my worst nightmare. Either by Barry or the police. Getting caught in that apartment simply would not do.

As I stood there vacillating, the only encouraging thought that sprang to mind, and it was small consolation indeed, was that a studio apartment would be easy to search. A studio apartment just didn't have that many places to hide.

I took a breath, pushed the door open.

For once, I was right. It was a studio apartment, and there weren't that many places to hide.

Barry was lying right there in the middle of the floor.

23.

"This is getting to be a very bad habit."

I think Sergeant Thurman enjoyed saying that. After all, it was the sort of remark he could handle. Not particularly original, but when delivered with the requisite amount of sarcasm—which Sergeant Thurman was able to apply—it made even him sound halfway intelligent.

I said nothing. There was nothing to say. I just stood there and waited while he had his fun.

We were in the street outside Cliff McFadgen's apartment. I was in the custody of two police officers. I was grateful for their presence. I was also grateful for the fact it was a bright sunny day. I would have hated like hell to have been alone with Sergeant Thurman in a dark alley.

Yeah, I'd called the cops. It had occurred to me not to. It had also occurred to me to call Sergeant MacAullif instead of Sergeant Thurman. It had also occurred to me to call

Richard before I called anyone. But in the end, I dialed nine-one-one like a good little boy. After all, I already had immunity on the blackmail, and I figured there was no reason to piss off the cops any more than I had to.

That was Richard's opinion too, when I called him after calling nine-one-one. He was on his way, but had instructed me not to wait for him and to cooperate fully with the officers on the scene.

Particularly if that officer happened to be Sergeant Thurman.

Thurman, having already delivered the cliché about this being a bad habit, now cocked his head to one side and delivered another.

"What's the matter?" he said. "Cat got your tongue?"

It flashed on me, yeah, after I skinned him and put him in pajamas. I fought back what would have been a very inappropriate smile and said, "It's your show, Thurman. Just tell me what you want."

"You gonna talk?"

"I called the cops, didn't I? I'm here waiting for you. Fire away."

Thurman had already been upstairs to see the body, which was lying facedown in a pool of blood and had obviously been killed by a gunshot wound to the left temple. At least that's where the body had bled from, and there had been a gun lying right next to it.

Thurman jerked his thumb in that general direction. "How'd you come to find him?"

I exhaled. "You're not going to believe this, but I saw him on TV."

Thurman squinted at me. "What?"

I told him the story of Alice recording the soap opera. From the expression on his face while he listened, I might have been trying to tell him the earth was flat.

"Gee," Thurman said when I was done. "That certainly explains everything, doesn't it?"

"It doesn't explain a thing."

"Oh, really? I thought you just made this whole thing make perfect sense. Let me be sure I got it straight. You're here today finding this guy's body on the floor because yesterday he had hemorrhoids on TV?"

Cooperating or not, I was damned if I was dignifying that with an answer.

Thurman glanced at the two cops from the patrol car who had been keeping me company. "Perhaps you're reluctant to talk in front of these other officers," he said. "Would you prefer I sent them about their duties so we could have a little chat?"

"That won't be necessary," I said. "I'm perfectly happy to talk in their presence. Now, what was your question again?"

"Do you expect me to buy this shit? That's my question. You tell me some fairy tale about seeing this guy on some TV show, and the next day you're in his living room and he's dead."

"You understand the process that got me from point A to point B? If not, I'd be glad to go over it again."

"This guy you knew as Barry is an actor?"

"That's right."

"There's no question that it's him? This is the guy, Barry? The one you saw, the one you paid the blackmail money to?"

"That's right."

"He showed you the porno pictures?"

"That's right."

"And you gave him the cash?"

"Yes, I did."

"The cash the dead woman gave you?"

"She wasn't dead at the time."

"Don't get wise." Thurman leveled his finger. "You're on thin ice here. Even if you *do* answer my questions. You're in deep shit. So don't get wise."

"Sorry, sergeant, but we're going over the same ground. Yes, the woman who was killed gave me the money, and I gave it to this guy, who was also killed. So we now have both ends of the transaction dead."

"All but the go-between," Thurman muttered.

"I beg your pardon?"

"Why didn't you call the cops?"

"I did."

"I don't mean now, I mean then. If you saw this guy on TV and knew it was him, why didn't you call then?"

"I had to be sure. It's hard to make an ID from a photograph. You know that. A thing like this, you're gonna tell the cops a guy's a blackmailer, you better be sure."

"I don't buy that," Thurman said.

"No?"

"No. I think you *were* sure."

"I *thought* I was."

"You sure now?"

"Yeah."

"It's him?"

"Yeah, it's him."

"You know, his face is pretty well covered with blood. And he's lying on his side."

"So?"

"You can't really get that good a look at the body. I would think you'd see him better on TV."

I shrugged. "Yes and no. An image flashes by on TV."

"I thought you had it on tape."

Damn, he was sharp for a dumb guy.

"I don't know what else I can tell you. I had to be sure."

"Yeah. Right. So how'd you get in?"

"The door was open. When I knocked and got no answer, I turned the knob and found him."

"Just like that?"

"Just like that."

"The same way you found the broad?"

It hadn't really occurred to me, but it was. That was a little unsettling. As if the whole thing weren't unsettling.

"How'd you get in the downstairs door?"

"With a key."

His eyebrows raised. "You got a key to the downstairs door?"

"No, I used my house key."

"What?"

"Actually, any key will do. There's enough space between the door and the frame. You can stick it in there, push the lock back."

"That's breaking and entering."

"Not really. According to my lawyer, there's a question of intent."

"You called him?"

"Sure. And he told me to cooperate with you fully."

"I bet."

"Hey, I'm answering your questions. Ask away."

"You knocked on his door, you got no answer?"

"Right."

"Then you tried the doorknob?"

"That's right."

"Then you *had* the intent."

"I beg your pardon?"

"To break and enter. You'd already knocked, so you knew he wasn't there when you tried the knob."

I shrugged. "That's a matter for the A.D.A. to debate with my attorney. Assuming it ever got that far. But just between you and me?" I shrugged my shoulders again.

"Well, I say you intended to break in."

"You're entitled to your opinion."

"Did you search the apartment?"

"No, I did not."

"Either before or after you called the police?"

"I never searched the apartment."

"Did you remove anything from the apartment?"

"No, I did not."

"What about the gun?"

"What about it?"

"Did you touch it?"

"Absolutely not."

"Then I won't find your fingerprints on the gun?"

"Not a chance."

"Or anywhere else in the apartment?"

"Not except the doorknob."

"Inside and out?"

"Outside only. I pushed the door open. When I saw what I saw, I closed it again."

"So, aside from the outside doorknob, which really counts as outside the apartment, you're telling me your fingerprints won't be there?"

I started to answer, then hesitated.

Thurman pounced on it. "Oh yeah? You suddenly remember they *would* be there?"

"No," I said. "I didn't touch anything and they wouldn't. However, if you should happen to find the pictures—"

"Pictures?"

"Yeah. The eight-by-ten color glossy pictures." I couldn't help myself. I smiled, added, "With the circles and arrows and a paragraph on the back of each one."

Thurman frowned. "Circles and arrows?"

I put up my hand. "Sorry. I take it you're not an Arlo Guthrie fan. Scratch it. I'm talking about the blackmail photos."

He frowned. "The ones you bought?"

"Yeah."

"Wait a minute. You bought those from this guy?"

"Yeah."

"And gave them to her? Patricia Connely?"

"That's right. I did."

He jerked his thumb. "Then why would they be there?"

"Because they're nowhere else."

"Huh?"

"They weren't on her body when she was found. And they weren't in her apartment."

"Who told you that?"

"Well, were they?"

"I'm asking the questions here."

"Right. And the cops aren't telling me anything, naturally. But I gotta assume you didn't find those pictures. Why? Because I saw 'em and you know that. If you found those pictures, first thing would happen would be you'd drag me in there to see if I could identify 'em. You haven't done that, so you haven't found 'em."

Thurman frowned. "You're talking a lot, but you aren't saying anything."

"Maybe because I'm trying to answer your questions."

"Huh?"

"You keep going off on tangents. The question was, how can my fingerprints be in that apartment. I'm trying to answer it, but you keep interrupting me with all this other shit."

Thurman's face darkened. "I'm having trouble following

you," he said, "because you're starting to talk crazy. You're not making a lot of sense. You know what that makes me think? Makes me think you might be drunk."

"Did I mention my lawyer was on his way over here?"

"I thought your lawyer told you to cooperate."

"He did, and I am. He's still on his way over here."

"Ain't that just swell." Thurman took a breath. "All right. Last chance. Talk straight. What's this crap about your fingerprints?"

"That's the only way my fingerprints could be in that apartment. If somehow this guy got the blackmail photos. Because I handled them, see? So if you find those photos, my prints may be on 'em. But it wouldn't mean that I'd been in that apartment."

I was watching Thurman's face as he tried to follow that one. It was almost comic. I wondered how much of it he'd actually absorbed.

Not much.

"What makes you think the pictures are in that apartment?"

"I *don't* think the pictures are in that apartment."

"You just said you did."

"No, I just said *if*."

"No, you didn't."

"Yes, I did."

I felt like I was back in grade school. Having a says-you argument with another school kid.

The medical examiner showed up about then, and Richard close behind him, which kind of killed the discussion.

Which was all right with me.

I wasn't sure whether I'd won the argument or not, but I can't say I really cared.

At least I hadn't wound up in the drunk tank.

24.

"This is getting to be a very bad habit."

Good lord. A.D.A. Baby-Face Frost quoting Sergeant Thurman? I suppose it was possible. He'd certainly spent enough time with Thurman before he got to me. But I doubted it. I think it was probably just an example of great minds running in the same direction.

Other than that remark, Frost had Thurman beat hands down. He was a much more adept questioner and had no problem at all dealing with the concept of my fingerprints on the photos.

"That's interesting," Frost said, when I brought it up. "This Barry—or rather Cliff McFadgen—winds up with the pictures again. And just what made you think of that?"

"Actually, Sergeant Thurman did. By insisting, was I sure my prints couldn't be in that apartment. Since I didn't go in, the answer would be yes. But then it occurred to me my prints could be, if something I touched was in that apartment. I thought of the pictures, naturally."

"Why not the money?"

"What?"

"The money. The blackmail money. You gave that to him. Paid it over. But you *got* the pictures from him. There was a reason why he'd have the money, and a reason why he *wouldn't* have the pictures."

"Yeah. So?"

"So why'd you think of the pictures? Why not the money?"

"I don't know. For one thing, I didn't touch the money."

"Oh? I thought you made the payoff."

"Yeah, but you'll recall the money was in an envelope. When I gave him the envelope he tore it open and dumped the money out on the bed. So I never touched it."

"You touched the envelope."

"Of course."

"When I say the money, that's what I mean. The package with the money in it. You gave it to him. So why wouldn't your prints be on that?"

"I didn't think of it."

"Why not?"

I turned to Richard, who was sitting next to me at the table. "How can I answer that?"

He frowned. "I don't know. It's a difficult question if you don't know the answer." He looked at A.D.A. Frost. "On the other hand, it is nothing my client and I wish to withhold." He looked back at me. "So I suggest that you go through your thought process and describe your thinking to the best of your ability."

I exhaled. "Great," I said. "Now, what was the question again?"

"About your fingerprints—why did you think of the photos rather than the money? Or the envelope with the money?"

"Right. I don't know." I thought. "Well, for one thing, why would he save the envelope?"

"What?"

"I saw him tear open the envelope and dump out the

money. So why in the world would he save the envelope? He'd just throw it out."

"It could be in the trash."

"What?"

Frost shrugged. "Say he *did* throw it out—it could still be in his wastebasket."

"In his apartment? He opened it in the motel."

"He could have brought it with him."

I held up my hand. "Hey. This is silly. I can rationalize why the envelope isn't important, but the fact is, I never even thought of it."

"Right. And the question is, why is that?"

I took a breath. Exhaled. "I suppose it's the surface."

"What?"

"I suppose you can get fingerprints from paper. Or so I understand. That technically it can be done. But I don't think that way. I think of paper, an envelope, you handle that, it doesn't leave fingerprints. But a glossy photograph is just the type of thing to hold 'em. So when I'm asked what I might have left prints on, the photographs spring to mind. Even though the photographs *wouldn't* be in his possession and the blackmail money would. *Was* it in his possession?" I asked.

Frost smiled. "If you don't mind, I'm the one doing the questioning. But, no, there was no money in his possession. At least, not the money you describe, a large amount of hundred-dollar bills. And no blackmail photos either. Unless there's some secret panel in the apartment we haven't found yet. But, no, neither the money nor the pictures were there."

"Then what's the big deal about?"

"I beg your pardon?"

"Why are we spending so much time speculating about my fingerprints being on those photographs if the photographs aren't there?"

"Because you thought of it."

"I beg your pardon?"

"The photographs may not be there, but it occurred to you that they might be. It's interesting that you thought that, and that thought process is what we want to pursue."

"I'm flattered," I said. "But that's all it was—a thought. The only reason I had it was because Thurman asked me.

Like, here's an impossibility, explain it. And then I start thinking."

"And you come up with that. This Cliff McFadgen having the photographs."

"I find it hard not to think of him as Barry."

"Call him whatever you like. The fact is, you thought he might have them."

"Someone had to have 'em."

Frost nodded. "That's absolutely true. But wouldn't the most likely person be one of the people in the pictures?"

"I suppose so."

"I mean, after all, who would have the most motive for wanting to get those pictures back?"

"Of course. And if those pictures aren't in his apartment, that's probably exactly what happened. You understand, I didn't say it was *likely* those pictures were in his apartment, I was just suggesting it was possible."

"I quite understand," Frost said. "Now, with regard to the murder weapon."

"That gun *was* the murder weapon?"

"It will doubtless turn out to be."

"Then I assume the other gun did. The one found with Patricia Connely." When Frost said nothing, I said, "Come on. You can at least tell me that."

"Yes, of course it's the murder weapon. Just as I'm sure this one will be."

"Right. And I assume it's a cold piece, or it wouldn't have been left near the body. So you won't be able to trace it."

"A cold piece?" Frost said. He raised his eyebrows. "Do you watch a lot of television, Mr. Hastings?"

"I'm sorry I'm not up on the lingo," I said. "I mean whatever you guys call it."

I'd hoped Frost would say something else about the gun, but apparently he'd only used the TV dig to put me off.

"Now, with regard to the gun," he said, "I assume you'd never seen it before?"

"As to that, I wouldn't know."

Frost raised his eyebrows. "You wouldn't know?"

"I'd like to be very accurate here. Since you're taking down my answers. While it is highly unlikely I've ever seen that gun before, the fact is, I didn't see it closely enough to tell. When I saw the guy was dead, I got the hell out of there and called the cops. I really didn't look at the gun. I think it was a revolver, but, frankly, that's a guess. But swear I never saw it before? I would have to say, to the best of my knowledge, I certainly wouldn't think so."

Frost looked somewhat pained. "You'll pardon me, Mr. Hastings, but that's the type of answer that could either be scrupulously fair or diabolically misleading. Do you see what I mean? Which means I have to dissect that answer and ask some more questions. For instance, did you ever see a gun *similar* to the gun on the floor? Or did you ever see a gun which *might* have been the gun on the floor? Or did you ever see such a gun in the possession of the decedent, Cliff McFadgen? Or Barry, if you will? Or in the possession of the other decedent, Patricia Connely? See what I mean?"

"The answer to *all* those questions is no."

"Or did you ever have such a gun in *your* possession?"

I frowned. "The word *ever* makes that question difficult. I believe I handled a gun two or three years ago."

"Then let me help you. I am referring to the time since you first met the decedent, Patricia Connely—have you had a gun in your possession since then?"

"Absolutely not."

"Have you seen one? Aside from the guns found lying next to the dead bodies—have you seen a gun in any other instance during the time frame we just mentioned?"

"No, I have not."

Frost nodded. "Well, that's pretty clear. And you did not handle the gun in McFadgen's apartment?"

"Absolutely not. I never went near it."

"So if your fingerprints should be on that gun, it would constitute some sort of miracle?"

I felt a cold tug in the pit of my stomach. "Are you trying to tell me something?"

"Oh, absolutely not. I'm just trying to pin the matter down. But the fact is, you never touched that gun?"

"That's a fact."

Frost nodded. "Fine. That helps. Now then, going back to the night of the first murder—the night you found Patricia

Connely dead. That was the night you spoke to this Barry. Who turns out to be Cliff McFadgen. That was the night you spoke to him on the phone."

"That's right."

"Are you sure it was him you spoke to?"

"I'm not. It certainly *sounded* like him. I *assumed* it was him. But I certainly didn't know him well enough to *swear* it was him. If you want my opinion, it's him. If you want me to stand up in court, I'll have to say I *think* it was him. In terms of your investigation and whatever conclusions you're trying to draw, I'd say you should assume it was him."

"And the last time you talked to him was approximately nine-fifteen at night, when you got a call at a pay phone in Queens?"

"Is that right? I think so. If that's in my statement, which was made when it was more fresh in my mind, I'm sure it's right. Let me see. He sent me out to Queens. I was in Queens when he called and sent me back to the motel. There were no calls after that because I got the note." I looked up. "What about the note, by the way? You find samples of this guy's handwriting in his apartment and compare it with the note?"

"That's an excellent idea," Frost said. "We'll be sure to do that."

I looked at him. "You mean you hadn't thought of it?"

Frost merely smiled.

"What's the point, anyway?" I said. "You think this guy was killed the same night?"

"That's another interesting observation," Frost said. "We'll be sure to keep all this in mind. Now, getting back to what *I'd* like to talk about. With the death of both parties to this blackmail, the identity of the people in the pictures takes on increasing importance. It has been suggested that you have another go with the composite-sketch artist." Frost shook his head. "Though, considering the job you did on the decedent, that would appear to be a waste of time. It's a shame we have no one else to work with."

As with Sergeant Thurman, once again my face betrayed me.

"Yes?" Frost said. "What is it?"

"You recall Barry—this Cliff McFadgen—tore open the envelope with the photos and showed me?"

"Yes, of course," Frost said.

"So the envelope was open when I brought it home. And I didn't give it to Patricia Connely till the next day."

"So what are you saying?"

"It didn't occur to me till you just brought it up. But, actually, my wife saw the pictures."

"Oh yeah?"

"Yeah."

I'd expected Frost to be upset. Instead he smiled.

"That's the best news I've had all day."

25.

She was fine.

I was afraid Alice would be upset, but she took to it like a duck to water. She also thought A.D.A. Frost's idea was reasonable and made perfect sense, and first thing next morning the two of us were downtown making our composite sketches.

Now, that's not exactly right. They weren't really *composite* sketches. They were separate sketches. With two separate sketch artists, Alice with one and me with the other. So we were working independently and not together.

I must say I found that somewhat distracting. Knowing my wife was off in a room somewhere with some policeman, describing some of the most extraordinarily inventive and athletic sexual practices you could ever wish to see. That made it a little hard for me to concentrate on my own sketch.

I shouldn't have worried, because Alice had no such trouble. And she was not at all distracted by the sexual acts these people were performing, but instead gave a rather accurate description of their physical features.

Their *facial* physical features.

I found that out at the end of the session, when the two of us were brought together to compare and comment on each other's drawings. An embarrassment I would have preferred to have foregone. I must admit, Alice had me beat hands down. For instance, the sketch of the woman made from Alice's description actually tended to resemble the woman in the pictures. The sketch made from my description tended to resemble a plastic blow-up sex toy.

Fortunately we weren't going home together, so I was spared a lengthy assessment of my performance. But I'd missed enough days' work since this thing started. Today I was taking cases for Richard.

Unfortunately, my first was a fourth-floor walkup in the Bronx that made a murder investigation look like a day at the beach. All I was investigating was a worn stair tread that had caused the client, one Jerome Harmon, to slip and fall on his keister, but that wasn't the point. Cases for Richard were never dangerous in themselves. What made them hazardous to your health were the places you had to go to do 'em.

Jerome Harmon's residence was on the fourth floor of a crack house. The occupants of the establishment, who were hanging out in force in the hallways and stairwells, were all black, ragged, strung out, openly doing drugs, and shocked as hell to see a white man in a suit and tie in their building. This was not surprising. White men in suits and ties didn't *go* in their building. If one did, he was either a cop or a *very* naive young man about to enjoy the last few minutes of his life.

I am by no means brave, but I've been in situations like that before, so I knew what to do. I just stuck out my jaw and barged on ahead as if I had every right to be there. And the junkies took me for a cop and made way to let me pass.

Jerome Harmon had a cracked fibula to show for his last trip down the stairwell, and it seemed to please him. Not the fact he was injured, but the fact it was a fibula. Jerome Harmon was an amiable black man of about thirty—twenty-eight, actually, I found when I filled out his fact sheet. His doctor at Lincoln Hospital had told him that what he had broken was his fibula, and he seemed to find that enormously funny. "Broke ma fibula, man," he said several times, and each time broke out giggling.

Despite the bursts of mirth, I eventually recorded the necessary information and went with him to check out the offending step.

There was a large black junkie sitting on it, smoking a crack pipe. That would have made one hell of a location-of-accident picture, but unfortunately I hadn't written up the cause of Jerome Harmon's mishap as, "Client tripped over junkie in stairwell." So, with Jerome's help, I shooed him away and shot the step itself. After that, it was just a cakewalk through the crack heads back to my car, and I was out of there and heading for my next sign-up in Brooklyn.

It was a project in East New York that made Jerome Harmon's establishment look like the Ritz. The client, one Wanita Perez, lived on the fourteenth floor. Which was too bad—I try to avoid elevators in projects because you never know who you'll get trapped in there with. On this occasion, it was a short, scraggly bearded, bad-smelling man with a bottle of cheap rotgut in one hand and a bible in the other. Which was nice. If I had to ride in the elevator with someone, I'm happy to have his hands occupied.

Wanita Perez began a long story about shopping in Macy's—which made me think I'd have to go there to get the accident photos—but turned out to have fallen on a city bus after leaving the store, which meant pictures wouldn't be required.

While I was signing her up my beeper went off, and when I called in, Wendy/Janet sent me to Kings County Hospital to sign up a hit-and-run.

By the time I'd signed up Yolanda Wilson, mother of hit-and-run victim Derek Wilson, it was five-thirty, my beeper was quiet, I'd done my duty, and I was heading home.

And feeling kind of good. Three cases undertaken, three cases done. Just my typical average day.

I had a long time to think about it on my way back from

Kings County. To sort the whole thing out in my mind. And the conclusion I came to was this: I had gone back to work.

I don't know. Maybe it was the joy of making money again. Or maybe it was the fact that I'd had three cases and handled them well. Particularly the one in the crack house. There had to be a certain satisfaction in that. Doing something you know most people couldn't have done. Or maybe it was the last case, helping a young mother worried about her child. But I think basically it was the fact that I was doing something someone *wanted* me to do on the one hand, and that I could do on the other.

Because nobody wanted me messing around in the murder. And with the demise of my chief suspect, Barry, I was really left with very little in the way to investigate.

See, I had to admit, as I bore right onto Flatbush Avenue, heading for the Manhattan Bridge, there certainly was something to what Alice said. That the only real reason I wanted to investigate was the thought of getting revenge. And to what end? So a stupid cop throws you in the drunk tank. What are you going to do? Spend the rest of your life getting even? No; you acknowledge the iniquity, put it behind you, and move on.

By the time I'd found a parking spot on 103rd Street and walked up West End Avenue to our home, I had come to the conclusion, not without some regrets, that it was time to let the whole thing go.

I knew Alice would be pleased, so I told her the minute I got in the door.

She looked at me with the look she has that tells me she knows she's dealing with a total asshole.

"What, are you nuts?" she said. "You gotta solve this thing."

26.

"There's been a second murder."

"No shit," MacAullif said. "You come in here to tell me that?"

"I had a feeling you might have heard."

"Your feeling was correct. Why are you here?"

"I got a problem with the case."

"*You* got a problem with the case? You gotta be kidding. *You* don't got no problem with the case. It ain't your case."

"That's the problem."

MacAullif took a deep breath. He blew it out again through clenched teeth. "Did I mention I'm not having a good day?"

"I don't believe you did."

"Yeah, well, bear it in mind. You also might consider that, compared to me, Sergeant Thurman could qualify as your best friend."

"So noted. Now, about the case—"

"Fuck the case," MacAullif said. "What are you, deaf? This is not your case. This is not *my* case. This is nothing we should be discussing."

"Actually, I know that," I said. "The problem is, my wife thinks I should."

MacAullif gawked at me. "Your wife?"

"Yeah."

"You're tellin' me you're in here bothering me because your *wife* wants you to?"

"Is that really so hard to understand? You got a wife, don't you? Don't you ever do what she says?"

MacAullif glowered at me. "Yeah, I got a wife," he said. "She tells me to bring home pot roast, I bring home pot roast. She tells me not to throw my clothes on the floor, I sometimes forget, but I try to remember. But if she told me how to run a murder investigation . . ." MacAullif shook his head. "No way."

I figured that was probably true. Still, I had made my point.

A while back, I had done MacAullif a favor, helped him out when he had had a personal problem. He'd since repaid it threefold. Still, mentioning family matters had to bring it to mind.

"Yeah," I said. "I'm sure that's how you work, and I'm sure you've had better days. Me. I've had worse. I may be saddled with a completely unsolvable double homicide, but at least I'm not the prime suspect this time. Of course, if I were, you might stop being such a hard-ass and see fit to help me out."

"Well, don't fret about it," MacAullif said. "Maybe you can implicate yourself in the next one."

"You think there's going to be a third killing?"

"I didn't mean this case," MacAullif said. "I meant the next homicide you're involved in."

"Then you think the killings are over?"

"I think there's going to be another one right here, if you don't get out of my office."

"Damn," I said. "And you know, I did what you always wanted me to do and interviewed the neighbors."

"Neighbors?" MacAullif said.

"Yeah. Cliff McFadgen's neighbors. First thing this morning I went by his apartment house and knocked on doors."

"And?"

"Can't say I got a lot. He's described as a quiet type. A loner. Perfectly nice gentleman no one can imagine this ever happening to."

MacAullif nodded. "Your typical serial-killer description."

"Exactly."

"Not that it helps much, since we're talking about the victim."

"Who was also a blackmailer. That's the wrinkle. The problem is, it's a bit hard to sort out without the facts. I had a nice talk with Patricia Connely's bereaved husband."

"Oh yeah?"

"Yeah. And he seemed a perfectly decent sort. Except the thought of hiring me to investigate his wife's death never crossed his mind."

"How disappointing."

"I thought so. Particularly since this Cliff McFadgen was single, I don't really know that much about him, and in his case I can't even come up with a friend, acquaintance, or relative likely to give a shit."

"All the more reason to butt the hell out."

"Yeah," I said. "Except for my wife."

"Oh, sure," MacAullif said. "Lay it all on the little woman. If you didn't want to investigate this sucker, you wouldn't be in here."

"Before my wife said anything, I'd decided to give it up."

MacAullif gave me a look. "I decided to give up cigars. You think that means I wouldn't like to smoke one?"

"I'm sure you would."

"Yeah. So don't give me this gave-it-up shit. Or any other explanation. The fact is, you're in my office."

"True."

"What the fuck do I have to do to get you out?"

"How about a little information?"

"Shit."

"You know what it's like working in the dark?"

"No. Do you know what it's like being a cop? Do you have the faintest fucking idea?"

"Probably not."

"Yeah. Probably fucking not." MacAullif jerked his thumb at the door. "There's cops out there. And you know what? Some of them know you're in here. Out of those, some of them probably know why. 'Cause you may not believe this, but they're not all dumb. And even the dumb ones ain't necessarily stupid." MacAullif glowered at me, pointed his finger. "Take Sergeant Thurman."

I couldn't help myself. Under my breath I muttered, "Please."

MacAullif caught it. Which could have been an absolute disaster. It probably would have been, if he'd managed to keep a straight face. But as it happened, I lucked out. Because his lip quivered, and before he could catch himself, he'd gone too far. He laughed out loud and said, "Shit. Henny Fucking Youngman. Right. Take Sergeant Thurman . . . Please. Well, that's the point I'm makin'. That's the whole deal." MacAullif jerked his thumb again. "The cops out there know this is Sergeant Thurman's case. They've also heard about the drunk tank—these things get around. You know what that means? It means they close ranks. They might not like what Thurman did—they might not do that themselves—but once it happens, they draw the line. Right. The line in the sand. You're either on one side or the other. Which side are you on? You side against Sergeant Thurman, you draw your bloody sword. See what I mean? See what I'm talking about?"

"Not exactly."

"Jesus Christ," MacAullif said. "Are you so fucking dumb? Thurman cut a corner. Threw you in the drunk tank. If you plan to nail him on it, you're up against the whole fucking force. If that's what you want, fine, only leave me out of it. You nail Thurman, and the guys out there think I had a hand in it, I'm suddenly the least popular cop on the force. And I'm not talkin' snubs, I'm talkin' ostracized. I'm talking getting into situations where the backup don't arrive."

"I told you. We cut a deal. I signed releases, for Christ's sake."

"Yeah. For your legal rights. So you can't prosecute and you can't sue. Big deal. There's more than one way to skin a cat."

Son of a bitch.

"What the hell you smilin' at?" MacAullif said.

"Nothing. I hear you."

"I hope you do. Let me spell it out. If you nail Thurman and it looks like I helped you do it, what he did to you is gonna seem like a day at the beach."

"I understand. Would you admit to a distinction between nailing him and showing him up?"

"Oh, absolutely. I've done that myself. In fact, some cops I know think it's practically their duty."

"Fine. So how about seeing your way clear to let loose with a few pertinent facts?"

MacAullif looked at me a moment. Then he sighed, shook his head, opened a desk drawer, took out two thick manila files, and flopped them down on his desk.

I looked at them and my eyes widened. How about that. And after being such a hard-ass too.

MacAullif had the case files all ready for me.

27.

"I don't expect this will help you much," MacAullif said. "The guns in both cases were stolen. One from a sporting-goods store, the other from a private home. In both cases a long time ago. We're talkin' years. Four in the one case, six in the other. Passing through many hands before reachin' the dealer in question."

"What dealer?"

"What dealer you think? The guy movin' hot guns our killer bought these two from."

"You figure it's the same guy?"

"Or girl. I wouldn't wanna be called a sexist for thinkin' only men commit murder."

"Keep calling 'em girls and they'll get you anyway."

"Huh?"

"Anyway, you think it's the same person?"

"Stands to reason. Or persons. That's the other wrinkle."

"You thinking of the blackmail photos?"

"Yeah. Kind of a shame I never got to see 'em."

"I track 'em down, you'll be the first to know."

"Great. You can add trafficking in pornography to your list of charges."

"I believe these things are legal."

"Let's not quibble. You come up with them, I'll take a look, tell you if they're legal or not."

"Great," I said. "Anyway, you were saying. About the gun."

"Not much to say. There's no prints on 'em, and their history isn't helpful. On the other hand, ballistics confirms they are both the murder weapons. One is a thirty-two-caliber revolver. The other is a thirty-eight automatic. Not that that mattered much to the victims—they both did the job."

"What about the time of death?"

MacAullif nodded. "Yeah. That's a biggie. For the Connely broad, it's pretty good. On account of you finding her so soon. Doc's got her listed between eight and ten, probably close to nine. Now, the other guy you got a problem, 'cause he'd been dead for days. But it sure looks like he bought it the same night."

"Shit."

"Yeah, but after that amount of time, the doc can't be that accurate. Between six that night and six the next morning is the best he'll do."

"I know he was alive at nine. I talked to him."

"But you can't be sure it was him."

"I'm virtually certain."

"Virtually is a big if."

"Yeah, but I'd been talking to him all night long."

"All night long? Wasn't it just twice?"

"Was it? Let me think. She sent me to the bridge. He called me there. Sent me to Queens. Called me there. Sent me to the motel. All right, only twice. But I'd talked to him before, when I met him."

"Exactly. And can you be sure the guy you talked to on the phone was the same guy you met at the motel?"

"Not entirely."

"There you are. And can you even be sure it was the same

guy you talked to on the phone both times that night? I mean that the guy you talked to the first time was the same guy you talked to the second time?"

I took a breath. "I can't be *sure* of anything. I have an opinion; I think it's valid enough to act on. I'm not ruling out possibilities, but I'm taking this as a strong indication."

"No need to get testy," MacAullif said. "I'm only trying to help."

"I appreciate it. For what it's worth, my opinion is the guy was alive at nine that night."

"He probably was. If the doctor says between six and six, the likelihood is near midnight, and the big spread is just the doc covering his ass."

"Which allows for another wrinkle," I said.

"What's that?"

"He killed her, someone else killed him."

MacAullif nodded. "Possible. I fail to see why."

"I fail to see a reason for any of it."

"True. But if he killed her, why send you there?"

"He was setting me up."

"Obviously. But for what? I mean, as a murder frame, it's clumsy as hell. It couldn't even convince as stupid a cop as Sergeant Thurman. Plus, with her bein' killed between eight and ten, and him callin' you at nine, that would make him one busy individual. Plus, she's killed way downtown in this loft, and he's killed uptown in his apartment."

"True. You don't suppose? . . ."

"What?"

"He called from there?"

"Called who?"

"Me. The calls we're talking about. At the bridge and in Queens. Can they trace shit like that?"

"Sometimes they can, sometimes they can't."

"You're kidding."

"Hey, no system's perfect. New York Telephone may have a record of the calls. On the other hand, they may not."

"Anyone look for it?"

"If it's in here, I didn't see it. It's not my case, and I just skimmed the file."

"It's a thought."

"Sure, it's a thought. But a clever blackmailer doesn't use his own phone."

"Or he might wind up dead," I said dryly.

"You have a point. You expect me to dance up and down because you have a point?"

"No."

"Good. I hope you don't expect me to trace those calls either. I can drop a hint in the right direction, but that's it."

"I understand."

"Just so's you do. Now, where were we? Oh yeah. The theory he kills her, someone else kills him. I think we can agree that's pretty bad. The blackmailer kills the blackmail victim. And even if we can stretch and find a reason for that, then he's coincidentally killed hours later? No way I can make that fly. No, the way I see it, the whole thing smacks of a sting that went bad."

"A sting?"

"Yeah."

"A sting of who?"

"Of you, of course."

"What?"

"Why is that such a surprise. You think you don't fit the part?"

"What the fuck are you talking about?"

"The way I see it, they gave you what—five hundred the first time and a thousand the second? Well, that's way out of line. It's too much for the job. A pickup and delivery. But it would make sense if they were buying a patsy. Uppin' the ante and suckin' you in."

"Into what?"

"How the hell should I know? But most likely a blackmail scheme. That's what they were conditioning you for. You're payin' blackmail, they're uppin' the ante, and before you know it you're payin' more."

"You mind explaining that to me so it makes sense?"

"Sure," MacAullif said. "If it's a sting operation, the broad and the guy are working together and the blackmail is a charade. She comes to you with her problem, gives you the blackmail money. You pay it to the guy, get the pictures. She's back with the bit about the negatives and they do it again. Once you've bought the negatives and they've got you conditioned to it, then they pull the hook."

"Which is?"

"The broad comes to you, says the guy's pulled the dirty again. There's more negatives, more pictures. And he wants to sell. The wrinkle this time is he's shakin' down the woman in the pictures."

I frowned. "What the hell."

"You still haven't got it, have you?" MacAullif said. "The broad says she's workin' for the woman in the pictures, tryin' to help her out. And we're talkin' big-time stuff here, maybe twenty-five, fifty thousand dollars. Which is why they're willin' to pay you two grand. Maybe even twenty-five hundred."

"For what?"

"What do you think? Pickup and delivery. Just like before. You pick up the blackmail money and deliver it."

"What's the point?"

"The point is, this time you pick it up from the woman in the pictures and you deliver it to them. To the guy, but of course they're workin' together."

"So?"

"So, this woman's never met the other two people. All she's ever heard is the broad's voice on the phone. But she don't know her from Adam. This broad ain't a friend of hers, and she ain't helpin' her. She just maybe sent her one of the pictures in the mail and then called her on the phone and said, 'How'd you like to have these back?' And the woman in the pictures is a rich, high-society woman with a lot to lose, who'd probably *love* to have them back. And she's probably willing to pay a fancy price to do so."

MacAullif held up one finger. "But on the off chance she's gonna go to the cops and pull a double cross and turn 'em in and the whole bit, this woman's never gonna meet 'em, never gonna know who they are. 'Cause the only one she's ever gonna actually meet is you."

I frowned. "So I'm really just a buffer for them."

MacAullif shook his head. "Still don't see how it works? Let me develop this for you a bit.

"The broad sets it up for you to handle the payoff for the

woman in the pictures. You gotta meet her for her to give you the money. You don't mind doin' it, you're bein' the intermediary like you were before. But once you've agreed to that and you're all set to do it, the broad tells you there's a switch. The problem is, this woman don't trust you. 'Cause it's an awful lot of money. On the other hand, Barry does, 'cause you paid off before."

MacAullif shrugged. "And that's the situation. The woman won't pay over the money until she sees the pictures and the negatives. So this time the payoff and delivery is the other way around."

MacAullif ticked it off on his fingers. "First, you meet Barry, he gives you the pix. Second, you show 'em to the woman. When she sees that they're genuine, she gives you the cash. Which you then take to Barry."

MacAullif pointed at me. "From your point of view, it's the same thing. You're just an intermediary makin' a pickup and delivery."

He shrugged. "But look at it from *her* point of view."

"Son of a bitch!" I said.

MacAullif looked at me and shook his head.

"So," he said. "You finally got it." He nodded. "That's right." He nodded again.

"You're the blackmailer."

28.

I stared at MacAullif. "You gotta be kidding."

He shrugged. "If you ask me, that's the way I see it."

"But . . ."

"But what?"

"You're doping this out from no information. You got nothing to go on."

"I got your story. The way I see it, this accounts for it."

"How?"

"For one thing, it explains why someone would pay you fifteen hundred bucks for basically doing nothing."

"What do you mean, nothing?"

"No offense meant, but what the hell made you so all-fired important?"

"She didn't want to meet the guy herself. Not alone at a motel. An attractive girl like that. It's perfectly understandable."

"Sure, if it's legit. But the odds are, she wasn't bein' blackmailed."

"Why?"

"Because both parties are dead. Plus, she wasn't the girl in the pictures. Which is a biggie. No, it works just fine the way I told you. It fits in with everything else."

"Like what?"

"The way they played it. You're told it's a pickup and delivery and you aren't to know what's in the package. This is stressed. So what's the first thing that happens? The guy rips the envelope open so you can see the money. Then what does he do? He rips the other one open and shoves the pictures in your face. To make sure you see there's no negatives, so you're all primed for the second buy. Plus he makes sure you get a good look at the woman. So once they set the hook and shake *her* down, you go along without thinkin'. 'Cause her *bein'* the woman in the pictures is corroborating evidence, makes you think the story is true. Actually it isn't, and the woman bein' her doesn't corroborate anything at all, but you'll take it as such. Yes, she's the woman bein' blackmailed, and was all along. But that bein' true doesn't make the rest of it true. The rest of it is bullshit."

"I see what you mean. I'm asking how you dope it out?"

"'Cause they're dead. If they weren't in it together, it makes no sense that they're dead. If they're in it together, the thing starts to play."

"How?"

MacAullif looked at me. "You want an awful fuckin' lot, considerin' this ain't my case."

"No, but it's your theory."

"It's my opinion." He shrugged. "You can't read a case file without havin' an opinion."

"That opinion must have a basis, whether you've actually thought it out or not."

MacAullif began unwrapping a cigar. It was the best news I'd had since he'd produced the file. He inspected it gloomily, then drummed it on the desk.

"Everything points to the fact these two people were in it together. The main thing is that they're dead. But the point is, nothing else contradicts it. If they were, it's a sting operation. And what we're dealing with is the result of a sting operation gone bad. If that's the case, this shouldn't be that hard to solve."

"I'm glad to hear it. How do you figure?"

"In that case, there's only two potential killers. One, a confederate who don't want to split the loot. Or, two, a victim who don't want to pay. The first case ain't that likely. Why? Because they ain't got the money yet."

"I paid five grand."

"Yeah, but it was their own money. They're in it together, remember? If my theory's right, the real money ain't showed up yet. If you'd picked up fifty G's from the woman in the pictures, the whole thing works just fine. The mastermind bumps off his henchmen and pockets the loot."

"Who's the mastermind?"

"How the hell should I know? Particularly since it didn't happen that way. The way things stand, the most likely scenario is number two. The victim saves fifty grand by wipin' the conspirators out and grabbin' the pix. In that case, there *is* no mastermind and those two are it. So the brains is one of them, either the guy or the broad. She look smart enough to pull it off?"

"If she was acting, who's to say?"

"Who indeed. Anyway, in that case your choice of killers is most likely limited to two. The guy and girl in the pix. Or any friend, relative, spouse, or hired employee acting in their behalf. But, basically, they're the two with the motive. Then there's another thing."

"What's that?"

"Long shadows. These pictures aren't dated. Could have been taken any time. Like a while ago. Even a *long* while ago."

"So?"

"So, this woman in the pictures—maybe it's her *son* trying to keep mommie out of the tabloids."

"Jesus Christ."

"Hey, just a thought. Anyway, that's the way it plays best. With the facts we now have." He shrugged. "We get some more facts, maybe we go back to theory number one."

"Which was?"

"Mastermind wipes out gang. In which case, mastermind is most likely an actor. I understand the broad's husband is an actor, which would make him suspect number one."

I frowned. "I see."

"You don't like that?"

"Having met the guy, I just can't see it at all."

MacAullif nodded. "With your track record, that should clinch the case. Shall I get the handcuffs ready now?"

"Fuck you."

"Plus, the guy gets five points for bein' her husband. That in itself makes him a logical choice."

"That's hard to buy in this case."

"True, but stranger things have happened. Besides, she had money."

"Oh?"

"Yeah. An inheritance." MacAullif shrugged. "Not that much, but enough she didn't have to work."

"Even so."

"Yeah, I know," MacAullif said. "The way things stand, I'd look to the victims. Particularly since it looks like a sting."

"You're really sold on that idea."

"Well, everything points to it. The money, for instance."

"What about the money?"

"We got this phony payoff to explain, right? The newsprint you were carrying around you thought was cash. Unless you still think Sergeant Thurman grabbed it."

"No. What about it?"

"Well, it fits right in. With it bein' a sting, I mean. Aside from the fifteen hundred bucks to you, no money's actually changing hands. These guys are playin' patty cake to suck you in."

"I saw the first payment myself."

"Sure. You were *supposed* to see it. But what did you see? A bundle of bills thrown on the bed. With a century note on top. You know what that was? Ten to one, it's a Jewish bankroll. You know what that is?"

"Aside from an offensive remark?"

"Get real. It's supposed to be five grand. Fifty hundred-dollar bills. Right? Wrong. It's forty-eight ones sandwiched between two hundreds. Two hundred forty-eight dollars that looks like a million. They rip it open, throw it on the bed, as far as you're concerned, you saw five grand."

MacAullif gestured with the cigar. "See? And that explains the funny money in the second package. The guy ain't gonna cut it open that time, so why use real cash? Besides, they probably spent their hundreds as part of the grand they gave to you. But that's no matter, 'cause you're not gonna open the envelope. So you won't see it unless he does, and he doesn't. And if things hadn't fucked up, as sure as you're sittin' here, you'd have sworn on a stack of bibles you paid the guy off."

I frowned.

"See?" MacAullif said. "It all fits right in. The only thing that doesn't wash is the timing."

"Timing?"

"Yeah. These people died too soon. Killed during the second milk run. While you're runnin' around with the funny money. Which is still part of the setup. They haven't even got to the main game. So, by rights, the victim who killed 'em shouldn't have even come into play yet."

"Right. So how do you rationalize that?"

"That they're rushin' things along. That they've already made the approach. Which makes sense, in a way. Once they got you hooked, they're not gonna want you to have time to think it over. Probably come back at you the next day. And they've already sent letters and phone calls to the woman bein' blackmailed. Or the guy, if that was the target. Either way, they're both targets. Both potential killers. They could be already putting the squeeze, and all they're negotiating is the final payoff. Which of course will be scheduled for the next day. With you. Only, the victim sees through it and makes sure that doesn't happen."

I frowned. Thought that over.

MacAullif rolled his cigar through his hands. "It's just my opinion," he said. "I'm glad you're so interested in it. But what you got in your lap there is a case file. I hate to break it to you, but it ain't leavin' my office."

I took the hint, paged through the file. It was mostly stuff I already knew. In fact, a lot of it came straight from me.

I found one point of interest.

"The loft was unrented," I said.

"Then how did they get in?"

I referred to the paper in the file. "According to the realty company, no one's been in the place in the last nine months. They haven't even shown it to anyone. Prior to that it was rented out for three months. Aside from that it hadn't been rented in over two years."

"Yeah. So?"

"The names of the renters are listed. I'm sure the cops checked with them, but maybe I should talk to 'em too."

"Why?"

"To see if I might happen to recognize 'em from their pictures."

MacAullif grimaced. "That's a real long shot. I mean, the guy's really gonna do it in a place that can be traced to him."

"Just a thought," I said. "Probably not a great one, but I guess it's something I ought to check. I should probably check the previous one too, and—I'll be damned."

"What is it?" MacAullif said.

"This rental two years ago. That was for three months too."

"Really? But not by the same party?"

"No."

"That *is* unusual. But what's the point?"

"A loft in SoHo rented for three months. Twice by different people. Unusual in one way, but when you think about it, it's not. And I bet the cops never bothered to ask."

"Ask what?"

"What these people were renting it for."

MacAullif scowled. "Are you enjoying this? Tell me what the fuck you mean. Rented it for what?"

After all the crap I'd taken, I think I *was* enjoying it. I smiled.

"To rehearse a play."

29.

"I assume you've been told?"

Bradley Connely nodded. "Oh, yes, of course. They took me down to see the body."

"Did you recognize it?"

He sighed, shook his head. "Wish I did. I've never seen the guy before in my life."

"He was an actor."

"I know. And so am I, and so was my wife. You might expect we'd have run into each other. But you know how many actors there are in New York City?"

"Actually, I do."

"Oh?"

"It's been a while, but I used to make the rounds myself."

"Oh. Then you know. The fact is, I never met him and I don't think my wife ever did either."

"She was never in a production of a play called *Foot-dance*?"

He frowned. "What?"

"You never heard of it?"

"No? What is it?"

"An experimental play. It had a showcase production last fall."

"Why is it important?"

"It was put on in the loft where your wife was found."

His face contorted slightly, but then he looked at me with interest. "When did you say?"

"Last fall."

He frowned. "Last fall?"

"I know it's a long time. But those were the last people to use the space."

"I see," he said. "I'm sorry. It means nothing to me."

"One of the actors in the production," I said gently, "was the late Cliff McFadgen."

He blinked. "You're kidding! Do the police know this?"

"They do *now*."

He looked at me sharply. "You sound like you told them."

"I did."

He looked at me a few moments. He seemed to be searching for the right words. "How is it," he said, "that you came up with this information and the police didn't?"

Just what I'd hoped he'd ask me. If the truth be known, I was trying to prod the gentleman into hiring me, a notion he somehow hadn't managed to come up with himself.

"Can I tell you off the record?"

He frowned angrily. "Off the record, on the record. Go on, man. My wife is dead."

"I'm sorry. This is somewhat delicate and I wouldn't want to be quoted. But the guy in charge of the investigation is not particularly swift."

"What?" Connely said. "What the hell! How do you know that?"

"I've run into him on cases before. And you'll witness the fact that I'm talking to you now, and the cops haven't yet. And you'd think, with you and your wife being actors, this is the sort of thing they'd want to check out."

I didn't mention that I'd come straight from telling Baby-Face Frost, so Sergeant Thurman was probably just hearing about it now. I figured the drunk-tank incident gave me poetic license to take a swipe.

I hadn't figured on Connely's response.

"My god," he said. "I've got to get him off the case."

"What?"

"This is my wife we're talking about. I can't have an incompetent investigating her death."

I put up my hands. "Whoa. Wait a minute. You can't just pull a homicide cop off a case."

"Oh yeah? Not if he's incompetent?"

"I said *off the record.* You can't go tell the cops I said Thurman was incompetent."

He looked at me and his eyes were wide. He blinked them, once, twice. "You can't do that to me," he said. "Tell me that I have no recourse. 'Off the record, sir, your wife's investigation is being botched. I'm sorry you can't do anything about it, but that's unofficial.'" He looked at me with pleading eyes. "How can you tell me that?"

"I'm *not* telling you that. There's a-lot of things you can do. Just don't quote me saying Sergeant Thurman's incompetent. That's a conclusion you can come to on your own. Believe me, it won't be hard. But that doesn't mean you can get him removed, and quite frankly I doubt if you can. But it's not the end of the world. Having him on the case doesn't mean it won't be solved. 'Cause there's other people working on it who'll be figuring out things he can't. I was only really responding to your observation that I got here ahead of the cops."

Damn. Instead of hiring me, he'd gone off on a tangent about firing Sergeant Thurman. Just my luck. If I was going to investigate this thing anyway, it sure would have been nice to have someone pay for it.

But he wasn't biting.

"I'm sorry," he said. "You're right, of course. It's just that I'm upset. Go on. What were you saying? About the loft and this guy being in a play?"

"As I said, it was a showcase, went on last fall in that loft. I spoke to the producer this morning. The whole thing's news to him. He hadn't recognized the address of the loft in the papers, or heard about Cliff McFadgen. But he did confirm McFadgen was in the show."

Bradley Connely frowned. "I see."

"Which would explain how he had access to the key."

"Yes, yes. That's obvious. But . . ."

"But what?"

"He wasn't the one found there."

"I know," I said. "But your wife wasn't in the showcase."

"No."

"Which reminds me. I could use a snapshot."

"What?"

"Of your wife. The producer assured me he didn't know a Patricia Connely. But I didn't have a picture to show him, to see if he knew her under any other name."

"Oh."

"So, would you have a picture?"

I don't think I could have given the guy a broader hint without straight-out asking him to hire me, but he still didn't tumble, just went in the bedroom and returned with a Polaroid of his wife.

"Here," he said. "Show him this. But I assure you, she wasn't in the play."

I took the picture, shoved it in my jacket pocket.

And decided to push the situation. I hated to intrude on the gentleman's grief, but I was never going to find anything out if I didn't ask questions. At least, that's the way I rationalized it. Surely I wasn't just being vindictive over not being hired.

"Too bad," I said. "It would have fit in with one of the police theories of the case."

He looked up sharply. "What theory?"

I put up my hand. "Please understand. I'm talking tentatively here. A lot of theories kick around. The police don't necessarily share all of them with you. Particularly, you being the husband and all. So don't take this as the official police theory. Or even one shared by the officer in charge of the case. All I'm saying is—"

"Jesus Christ!" Connely cried. "What is it? Stop equivocating and get on with it! Can't you see you're driving me nuts?"

"Sorry," I said. "Basically the theory is this. Cliff McFadgen wasn't really blackmailing your wife. The two of them were actually working together."

Connely's eyes narrowed. "Excuse me?"

"That's the theory. That it was all an act. What your wife told me about being blackmailed."

"What are you saying?"

"It's not what *I'm* saying. It's one of the police theories. That your wife and this Cliff McFadgen knew each other and were confederates. And they were mixed up in something together and that's why they were killed. I take it the police didn't mention this to you?"

Connely slammed his fist down on the coffee table, lunged to his feet.

"Damn it!" he said. "Damn it to hell! Are you saying my wife was mixed up in something?"

"Not me. The police."

"I don't care who's saying it," Connely said. "I don't want to hear it. I don't want to listen to it, do you understand? First you say my wife was paying blackmail. Now you try to tell me she was involved? I'm sorry, but I don't have to listen to that."

I knew he was about to throw me out, so I played my trump card. I opened my briefcase and took out a sheet of paper, printed on and folded in half.

"What's that?" Connely demanded.

"Program," I said. "For the show. The producer gave it to me." I opened it up, pointed. "There's six actors in the show, plus a producer, director, lighting man, and stage manager. As you can see, Cliff McFadgen's name is in the cast. Your wife's is not. The producer and director claim they never heard of her. The other actors are yet to be contacted, but are likely to say the same."

"Let me see that," Connely said.

He practically snatched it from me.

"Do any of those names mean anything to you?" I asked.

Connely looked up, shook his head. "I don't know any of

them." He looked back at the program. Frowned. "The name Jack Fargo is familiar. I've heard the name, but I've never met him."

"Is it possible you heard it from your wife?"

He waved it away. "No. I'm sure she never knew him. I mean *heard* like in a review. Or like some other actor was in a show with him."

"And you heard that mentioned?"

"It's possible."

"Who might that other actor be?"

"I have no idea. You understand, I have no specific recollection. Just a feeling I've heard the name." Dealing with the program had calmed Connely down. Now he even smiled slightly. "I could even be thinking of *Wells* Fargo and just *imagining* I've heard the name."

"I see," I said. "And none of these other names are familiar?"

"No, they're not."

"Nor the names of the technical crew?"

"No."

"And the show doesn't ring a bell? *Footdance*?"

He shook his head. "No. Except it sounds like half-a-dozen other shows of that type."

It sure did. The whole New York actor showcase routine was a familiar and depressing syndrome.

Things were not going well. The guy didn't know anything, and wasn't about to hire me. Pretty depressing for a day that had started off with such promise. I took the program back from him, folded it, and put it in my pocket.

"Sorry this doesn't help," I said.

I was gone shortly thereafter, neither having gained employment nor learned anything useful.

I did make a mental note, however, to be sure and let MacAullif know just what Bradley Connely thought of his theory.

30.

Jack Fargo was unemployed. That was why I was able to find him home at two o'clock on a weekday afternoon. Jack was an actor obviously suited to character roles. Evidently, there was no role for a short, plump, genial type available at the moment, but there had been one in the showcase *Footdance,* and Jack Fargo had beat out twenty-six other actors for the part.

"That's right," he said. "Twenty-six. I got friendly with the director, and after we were running, he went back and looked it up. They had records from the auditions. Well, not records, really, but the résumé photos. They'd sorted them out into the actors they were considering for particular parts. The part of Sam, the part I played—there were twenty-seven photos in that pile. Just for that one part. Shows you what you're up against, huh?"

"Yes, it does," I said. "Now, about Cliff McFadgen . . ."

He shook his head. "Boy, that's a shock. Couldn't believe it when you told me. Damn shame. Not that I really knew the guy, but even so."

"You hadn't heard then?"

"No. Didn't I say that on the phone? I think I did. It was news to me. Kind of sad, don't you think? An actor dies and nobody hears about it. Even people he's worked with. Death of a nobody. Kind of makes you stop and think."

"Right," I said. "When you say you didn't know him well? . . ."

"Hardly knew him at all. Just that one production. Quite a nice enough guy. Not that talented, maybe. Not that great an actor. I don't know how many guys he beat out for his part. But that was a different type of role. I'm sure he was just typecast in it. Beefy, overbearing redhead."

"Overbearing?" I said.

Fargo smiled. "Well, that was the role."

"Yes. But you said it was typecast. Did you find Cliff McFadgen overbearing? I thought you said he was a nice guy."

"Well, one hates to speak ill of the dead."

"Of course," I said. "On the other hand, this *is* a murder investigation. Anything you know that might be helpful, please don't withhold it on the theory that the ghost of Cliff McFadgen might be offended."

Speaking of offending people, I made another mental note to work on my patience and tact, which, it occurred to me, I seemed to have much less of now than before I'd been thrown in the drunk tank.

Fargo bristled, said somewhat stiffly, "I'm not withholding anything. The fact is, I didn't know the man well, and my impressions are probably not that helpful. If I say *overbearing,* that was merely an impression I got. I can't think of a single instance to base it on. We didn't have that much contact. We weren't really friends."

I imagined it was exactly that which had led Jack Fargo to form that impression.

"I understand," I said. "It's just a baffling situation, and I need all the help I can get. You didn't know Cliff McFadgen well. I didn't know him at all. So far I haven't been able to find anybody who *did* know him well. I apologize if I speak out of my frustration."

That seemed to mollify him. Fargo relaxed somewhat, settled back in his chair, crossed his legs.

Fargo lived in a studio apartment on West Eighty-eighth Street, fairly similar to the one where I'd found Cliff McFadgen. It was also as poorly furnished. Between that and not having a job, so far the only thing Jack Fargo had up on Cliff McFadgen was in being alive.

I smiled at Fargo. "So you can see my problem. I need to get a line on this guy, and no one knows him. So when I hear a word like *overbearing*, it may not seem like much, but at the moment it's all I got."

Fargo nodded. "Right. But then you gotta understand, I didn't know the guy personally. If I got an impression of him, it came from rehearsal."

"What did he do in rehearsal?"

Fargo frowned, considered. "That's just it. He didn't take direction well. If the director told him something, he didn't just do it. He'd stop and think about it, with this intense look on his face, as if he was going through some artistic agony. It was like he couldn't do it unless he could justify it to himself. To his character, I mean.

"And if he *couldn't*, he'd turn back to the director and say, 'Fred wouldn't do that.' And then they'd have to talk him into it."

"They?"

"The producer and the director. Phil and Charlie. They were really like co-directors—did everything together. They'd work on him, talk him into it."

"Could they do that?"

Fargo shook his head. "Not all the time. Most of the time, yeah. But some of the time the bastard wouldn't budge. That's what I mean by overbearing. There were times he'd get an idea in his head and just wouldn't budge."

"Why didn't they fire him?"

"I asked myself the same question. But, you know, a showcase, you do it on a shoestring. There's no extra money, no extra time. And once they're into rehearsals—to write those days off, bring in someone else—it's an iffy thing. I know there were times they'd have *liked* to fire him."

"Thanks. That's very helpful," I said. "Can you think of anything else you noticed about him? Anything at all?"

Fargo hesitated a moment. "Well, I don't know if it's what you want, but he wasn't good at learning his lines. He was awful, in fact. He was on the book longer than anyone, and when he came off it, he didn't say them as written. He paraphrased, you know. Gave you the general idea. Well, that's damn hard to work with. You never know when your cue's coming, 'cause you never know when his line's gonna end."

I nodded. "Despite all that, this play went on?"

"Oh yes, it went on."

"How was he in performance?"

"Same thing. You could never be sure what line he was gonna throw."

"What kind of reviews did it get?"

Fargo looked pained. "We didn't get reviewed. I know Phil tried to get 'em down there, but he couldn't pull it off. Damn shame. It's not like I did it for the money, you know."

"Yeah. Too bad," I said. "Tell me, does the name Patricia Connely mean anything to you?"

"Patricia Connely?"

"Yeah."

"Is that the woman who was killed?"

"That's right."

He shook his head. "Never heard of her. You say she was an actress?"

"That's right."

He shrugged. "In New York City, every woman's an actress. Unless I worked with her, I wouldn't know."

"What about Bradley Connely?"

"Bradley Connely?"

"Yeah. Name mean anything to you?"

He wrinkled up his nose. "It's a bad stage name. Both names ending in *lee*. It should be *Brad* Connely. If the guy's an actor. Is he?"

"As a matter of fact, he is."

Fargo shook his head. "Then I don't understand the name.

With a one-syllable last name *Bradley* is fine, but with Connely?"

"I meant had you ever heard of him?"

"No, I haven't."

"Are you sure?"

"A name like that, I wouldn't forget."

"Un-huh," I said. "Now about the woman—I'm wondering if you might have known her without knowing her name. Seen her out at auditions somewhere, or just making the rounds."

I reached in my jacket pocket, pulled out the photograph of Patricia Connely, and handed it to Jack Fargo. He took it, studied it.

"This is the dead woman?" he said.

"That's right."

"Attractive."

"Yes. What about it? Did you ever see her?"

He shook his head. "No, I haven't."

Fargo handed the picture back. I took it, wishing like hell I'd been able to dream up a reason to ask Bradley Connely for a picture of the two of them.

"Is that all?" Fargo said. "I don't mind helping, but I've got things to do."

"I think that's about it," I said.

I got up and went to the door. Fargo followed to let me out.

I turned back in the doorway. "Just one thing," I said.

"What's that?"

"I was wondering if you'd know of any actors who would be working legit now—but who might at one time in their career have posed for pornography."

Fargo's face drained of color.

"No," he said. "I can't think of anyone."

And he closed the door behind me.

Son of a bitch.

I figured it probably had absolutely nothing at all to ao with my investigation, but still I couldn't help wondering just what sort of pornographic pictures Jack Fargo had been involved with at some point in his career.

31.

Alice was not happy. "You're getting nowhere," she said.

"Excuse me?"

"Nothing adds up. There's got to be a link somewhere, and you haven't found it."

"What more could I be doing?"

"You only saw this one actor."

"That was the one the guy mentioned."

"What guy?"

"Her husband."

"You said he didn't know him. He just thought the name was familiar."

"Right."

"This actor probably wasn't any more important than anyone else in the cast."

I exhaled, rubbed my head.

We were sitting at the kitchen table. In the living room,

our son, Tommie, was playing Super Mario World on his Super NES, the new, improved, more expensive Nintendo system that all the kids simply had to have. The graphics were better and Mario got to ride on a dinosaur named Yoshi, and I had to admit the whole thing was indeed incredibly cute, but right now the bouncy music from it was getting on my nerves.

"Tommie, turn that down," I yelled.

There was a pause, then moments later the volume level dropped almost imperceptively.

I groaned, rubbed my head again.

"I'm not blaming you," Alice said. "It's just very frustrating."

It was indeed. What was even more frustrating was the fact that she *was* blaming me, but wouldn't admit it. A situation calculated to drive me crazy.

"The way I see it, Alice," I said. "If we're going to consider MacAullif's theory—" Here I paused and looked at her.

"Which of course we should," Alice said.

"Well, if we're going to do that, I think the important thing would be to find a link between Patricia Connely and Cliff McFadgen. So far we haven't been able to do it. And neither have the cops. We got nothing. Cliff McFadgen was in a show. And her husband thought one of the other actors in the show sounded familiar. Doesn't that make him a lead?"

Alice shook her head. "No."

"Why not?"

"Because whatever she was mixed up in—whether it's MacAullif's theory or what have you—her husband didn't know about it. So if there's a link between her and Cliff McFadgen, her husband didn't know about it. So if this is an actor her husband's heard of, I would say that makes him the *least* likely suspect."

I blinked, rubbed my head again. Looked up to find Alice waiting for a response.

"Well," she said. "Doesn't that make sense?"

I exhaled. "I suppose so."

"Don't humor me."

"I'm not humoring you."

"Well, don't say you suppose so if you really don't."

"Alice, I'm not having a good time here. Today I interviewed this actor. I interviewed her husband. And I interviewed the producer and director of the show. I got a picture of the woman to show around—"

"A picture of who?"

"Patricia Connely."

"You didn't tell me that."

"I forgot to mention it."

"Where is it? Let me see it."

I took the picture out of my jacket pocket, passed it over.

Alice inspected it critically. After a few moments she shook her head. "Figures."

"What does?"

"Your description of her. She doesn't look anything like it."

"Oh, come on," I said. I was afraid I was due for another composite-sketch-incident bashing.

But Alice merely frowned and said, "Poor woman." She looked up and said, "We've gotta do something."

"If you want me to interview the other actors, I'll interview the other actors. You gotta remember I'm fitting this in around my job. I got two cases for Richard already tomorrow. Who knows how many more will come in."

"I know," Alice said. She thought a moment. "Maybe *I* should interview those actors."

That was all. Just that simple flat statement.

I felt an absolute rush of panic.

It was incredible. Like I was suddenly hollow inside.

I'd like to think that it was fear for Alice. Not just fear that she was encroaching on my territory. Usurping my position and taking away my job. I mean, this wasn't castration anxiety, was it?

At any rate, I'm sure my face drained of color just as Jack Fargo's had when I'd mentioned pornography.

"You can't do it," I said.

Alice looked at me. "Good lord, what's the matter?" she said.

"I just had a panic attack at the thought of you doing that. Look, it's fine you making composite sketches and thinking this thing out. But it isn't just a game. Someone killed two people. And one of them was a woman. This person kills women. See? We don't know who and we don't know why, but we're asking these actors to find out.

"And if we do find out, if we do find the connection, we could be next. 'Cause any one of these actors could be the killer, see?"

Alice smiled. "I think you're being overprotective."

"I don't. I'll see them myself. In between jobs. I'll fit them in."

"Okay," Alice said. "And what about this Fargo?"

"What about him?"

"You gonna tell the cops about him?"

"Tell 'em what?"

"What you said. About pornography. How he reacted."

"That probably doesn't mean anything. Most likely he dabbled in it once."

"Yeah, but maybe not. Maybe the word *pornography* made him think of the pictures."

"You mean he's involved in the blackmail?"

"Right."

"And the murder?"

"Could be."

"Not likely. We discussed all that. Blackmail doesn't bother him. Murder doesn't bother him. Pornography does. I figure it's personal, not part of some scheme."

"Okay," Alice said. "But if he was involved in pornography, he could *know* the people in the blackmail photos. Without being involved in the scheme, he could be a witness of some sort. See what I mean?"

I frowned. Grimaced. "It's very farfetched, Alice."

"Then you don't think you should tell the cops?"

"Why should I? I already gave them the lead to the show. They'll talk to the producer, director, all the actors themselves. They've probably even done it already. When I talk to the actors tomorrow, they'll have already talked to the cops."

"I *suppose* so," Alice said.

She said it rather grudgingly.

But I didn't ask her if she *really* supposed so, or if she was just humoring me.

32.

I never got to talk to the actors.

I had a sign-up in the Bronx at nine o'clock. I'd planned on knocking it off real quick, which would leave me time for a little snooping before my two o'clock in Brooklyn. But I hit a traffic jam on the Cross Bronx Expressway and got beeped in the middle of it. By the time I got off and got to a phone I was already late for my nine o'clock, and Wendy/Janet gave me another sign-up in the Bronx for eleven. And just because two appointments are in the Bronx doesn't make them close together—the Bronx takes in a lot of territory. Anyway, I took care of my nine o'clock and was racing toward Co-op City for my eleven when she beeped me off the Hutchinson River Parkway to give me one in Queens. I actually managed that and was heading for my two o'clock in Brooklyn when she beeped me off the Interboro to give me a four o'clock back in the Bronx.

When she beeped me off the Triboro Bridge on my way there, I was ready to kill her. Failing that, I was certainly going to tell Wendy/Janet what she could do with her damn sign-up.

I never got a chance to.

Because this time she'd beeped me to tell me someone was dead.

33.

There were cop cars all around Jack Fargo's apartment. When I pulled up behind one, the officer on the sidewalk tried to wave me away. I pissed him off by stopping anyway and getting out of my car.

The officer, a bullnecked type of the Sergeant Thurman school of law enforcement, said, "Hey, buddy, I told you to move it."

"I'm Stanley Hastings," I said. "Sergeant Thurman wants to see me."

That meant something to him. He cocked his head, said, "Oh, *you're* the one." Then he looked at me the way I could imagine Romans looked at Christians just before marching them in to the lions. "Stay right here," he said. Then he turned and bellowed, "Hey, Marty. Tell the sarge he's here."

Richard showed up just then. I don't know what would have happened if he hadn't, but I was damn glad to see him.

I'd called him, of course, right after I'd talked to the cops and been instructed to come here. No one had said the name Jack Fargo, but I recognized the address, so I knew the news wasn't good.

Sergeant Thurman came out the front door and demanded, "Where's the asshole?"

When he spotted me his face got red. When he spotted Richard, it purpled. I had a feeling that not being able to beat me up was almost more than he could bear.

Thurman came thundering down the front steps. "So you got your lawyer here," he said. "Good for you. You need a lawyer."

"Now see here," Richard said.

"Shut the fuck up," Thurman said. "You wanna sue me, sue me. I don't give a shit. I'm not gonna hassle your client any, or deprive him of any of his fuckin' rights, but I'm damned if I'll listen to you." He turned to me. "Now, asshole, I need you to make an identification." He wheeled back on Richard. "You got any objections to that?"

Richard smiled. "None whatever. And thank you for phrasing it so politely."

Thurman grabbed me by the arm. "Come on, asshole."

"If you manhandle my client—" Richard said.

"Get fucked," Thurman growled, and dragged me inside.

It was Fargo, all right. I took one look and almost threw up. I think the only thing that stopped me was not wanting to give Sergeant Thurman the satisfaction.

They hadn't told me anything, so I hadn't known what to expect. I'd been prepared for a dead body. Shot, like the others.

Jack Fargo hadn't been shot.

He'd been butchered.

He'd been stabbed several times in the body.

His throat had been slit.

There was blood everywhere.

Fargo was lying on his back with his head twisted to the side. His eyes were wide and glassy. His face was white and drained of blood. Just as it had been when I'd asked him about pornography.

Jesus Christ.

"Well?" Sergeant Thurman demanded. He was looking at me closely. I got the impression he was disappointed I hadn't blown lunch. "You ever seen this man before?"

I took a breath. "Yes, I have."

"When?"

"Yesterday afternoon."

Thurman exhaled noisily. "Shit," he said. "You know his name?"

"Jack Fargo."

Thurman exhaled again. "Great," he said. "Just great." He turned, jerked his thumb at the crime-scene unit and the medical examiner. "Okay, boys," he said. "Sorry to bother you, it's all yours again."

Thurman grabbed my arm, jerked me out of there.

I was relieved to see Richard still standing on the sidewalk out front. Thurman dragged me up to him.

"Your client's involved in another homicide. I need to ask him some questions. You intend to let him cooperate?"

"Absolutely."

"Fine," Thurman said. "I got a few questions myself, but I been instructed to bring you in. And I'm sure as hell going along. So let's move it."

We moved it, and not twenty minutes later, Sergeant Thurman, Richard, a stenographer, and I were all sitting at a conference table with Baby-Face Frost.

Who didn't look happy. "Mr. Hastings," Frost said, "I understand that you called on Jack Fargo yesterday afternoon."

"Yes, I did."

"What time was that?"

"Around two o'clock."

"Why did you call on him?"

"You know why. Because the last people to use the theater space where Patricia Connely was found dead were a theater group, and Cliff McFadgen happened to be in the production. I was checking on the other people who were in the production."

"On the actors?"

"And the producer and director."

"Yes, I know you talked to them. But I'm now referring to

the actors. How many actors in the production did you talk to?"

"Just one."

"Jack Fargo?"

"That's right."

"Why him in particular?"

"When I spoke to Patricia Connely's husband, that was the only name he said sounded familiar."

"And when did you speak to Mr. Connely?"

"Yesterday."

"What time?"

"That would be around one o'clock."

"Just before you went to Fargo?"

"That's right."

Frost took a breath, blew it out again. "Mr. Hastings. Yesterday at twelve noon you were in this very office. Sitting at this very table. Discussing the case."

"Yes, sir."

Frost picked up a folded paper from the table. "At that time you gave me this program from the show Cliff McFadgen was in. Said that you had received it from the director of the show."

"That's right."

"Among the cast listed is the decedent, Jack Fargo."

"This is true."

"Are you telling me you took a copy of this program to Patricia Connely's husband, showed it to him, asked him if it meant anything to him?"

"Yes, I did."

"You had no right to do that."

"I think I'd like to jump in here," Richard said. "That is not a question."

"I retract it," Frost said. "Mr. Hastings, when you were in here yesterday and presented me with this program, you didn't mention that you had *two* copies of it. Did you?"

"No, I did not."

"Did you mention that you were going to call on Patricia Connely's husband?"

"No, I did not."

"Mr. Hastings, you are a private detective, is that right?"

"Yes, it is."

"Are you employed by anyone at the present time to investigate this crime?"

"No, I am not."

"Or the deaths of Patricia Connely or Cliff McFadgen?"

"No, I am not."

"You are employed by Mr. Rosenberg here, are you not, to investigate accident cases?"

"Yes, I am."

"I wanted to get that cleared up," Frost said. "So you have no official standing in this case?"

"I'm a witness."

"That you are. Do you understand the difference between a witness and an investigator?"

"Once again," Richard said, "I feel the need to step in. While that *is* a question, it is not one designed to elicit any information. Need I say more?"

"No," Frost said. "Let's move on. Mr. Hastings, were you aware that, yesterday afternoon, Bradley Connely lodged a formal complaint against the way the investigation into his wife's death was being handled?"

Oh, shit.

"No, I was not," I said.

"Is that so?" Frost said. "For your information, he first demanded to see the officer in charge. When Sergeant Thurman was not available, he demanded to see me. I actually met with the man, not that I really had the time or the inclination to do so."

I said nothing, just sat there and took it. Everything in the world was blowing up in my face.

"Now then," Frost said. "Mr. Connely didn't indicate what prompted him to pay this call—he was actually rather evasive as to how he formed his opinion. Not that I thought that much about it at the time. With a widowed husband, this reaction is fairly typical. The police are never doing enough, the investigation is being bungled, etcetera, etcetera. Frankly, I was busy and tried to brush him off and get him out of here.

"But it wasn't easy. Because you'd told him about Cliff McFadgen being in that showcase production. So the guy had a legitimate gripe, wanting to know how the hell you got that ahead of the cops."

I stole a glance at Thurman. Visions of drunk tanks danced in my head.

"This was late afternoon," Frost said. "Sergeant Thurman was already out chasing down leads from the names in the program. Which is why we hadn't got to you yet. Because, otherwise, believe me we would."

"I believe you," I said. I shouldn't have. I should have just sat there with my mouth closed. I made a mental note to do so, and Richard shot me a glance that clearly meant the same thing.

Frost took a breath. "The thing is, no one knew you were calling on these actors. Thurman was calling on them, and he never crossed your back trail. Of course he never got to see Jack Fargo, because Fargo wasn't in. There was nothing crucial about these actors, so we naturally called on those who were in. Only, Fargo was in, he just wasn't answering the bell."

"When was he killed?" I said.

Richard shot me another glance, but Frost merely ignored my question and went on as if I hadn't asked it.

"What's the wrap-up?" Frost said. "By this afternoon we've talked to all the actors except Fargo. When he's still a no-show, we checked with the super and went in. You know what we found."

That was not a question, so I kept quiet.

"One of the first people we contacted was Bradley Connely. Dragged him down there to see if he could make the ID."

I sat on the impulse to say, "Did he?"

Frost told me anyway. "Connely says he never saw him before in his life. But tells us the name is familiar. Tells us he told *you* the name was familiar. A thing he hadn't *remembered* to tell us when he was in here yesterday making all the fuss."

Oh boy. What a fucking mess.

Frost took a breath. Went on. "Well, that booted contacting you from being a rather low-to-middling priority way up to the top of the list. Which is why you've been to see the body, and why you're here now.

"Now," Frost said. "The reason I'm being such a nice guy and telling you and your attorney all this is because I want you to be fully aware of just how important all of this is. I wouldn't want you to say you were acting out of ignorance of the facts. The facts are these: Since you say you called on Jack Fargo yesterday afternoon, you were probably the last person to see him alive. You were certainly the last person we are *aware* of to see him alive. So the importance of that particular visit is clear. Do you understand?"

"Yes, I do."

He turned to Richard. "Do you understand what I'm telling your client?"

"I have a certain grasp of the English language. But if that was a threat, I certainly didn't hear it. Because I'm sure no reputable A.D.A. would ever make one."

I tried to catch Richard's eye. I knew he couldn't let himself be pushed around, but at that point I just wanted them to get on with it.

Frost did. "Now, Mr. Hastings," he said. "Could you please tell us the sum and substance of your meeting with the deceased, Jack Fargo?"

"Certainly," I said. "As you might expect, I went there for the specific purpose of finding out how well acquainted he was with Cliff McFadgen. I also endeavored to find out if he had any knowledge whatever of Patricia Connely or her husband, Bradley Connely."

"Had he?"

"None at all. Neither of the names meant anything to him, and he didn't recognize her picture."

Frost looked up. "Picture?"

"Yes. Patricia Connely's picture."

"Where did you get that?"

"Her husband gave it to me."

As Frost and Sergeant Thurman exchanged glances, I said, "I take it he didn't mention that either?"

"So you have her picture," Frost said. "May we see it?"

I looked to Richard.

He said, "You may *see* it. You may not *have* it."

Frost thought that over. "Very well," he said. "At this point, I am asking only to inspect the photo."

Richard turned to me. "Show it to him."

I took the picture out of my pocket, passed it over. Frost examined it, passed it to Thurman.

Richard extended his hand across the table.

Thurman glanced at Frost, who nodded, then grudgingly handed it back.

Richard gave me the picture and I put it back in my pocket.

A small victory, but one's own.

"You say he didn't recognize the picture?"

"Not at all."

"Or either of the names?"

"That's right."

"What about Cliff McFadgen? How well did he know him?"

"He *claimed* he didn't know him at all. The only evidence he gave to the contrary was in describing him as overbearing."

"Overbearing?"

"That's right. When I questioned him on it, he said that was an opinion formed from rehearsal and from the guy's refusal to take direction. But he claimed he didn't know him socially at all."

"Did you believe him?"

"Is that relevant?" Richard asked.

Frost shrugged. "Maybe not. I'm not trying to bind your client to anything. I'm just interested in what he thought."

"On that basis, you may answer," Richard said.

"Did you believe him?" Frost repeated.

"Actually, I did."

"I see," Frost said. He thought a moment. "Did you learn anything else from Jack Fargo which you considered to be significant?"

I hesitated.

Frost pounced on it. "Yes? What is it?"

"I asked about pornography. Because of the blackmail pictures. I asked him if he knew of any actors working legitimately now, who used to be involved in porn."

"Did he?"

"He said no. But the question bothered him. I could tell. His face actually went pale."

Frost stared at me. He blinked. "And you didn't communicate this to the police?"

"Now, hold on a minute," Richard said. "Are you making the charge my client *should* have communicated this to the police? Are you indicating some *law* was broken here?"

"I'm not saying it was," Frost said. "I'm not saying it wasn't, either."

Richard turned to me. "Under those circumstances, don't tell him a thing."

"Whoa. Hold on here," Frost said. "Let's not go off the deep end here."

"Deep end, hell," Richard said. "You're giving me a maybe-if about suspecting my client of a crime? Then our cooperation is over. My client's been quite frank and forthcoming. He's come in here of his own volition and given his statement. That statement is now over. Unless you care to retract what you just said, our cooperation is withdrawn. And since the statement is over, I suggest we go off the record."

Frost nodded to the stenographer. "That will do." He turned to me. "Now, speaking informally and off the record, why the fuck didn't you tell somebody?"

"Let me answer, Richard."

He shrugged. "Off the record, fine."

"Because I didn't think it had anything to do with the case. The way the guy acted, he gave the impression that *he'd* been involved in porn some time ago. He found the subject embarrassing. Like it touched a nerve. Sort of related only to him."

"That's why you didn't see fit to relate this to the police?" Frost said.

"That's right."

Frost cocked his head, looked at me. It was hard to imagine a baby face looking so hard. "And this was yesterday?" he said. His eyes bored into mine. "Yesterday?" He paused, then rammed it home.

"While Jack Fargo was still alive?"

34.

Alice was devastated. She took it worse than I did, which was saying something. Which was pretty unfair, since she was the one who had insisted Jack Fargo's reaction to pornography had to mean something. I was the one who had pooh-poohed the idea, said it meant something else. But she didn't throw it in my face, like nine out of ten other women would have done. She didn't blame me.

Which was good, 'cause I was doing a pretty good job of blaming myself.

"It's not your fault," Alice said. It was not the first time she'd uttered those words.

Or the first time they'd fallen on deaf ears. "I wish you'd stop saying that," I said.

"Why? You *want* it to be your fault?"

"Alice."

"That's understandable, because it's easier," Alice said. "Just accept the fact it's your fault, and wallow in it."

"Damn it."

"Not that I'm accusing you of wallowing," Alice said. "But it's perfectly understandable that that's how a person would naturally feel."

I wanted to strangle her. Why couldn't she be like those nine out of ten other women and tell me it was my fault? But, no, I had to go through pseudosupportive psycho-babble. Only, *pseudosupportive* is unfair, since I'm sure Alice really means it. Not that that makes it any easier to live with. Harder, in fact, since I can't blame her for it.

"Alice," I said. "Thank you. I know you mean well. But the fact is, I fucked up. I should have listened to you yesterday. If I had, maybe this wouldn't have happened."

"Nonsense," Alice said. "Don't you remember what I said? I told you this one actor wasn't any more important than the rest of them."

"No, you didn't."

"Sure I did. Wasn't I bitching and moaning 'cause you'd only called on this one guy?"

"Well . . ."

"You don't remember that?"

"Bitching and moaning is not the way I'd have phrased it."

"No, but you get the idea. Don't you remember discussing that?"

"Yes, of course."

"There you are."

"Alice, you also said his reaction to pornography was important. You even suggested I take it to the cops."

"I didn't suggest that."

"Yes, you did."

"No, I didn't. I asked you if you were *going* to take it to the cops."

"Isn't that the same thing?"

"Not at all."

Which is another excellent example of why I can't argue with Alice. If she had *wanted* it to be the same thing, it would have been.

"When was he killed?" Alice asked.

"They didn't say."

"But you got a feeling, didn't you?"

"Only generally."

"Wasn't the impression you got that the cops tried to call on Fargo yesterday, but they couldn't reach him because he was dead?"

"That's right."

"See? So when we were talking about it, the odds are he was already dead. Isn't that right?"

"It's possible."

"It's more than possible. It's likely. And if you'd gone to the cops, no difference."

"Maybe not then. But I'm a big boy. I didn't need you to point that out to me. I could have gone to the cops right away."

"Maybe they listened and maybe they didn't. And maybe while they were listening, Jack Fargo was getting killed. So the end result—no difference."

I took a breath, blew it out again. "There's the other thing, Alice."

"What's that?"

"However you want to slice it, basically the guy got killed because I called on him."

Alice shook her head. "See now, there's another example of wrong thinking."

Wrong thinking. How does she do it?

"I beg your pardon?"

Alice spoke to me as if addressing a small child. "Stanley. Jack Fargo did not get killed because you called on him. Jack Fargo got killed because he got involved in blackmail and murder. He may have got involved in pornography too, but that's somehow beside the point."

"Not if he knew the blackmail victims."

"Big deal. There's no evidence that he did. That's mere supposition on your part."

"It's a logical inference."

Alice shrugged. "Well, if you're determined to wallow."

"Damn it, Alice."

"No, no. I quite understand," Alice said. "It makes perfect sense that you would want to. And I suppose you can make a case for feeling guilty. Even if you have to stretch the facts a bit to make it hold water."

Jesus Christ.

I had to hand it to Alice. If I wound up solving this crime, I would owe it all to her.

I'd have done it in self-defense.

35.

MacAullif looked up from his desk. "What's the matter?" he said. "You avoiding me?"

"What do you mean?"

"There was another murder yesterday. It's been a whole day and you haven't been in."

"I've been busy."

"So I heard. Star witness. You and Baby-Face must be getting to be real buddies."

"I don't think Thurman likes me much."

"Really? Give him time. By the fourth or fifth murder, maybe he'll come around."

"Yeah. You pull the case file on Fargo?"

"Sure did."

"Mind telling me the time of death?"

"Day before yesterday between two and four in the afternoon."

"Shit."

"Yeah. Includes the time you were there, doesn't it?"

"That's not what bothers me."

"Feel like you killed him?"

"Feel like I caused his death, yes."

"That's stupid. You do what you do, and what happens, happens. If I figured like that, I probably caused a lot of deaths. You can't figure like that."

"I can't see why not."

"Bullshit. If the guy got croaked, it's 'cause he was dirty. It's not your fault if he was dirty."

"No? And if I don't go see him, what are the chances he's alive today?"

MacAullif shrugged. "Better than they are now. But there's no way you could know that."

"That doesn't make it any better."

"I know that. Nothing makes it any better. Which is why you have to let it go. At least deal with it on a nonpersonal level. Say, 'Yeah, that's the fact. I call on this guy and now he's dead. Is this cause and effect? And if so, I wanna figure out why.' See what I mean?"

"Easy for you to say."

"Bullshit. You think this doesn't happen to me? It happens to me all the fucking time. And you know what? Sometimes it's my fault and sometimes it ain't. And I can't spend all my time trying to figure out if it is.

"Now, in your case, I can't see how it's your fault at all. Not that that's gonna make you feel any better, knowing you. But there you are. Anyway, you call on this guy and now he's dead. That's a fact. You can either examine it or wallow in it."

I blinked at the echo of Alice.

"What is it?" MacAullif said.

"Nothing. All right. Let's examine it."

"Okay," MacAullif said. "The way I see it, you call on a guy and now he's dead. That makes you a living-poison, rotten scumbag son of a bitch."

"Hey."

"If you don't like that interpretation, that makes *him* a living-poison, rotten scumbag son of a bitch. Which is why he got killed. And the interesting part of him getting killed is it followed right on the heels of you calling on him."

"Nice of you to say so."

MacAullif raised his eyebrows. "Oh?"

"Rather than concluding he was killed while I was there."

"Don't be dumb," MacAullif said. "Even Thurman doesn't think that. The point is, your visit triggers Fargo's death."

"You have to keep harping on it?"

"That's the premise. If that's true, we gotta figure out why. 'Cause the *why* is hard, let's figure out how. You called on him, you dropped your bombshell about pornography, and you left. Within two hours the man is dead. Now how'd he get dead?"

"Like you said. Because of what I told him about pornography."

"Right," MacAullif said. "But how did anybody know that? I don't recall any other people present at this conversation."

"True."

"So are they psychic? How do they know this revelation is taking place?"

"Fargo must have called someone."

"That's one possibility," MacAullif said.

"You got another?"

"Always. You always got another. 'Cause there's no such thing as a sure thing."

"Oh, please."

"It's a good bet he called someone. Though that is as yet unconfirmed by the phone company. But say he *did* call someone. Who's he gonna call?"

"The people in the pictures."

"Of course. That's the only thing that makes sense. That's the only way he winds up dead. Plus, it fits in with the theory of the other murders—people bein' blackmailed kill rather than pay off."

"If it's that easy, why can't we solve this damn case?"

"Maybe 'cause the moron who saw the pictures couldn't describe his own ass."

"Fuck you. It happens my wife gave a pretty good description."

"Of your ass?"

"I thought we didn't have time to fool around."

"No. *You* don't have time to fool around. I'm in charge. I got time to do any fuckin' thing I want."

MacAullif had a cigar on his desk, already unwrapped. He picked it up, sniffed it.

"Where were we? Oh yeah. The only people it makes sense he calls are the people in the pictures. If that's true, they came and killed him."

"Which one?"

"What's the difference? This is all supposition. But as a guess, probably the guy. A mess like that. A bunch of knife wounds. If he's shot, it's just as easy a woman. But a guy gets stabbed, it's usually another guy. Unless it's in the back, and this wasn't in the back. Anyway, that certainly would seem to be the way it plays out. There's only one other scenario that makes sense."

"What's that?"

"You were followed."

"What?"

"You were followed to Fargo's. The killer sees you got a line to Fargo, he knows Fargo's gotta go."

"Oh, shit."

"Whatsa matter? Make you feel *more* guilty? I thought your guilt level was already at the max."

"It's a disturbing thought."

"Hey, this whole thing's disturbing. But the way I work it out, that's the only other solution. If Fargo didn't call the killer, then the killer followed you."

"Yeah, but . . ."

"But what?"

"Well, nobody knew I was going to Fargo's. Except Bradley Connely. And he's the one who gave me the lead."

"That don't mean he didn't kill him. I admit it makes no sense. I see what you're saying—if Jack Fargo's the guy he's trying to keep you away from, there's no reason to tip you off to him. Unless it's an elaborate double bluff to draw suspicion away from himself." MacAullif shook his head. "But that doesn't fly."

"Why not?"

"Because he kills him *after* you go to see him. If Fargo's going to spill the beans at all, he's likely to do it the first time. You ask him and he talks. Or you ask him and he *doesn't* talk. The only scenario that killing him after your first visit guards against is, you ask him, he doesn't talk, but he's likely to later. But you got a killer figuring like that, you really got no problem, 'cause the dumb boob's gonna fuck up all over the place. So, yeah, the idea of the husband is rather farfetched. Not impossible, just not likely. But you see where you fuck up?"

"No, but I'm sure you're going to tell me."

"Hey, who came to whose office? Now look here. You say, like a moron, that nobody but this Connely guy knew you were going to Fargo's. The point is, who gives a shit? You've been involved in this blackmail scheme from the beginning. You're the murderer's tool. So you got one or two possibilities. Either the murderer's keeping tabs on you, or the murderer ain't done playin' with you. Either way, say he's following you. He's not following you because he knows you're going to Jack Fargo's apartment. He's following you because he wants to see *where* you go. And believe it or not, he doesn't *start* when you leave the Connely apartment. Most likely he's been followin' you all day. Now, what did you do in the morning?"

"I called on the producer and director. I got a program from the show."

"Right. And the killer's following you and sees you doing all that. He's interested, 'cause this shows you're on the right track. Then you go see Connely, obviously lookin' for a lead. He wonders if Connely gave you one. You leave Connely's and where do you go? Straight to Jack Fargo. Bingo. Bump-off time. Can we conclude? Producer and director have no information of any importance. Fargo did."

"Damn."

"Hey, it's not necessarily lost forever. Most likely what he had was a lead to the people in the pictures. But that's only the one possibility. There may be a lot we don't know. Then there's the other possibility."

"What's that?"

"That the killer is *not* the people in the pictures, but the mastermind behind the blackmail. The conspiracy theory, right? Everyone setting you up. Though why he would bump off his henchmen before the sting went down—that's a little hard to figure. Afterwards, sure. But before he got the money?" MacAullif shrugged. "Makes no sense." He drummed the cigar on the desk á couple of times. "Anyway, you call on any of these other actors?"

"Actors from the showcase?"

"No, the cast of *Chorus Line*. I know you've had a hard day, but get with the picture."

"No, I didn't. But Thurman did."

"Yeah, but so what? This guy doesn't have to be the swiftest thing in the world to realize Thurman ain't no threat. His talkin' to these actors doesn't have to scare him. On the other hand, if *you* talked to them . . ."

"Are you suggesting I should?"

"No, I was just wondering."

"Wondering what?"

"If you were to talk to another actor in the show . . ."

"Yeah?"

"Whether he'd die."

36.

It was kind of tough after that. The thing is, I'm basically a nice guy. And I *did* want to talk to the other actors. But after MacAullif saying that, I just couldn't do it. Because if I called on one of them and he got killed, I could never forgive myself. I was having a hard enough time over Jack Fargo. And I didn't know anything when I went to see him. But with the idea in my head, to deliberately go see someone—I just couldn't bring myself to do it.

Maybe with police backup I would have. With cops there to protect the guy. In fact, it might have been a fine idea. Setting a trap. But somehow I couldn't see Sergeant Thurman going along with me.

I thought of calling them on the phone, which would be next to useless—no one tells you anything on the phone. So talking with the actors was out.

Fortunately, I had other fish to fry.

Sergeant Thurman had come up with one solid lead. *Come up with* is probably too strong a phrase—it was actually dropped in his lap. It wasn't in Jack Fargo's file. It was an addition to Cliff McFadgen's.

His girlfriend.

Her name was Martha Penrutti. She was—what else?—an actress. She lived with four other actresses in a six-room apartment on Riverside Drive.

The first thing that struck me about her was she had red hair. I couldn't help picturing her with Cliff, imagining them with little red-haired kids.

She had green eyes that welled with tears every two or three minutes, which made conversation slow. At least she was willing to talk to me. I imagined I owed some of that to Sergeant Thurman—after chatting with him, I probably seemed somewhat pleasant.

The fact that I had no real status in the case didn't matter a bit. I admitted right up front that I wasn't a cop, just a private detective. Martha couldn't have cared less, but her roommates were downright thrilled. Apparently they didn't know Cliff McFadgen that well, and his demise was pretty exciting to them. Having a real-life P.I. in their living room was just the icing on the cake.

The actresses were young, attractive, and impressionable. They were also apparently unemployed, since all of them were home at eleven o'clock on a weekday morning. Anyway, I found their attention flattering. At least until it occurred to me to wonder if my being there was putting *them* in danger. But by then it was too damn late—if I'd done it, I'd done it, and I might as well ask my questions.

Which I did.

Not that Martha Penrutti was particularly helpful. Naturally, she knew nothing whatever of any blackmail scheme.

"Cliff wouldn't do that," she said, then had recourse to tears.

It was several minutes before I could get her back in the frame of mind to discuss what Cliff *would* do. Which was basically act. According to Martha, it was all the guy talked about. It was certainly all *Martha* talked about. Classes, auditions, casting agents. A world I knew well. A world I'd left behind.

A world I didn't give two shits about now.

"Did you notice anything different about him recently? Say, in the last two weeks?"

"No," she said. "Why should I?"

That was the type of stupid question I could think of no response to that wasn't devastatingly cruel. I said gently, "In light of what happened."

Which was devastatingly cruel, and brought on a fresh torrent of tears.

That was sort of the way it went. Me tiptoeing through the tulips and treading on each tender blossom, until the poor damsel could take it no more and retreated to the bathroom.

Which was actually helpful, because it left her roommates free to talk.

When the bathroom door shut, as if on cue, all giggled.

One of them, a brunette in a purple tank top, said, "The tragic heroine. You think she does it well?"

I frowned. "I beg your pardon."

"Really," a long-haired blonde said, with a glance at the door. "To hear her talk, you'd think she and Cliff were lovers."

I blinked. "Weren't they?"

All the girls giggled again.

"Please," I said. "Before she comes back. What do you mean by that?"

The brunette, a perky young thing who seemed to be the ringleader, shut the others up and took charge. "Come on, give me a break," she said. "She dated the guy a couple of times. Big deal." She jerked her thumb at the blonde. "He's asked Carol out too."

This was not surprising. Carol, apparently a late riser, was wearing a sheer nightie covered by a silk kimono with a tendency to gape.

"Oh?" I said, raising my eyebrows and fighting my own tendency to gape.

"I didn't go," Carol said. "But Jean's right. He asked me, yeah."

"And, come on," Jean said. "It's not like they were living

together. She's living here with us. And seeing the guy maybe once a week."

"If that," a third girl put in. Her hair was also blond, but short and curly. She was wearing a white sweater and her breasts were quite large. It occurred to me that last observation probably had nothing to do with my murder investigation.

"Right," Jean said. "But according to her, they were practically engaged."

"I see," I said. "So when she says she doesn't know of any scheme he could have been mixed up in? . . ."

Jean shrugged. "Right. How would *she* know?"

Shit. My promising lead had come to absolutely nothing.

"You're saying she wouldn't know any better than you guys?"

Jean nodded. "That's the truth."

"Well," I said. "What about it? Did any of *you* notice anything different about him in the last weeks."

"I did."

I looked around in surprise.

When I said the girls were attractive, I was making a general statement. Some, of course, were more attractive than others.

This was one of the others. Your basic wallflower. A shy young thing with straight hair and glasses who had faded into the woodwork early on and had not uttered a word till now.

"Oh? And what was that?" I asked her.

The girl seemed rather pleased with herself. "He had money," she said.

The other girls were all over her in a moment, ridiculing that suggestion and asking her how she knew that.

The girl held her ground. "I saw him flash it," she said. "Last week. When he picked her up for the date."

That remark was greeted by cries of, "Oh yeah," "Go on," "No such thing," as well as the name "Bernice," uttered disparagingly with a heavy accent on the second syllable.

Jean smiled. "The reason we're so sure is Cliff was cheap." With a glance at the bathroom she lowered her voice and said, "The dates they went out on, they were dutch."

"But he *had* the money," Bernice said. "I saw it."

"Go on."

"No, I did."

"Nonsense," Jean said. "If he'd had money, Cliff would have said so. Remember how he bragged about how much he made on that commercial?"

"But I *saw* it."

"Oh, pooh."

"No, wait," I said. "What do you mean by that?"

Bernice stuck out her chin defiantly. "When he called on her, when he came to pick her up, she was still getting ready. He was waiting in the living room. I was in the kitchen and I saw him through the door. He pulled a wad of money out of his pocket, looked at it, and stuck it back."

"Bernice," the blonde named Carol hissed. "Don't make things up."

"I'm *not* making it up," Bernice said angrily.

"Bernice makes things up," Jean said.

"I do not!"

"She doesn't mean to, she just has a vivid imagination. If she says she saw the money, it means she *thinks* she saw it."

"I saw it," Bernice insisted, "and what's more, he saw me."

The girls tried to pooh-pooh that, but I shut them up. "What do you mean?"

"He saw me. In the kitchen door. He saw me when I saw him open his wallet."

"You mean he knew you saw him?"

"Exactly," Bernice said. "Because he grinned and put his finger to his lips like this. Then he beckoned me out of the kitchen, and he made me promise not to tell anyone. He was really insistent, so I did."

"Then why are you telling?" Carol said.

Bernice gave her a look. It occurred to me it must be hard to be picked on all the time. "Because he's dead," she said witheringly. "It's different now he's dead." She looked at me. "Isn't it?"

"Yes, it is," I said. "And this is exactly what I need. Listen, what did he say about the money? Did he explain where he got it?"

"Yes, he did. He said he got a job."

"What kind of job?"

"Acting, of course. He said he had an acting job, but it was a surprise, he didn't want anyone to know about it. He made me promise not to tell."

"He didn't say anything about blackmail?"

"Of course not."

"He let you think he got a part somewhere?"

"That's right."

"He say what it was? Dinner theater, off-Broadway, summer stock, what?"

"No. He just said he got a part."

"Did you ask him?"

"Yeah, but he said it was a secret. Then Martha came in and we had to stop talking about it."

At that moment the bathroom door opened and Martha came in and we had to stop talking about it. I suppose we could have continued, but I wasn't up to the histrionics that would have resulted from that. So I decided to hang it up.

I was about to go when something occurred to me. Which I suppose should have occurred to me before. But at the rate this case was popping, there was at least some excuse for getting confused. At any rate, since no one had mentioned him, it occurred to me to wonder if Sergeant Thurman had been here before or after the demise of Jack Fargo.

Whichever it was, he sure hadn't mentioned him. Because when I asked, no one reacted to his name.

But then one of the girls, the curly-haired blonde whose name I didn't know, frowned and said, "Oh yeah. The name's familiar. Didn't we see him in something?"

"He was in a showcase with Cliff," I suggested.

"That's it, that's it," she cried. "Remember, we knew we'd seen Cliff in something and that was it? Well, same thing. That's where we saw him." She looked at me. "Little dumpy guy, right?"

"Yeah. That's him."

"Oh, I remember him now," Jean said. "I've seen him at auditions."

"You know anything about him?" I said. "Any connection between him and Cliff?"

"Why? Was there any?"

I saw no reason to drop the bombshell. "Not that I know of," I said. "I'm just interested in any information. None of you know him well? He never asked you out on a date or anything?"

That produced a sputter of laughter, even from the grieving Martha.

"Gosh, no," Jean said. "Him?"

"A guy doesn't have to be the most attractive man in the world to ask a girl out."

"But not him," Jean said. "Heck, he's gay."

I was out of there shortly after that, having neither enlightened them about the demise of Jack Fargo, nor having been enlightened by them, except in the revelation that Fargo was gay. I suppose I could have figured that out for myself, if I'd stopped to think about it. But I hadn't. It had never occurred to me. Not that it was particularly important.

Or was it?

It was not until I was driving away from the place that the thought occurred to me.

If Jack Fargo was gay, the pornographic past that so embarrassed him was probably gay porn.

Which kind of screwed up the idea of him having once been involved with the people in the blackmail photos.

37.

MacAullif looked like he had a severe case of indigestion.

"Twice in one day?" he said. "To what do I owe this honor?"

I told him about the actresses. What I'd found out about Cliff McFadgen being flush, and Jack Fargo being gay.

The news did not thrill him. "You came in here just for this?"

"It's important," I said.

"It's important the guy's gay? Where's your bleeding-heart liberalism, sayin' a man's sexual orientation shouldn't matter one way or another?"

"Give me a break. If Fargo was involved in pornography, his death made sense. He was involved with the people in the blackmail photos. He's a threat to them, so they kill him."

"Please."

"It fit well enough. The guy practically had a coronary when I mentioned porn."

"It fit well enough because you *made* it fit. You took two vaguely related facts and jammed them together. They don't have to mean shit. If the guy's gay, they probably *don't* mean shit. There's no connection."

"The connection is, Fargo died."

"That I admit. But he didn't necessarily die because he did porn."

"You think it's coincidental?"

"I think there are probably a lot more starving actors in New York City fall into dirty pictures than one might think. Actresses make fuck films and dance in topless clubs. So a gay guy does porn. Probably not that unusual."

"Are you telling me it doesn't mean anything?"

"No, no," MacAullif said. "Everything means something. I'm telling you it probably doesn't mean what you think it means. Most things don't. You gather your information, you form your theories. Most of them explode in your face until one pans out."

I gritted my teeth. When MacAullif was expounding on *his* theories, I couldn't recall him talking as if he expected them to explode in *his* face.

"Fine," I said. "But where does that leave us?"

MacAullif looked puzzled. "That leaves us right where we were this morning. With a bunch of theories to test and data to check out. As for Fargo bein' gay, I'm sorry it upsets you so much. Me, I can't see it's a big deal. But this other thing you learned—about Cliff McFadgen bein' loaded—hey, that fits right in just fine. He was makin' money on the blackmail scheme. Of course he won't let on. This actress sees him with it, he makes up a story about the acting work he's gotten, then swears her to secrecy. Because he doesn't want the babe he's going with to know about it. Particularly since you say he's not really going with her, just takin' her out once or twice. For my money, this is a fairly good piece of corroborating evidence, and you ought to be pleased instead of grousing all over the place."

"Oh, come on."

"And you sure as hell shouldn't be running into my office

as if it were the end of the world. So Jack Fargo's gay. Big fuckin' deal. You know why it upsets you so much?"

"'Cause I have doubts about my own masculinity?"

"No, asshole. Because you're obsessed with the idea you killed him. You think this fucks it up. Or it doesn't. I don't know. Either way. Maybe that's it right there. You can't tell whether his bein' gay confirms the fact you killed him, or exonerates you from guilt. You're desperate to know, so it makes you a little crazy."

"I'm not crazy."

"You're not the sanest son of a bitch I ever saw. Look, do me a favor. Go play in traffic or something. Till something else happens. This shit you're bringin' me ain't worth the trip."

"I take it nothing's come in from your end?"

"Sergeant Thurman is *not* close to crackin' the case, no. Go on, get the hell out of here, do something useful. Maybe you can capture this guy before he kills again."

"You think he will?"

"How the hell should I know?"

"I'm serious. These actresses I talked to—you think they're in any danger?"

"*Anyone* could be in danger. Because we don't know who we're dealing with. We can't stop living because of that. Is that your idea? That everything you do makes things worse? You could be right, you could be wrong. But you can't think about it. You pick one way or another and you hope you're right. Investigating the crime could cost lives. It could save lives. Who's to know?"

"That's a hell of an attitude for a police sergeant."

"Sorry to disillusion you. But I can't solve your problems. A team of *shrinks* couldn't solve your problems. Get out of here and let me do my work."

"Come on, MacAullif. Just between you and me. You think I'm putting people in danger?"

MacAullif made a face. "What a pain in the ass. You can't tie your shoes without advice? Okay, you want advice, why don't you talk to the husband."

I frowned. "Why do you say that?"

"To get you out of my office."

"No, MacAullif. Why him?"

"You're so damn obsessed about putting people in danger."

I frowned. "Yeah. So?"

He shrugged. "So there you are. You talked to the guy twice already, and he's still alive."

38.

Bradley Connely seemed animated. The most I'd seen him since his wife died. Of course I'd *only* seen him since his wife died, so it was the most animated I'd ever seen him. He'd been upset before, but this was different. There was light in his eyes.

"The right track," he said. "We're on the right track. Jack Fargo. I *knew* the name was familiar."

"But you didn't see the showcase?"

"No."

"You still have no idea where?"

"I'm trying to think. Christ, I've been doing nothing else. It just won't come to me."

"And Cliff McFadgen—still no connection there?"

He grimaced. "None whatever. But it must exist, see? Because of Fargo."

"I understand you saw the body?"

His face contorted. "Yes. Yes, I did. Horrible. Hard to think about."

"So hard you couldn't look at it?"

"No. I had to know. And I'm sure. I'd never seen him before. It was just the name."

"And you have no idea who mentioned it?"

He shook his head. "How many times can I tell you? No."

My hand reached into my inside jacket pocket. Then I hesitated, torn.

The action was too familiar. It reminded me of reaching in, pulling out the program, showing him the names. Hearing him say Jack Fargo sounded familiar.

In my hand now was the list of names of the actresses I'd just talked to.

And I could see it happen. Me pulling it out, showing it to him. Him telling me he didn't know them, but one of the names sounded familiar.

And her winding up dead.

So I almost didn't.

But I had MacAullif's little talk prodding me, giving me a much-needed kick in the ass. A voice kept telling me, *it's not cause and effect, it's not your fault.*

I took out the list, passed it over.

"You know any of these women?" I asked him.

He frowned. "Women?"

"Yes."

He looked at the list. Read it over.

He shook his head. "No, I don't."

You can't imagine my relief.

I exhaled, took back the list.

"Who are they?" he asked.

"Actresses who knew Cliff McFadgen," I said. It was all I was going to tell him. I wasn't going to single one out, make her special. I smiled, tried to pass it off lightly. "I didn't expect you to know them."

He frowned. Seemed to be trying to think of something to say.

The phone rang.

I expected Connely to get up, but with a clack the phone answered itself.

I looked.

At the far end of the room, as part of an L-shaped turn that was probably another room, was a long narrow table on which rested a computer setup, including a printer, a modem, and every available accessory. Also on the table was a phone line attached to a fax machine. It was this that had just answered and clicked on; a fax was coming through.

"Excuse me a minute," Connely said. "I think I mentioned I run my business from home. I've gotta get that."

As he stood up to get the fax, I got up and trailed along behind him. I'd like you to think it's because I'm an ace detective and keenly observant, but if the truth be known, I had never seen a fax machine in operation before. Can one say that in this day and age without risking social disgrace? But it happened to be a fact. I was a fax-machine virgin. Which is why I was a few steps behind Connely when he took it out of the machine.

He read the fax, frowned. He looked up, saw me, then glanced at the computer setup.

The cover for the monitor and keyboard had been pulled off and was lying on the printer.

Connely gave the monitor a glance, then casually picked up the cover from the printer and draped it over the back of the chair.

Bad move.

If he hadn't done it, I probably wouldn't have noticed a thing. But moving the cover for no apparent reason drew my attention right to it.

Hung over the back of the chair, where Bradley Connely had placed the computer cover in an attempt to hide it, was a woman's purse.

39.

"Bradley Connely's got a girlfriend."

It was not MacAullif I was torturing with the news. Three times in one day and the guy might have had a stroke. No, I decided to pick on Alice. Spicy tidbit, right up her alley. The type of stuff her soap opera was made of. The soap opera that ran Cliff McFadgen's commercial. I wondered if it was still running. Ironic. The good old days. When the man's only worries were hemorrhoids. And not even real ones at that.

"A girlfriend?" Alice said.

"Well, that's a conclusion on my part," I said. "I didn't actually see her."

"How do you know?"

I told her about the bit with the purse.

Alice wasn't impressed. That figured. I just hadn't been that impressive lately.

"Doesn't mean he has a girlfriend," Alice said.

"What else *could* it mean?"

"What if it's his wife's purse?"

"Then why would he hide it?"

"A guilty reaction. He doesn't like the idea of you knowing he's been going through his wife's purse."

"She's dead."

"So what? He could still have that reaction. Maybe even more so. Rifling his *dead* wife's purse."

"I really can't see it," I said.

Alice shrugged. "It may not be true. You may be perfectly right about the girlfriend."

We were in the kitchen and Alice was cooking. Alice is hard to argue with in general, but she's *invincible* when she's cooking. It's as if no one preparing anything that delicious could be wrong.

"Say I'm right," I said. "About the girlfriend."

"Say you are."

"What does it mean?"

"The man is horny."

"His wife was just killed."

"True. Are you suggesting that should make him *less* horny?"

Unbelievable.

If *I* were suggesting the man were horny, Alice would be all over me, blasting me for being obsessed with sex.

"You're missing the point. If Connely had a girlfriend, it redefines his interest in the case. Particularly if he were involved with her *before* his wife died."

Alice paused in the midst of mincing a clove of garlic. She looked up at me. "Are you suggesting he killed his wife because he was involved with another woman?"

"Uh . . ."

"Well?"

"Not exactly."

"What exactly *are* you suggesting?"

"Nothing. It's just a factor to be considered. That the man had an outside interest."

"So what?"

"Alice," I said. "Come on. Weren't you the one who said

he did it? That was your first reaction, right? Don't you remember that?"

Alice looked at me as if I were an idiot. "Don't be silly," she said. "That was when it was just his wife. The murder might have been completely unrelated to the blackmail scheme. Now you've got three people dead, including the blackmailer. A slightly different situation, wouldn't you think?"

I blinked, tried to think of an appropriate response. There was a flaw in that logic somewhere, I was sure of it. Unfortunately at that moment Alice threw the chopped garlic into a frying pan of sizzling butter, and any hope of coherent thought evaporated in the fragrant mist.

"No fair," I said, fighting for time. Then I had it. "How can you say her death was unrelated to the blackmail scheme? Back then, I'm talking about. Regardless of the other murders. She was killed as part of the blackmail scheme."

"Who says she was?"

"Come on. That's how I found her body. I followed their directions, went where they told me to go, and there she was." Damn. I had her. "See? Killed as part of the blackmail scheme."

Alice shook her head. "Not at all. She may have gone there as part of the blackmail scheme. It doesn't mean she was killed because of it. Say she goes there as part of the blackmail scheme. Her husband, who's been keeping tabs on her and looking for an opportunity to kill her, follows her there. And says, 'Hey, here's my chance. What could be better? If I kill her here, it will look like something else.'"

See what I mean? Invincible when she's cooking.

I exhaled. "How do you account for the other two murders?"

Alice looked utterly surprised. "I *don't* account for them. We're not talking about my *present* theory. You were asking me to defend what I said way back then. Of course it doesn't make sense *now*."

"What is your present theory?"

"At the present," Alice said, "I don't have enough data to make an assessment."

Good lord. She had no data whatsoever when she made her Bradley Connely–guilty pronouncement. The logic of which she had just successfully defended.

"I see," I said. "And I suppose this is my fault? In not supplying you with sufficient data to crack the case?"

"There's no need to be so defensive," Alice said. "I wasn't blaming you."

"Maybe not. But tell me. Is there anything you think I should be doing? I mean something you feel I should be doing, that I'm not?"

"What do you think you're not doing?"

"Nothing. I just—"

"Then I don't understand the question."

I rubbed my head. "Alice, let me phrase this another way. You mentioned that you didn't have enough data. Could you suggest any way I might be able to get you some more data?"

"Sure," Alice said.

I blinked. Mentally shot myself. Wondered for maybe the hundredth time in our marriage if Alice *really* understood the fine line she drew between what she felt I should do and what she felt me deficient for not doing.

I did not bring any of that up, and I swear there was no edge in my voice at all as I asked, "And what would that be?"

"The people in the pictures," Alice said. "We still don't know who the people are in the pictures."

I exhaled. "That's right," I said. "I don't know. You don't know. The police don't know. Baby-Face Frost doesn't know."

"You suppose he knows they call him that?"

"I don't know, Alice," I said. "And I don't know who the people in the pictures are. But aside from what I'm doing, I can't think of a practical way to find out."

"I know," Alice said. "It's frustrating. But I was thinking."

"What?"

Alice had moved on to chopping onions. I found my eyes tearing. Magically, hers appeared clear and bright. Somehow that figured.

"It occurred to me you should trust your first instincts more."

I frowned. "What do you mean?"

When you saw those blackmail pictures, what did you think?"

"Huh?"

"What did you think when you saw them?"

"That's a complicated question."

"Why?"

"The guy'd just tore the thing open, showed them to me. I wasn't supposed to see them. I—"

"No, no, no," Alice said. "I don't mean that. Never mind all that emotional baggage. I mean, what did you think about *them*? In terms of what they were?"

"Dirty pictures."

"Yes, but more specific. What kind of dirty pictures?"

"I don't know. They weren't S and M, but they seemed to feature everything. Well, not golden showers, but you certainly had your—"

Alice wheeled around brandishing the knife with which she had been cutting onions. I don't think she intended it as a weapon, but still I instinctively stepped back.

"Stanley," she said. "Don't go off on a tangent. That's not what I mean. Don't you remember when you brought the things home? What you said they looked like—the people in the pictures?"

Under normal circumstances I would have remembered. But as so often happens under Alice's cross-examination, my mind blanked out.

"No," I said. "What did I think they looked like?"

"Porno actors."

40.

I must admit I've been in porno shops before, but not in many, many years, and never because my wife asked me to. If that wasn't enough to make me feel like a fool, add in the fact I was looking for something that on the one hand they wouldn't naturally have and on the other there was no way to ask for without sounding like a total idiot.

The bald fat guy with the mustache and the stubby cigar squinted at me through the smoke. "Pictures?" he said. "Are you kiddin' me? Buddy, we got nothing *but* pictures."

"No, no," I said. "I'm not talking about magazines. I'm talking about photographs."

"What do you think are in the magazines?"

"You don't understand. I mean eight-by-ten color photographs."

"Eight-by-ten?"

"Yeah."

"If it's size you want, we can do better than that."

"I don't want better than that. I'm looking for a store that sells eight-by-ten pictures. Not in a book. Not in a magazine. Just the pictures. The photographs. The separate photographs. Loose."

He frowned. "You want the artwork?"

Jesus Christ. My head swirled. Here, in a porno shop on Forty-second Street, the proprietor, who looked very much as if he'd just been sent over by Central Casting to *play* a proprietor of a porno shop, refers to the photos shot for a skin mag as "the artwork," just as if he were a Madison Avenue type discussing the layout for *Cosmopolitan.*

"Right," I said. "The artwork. The photographs. Where could I buy the photographs themselves."

He shrugged. "From the photographer."

"You don't sell 'em?"

"Nah."

"Suppose I don't know the photographer—is there any place I could look—any place might have 'em."

"You talkin' hard core or soft?"

"Hard."

He shook his head. "I wouldn't know."

"But soft you would?"

"I wouldn't know that either."

"Then why'd you ask?"

"To find out what you want. Now if it's hard core you want, I got plenty of stuff here. So the pictures aren't loose. Big deal. You want single shots, take a scissors, cut 'em out."

"Thanks for the suggestion."

The second shop I tried was much the same thing, except the proprietor didn't speak as good English and wasn't nearly as friendly. I got the impression he thought I was a cop. What the hell he thought I might be busting him for—since as far as I know all that stuff was legal—was beyond me. Unless the guy had kiddie porn in the back somewhere. At any rate, he was hostile and noncommunicative, and his shop was a total washout.

Third shop, I met the Crazy Eddie of the porn world, with prices so low he must be giving it away. A little old man with greedy eyes and an ingratiating smile, he seemed to take the idea that someone might leave his store without buying something as a personal affront, and *would* not be undersold. If I wanted dirty pictures, I was gonna *have* dirty pictures, even if he had to get a girl and a camera and take them himself. Which he would have had to do, since he didn't happen to have any in his shop. All he had were magazines and video tapes, just like everybody else. But what was the big deal, he wanted to know, whether I saw the pictures before they were put in the magazine or after? "Pictures are pictures," he said with a shrug. "Come on, I give you a good price."

It wasn't till I got to the next shop that I realized what the guy said made sense. If the pictures I was looking for really were porn pictures of porn actors posing for a photographer, what would be more logical than that they would eventually wind up in a porn magazine?

So I started looking at magazines.

Oh boy.

Even having a noble purpose could not make up for the funny feeling I felt standing there flipping through the mags. It occurred to me, what if the principal of Tommie's school should walk in and see me doing this? I'm such a jerk it took a while before I realized if that actually happened, the man would be hard pressed to fault me.

I found that small consolation.

It was maybe five shops and I can't tell you how many sexual organs later when I found it.

It was a dive on Eighth Avenue, a grungy place even by porno-shop standards. It was a hole-in-the-wall affair boasting no live girls, no peep show, no films, videos, or what have you. Just dirty magazines, and from the looks of them, recycled ones at that.

In the back of the store was a bin. On the front of the bin was a sign. Old. Faded. So much so you could barely read it anymore. The sign said: 3 for $1.00.

The proprietor of the store was a little guy with a runny nose, who looked like a rat who had survived by being just barely smart enough not to eat the poison. I pushed by him to the back of the store and looked down into the bin.

It was filled with pictures. Old, glossy eight-by-ten photographs. Here it was, the answer to what became of porno photographers' old pix. Ratface sold 'em three for a buck.

41.

"It's her," Alice said.

"Are you sure?"

"Sure I'm sure. Can't you tell it's her?"

"I thought it was."

"Well, you're right. Good for you. You're usually not good at recognizing faces."

I said nothing. I wasn't about to point out to Alice it was in the woman's distinctive erect nipples that I had first noticed a similarity.

"Her hair's different," I said.

"Yes, of course, her hair's different."

"But it is her?"

"Of course it's her."

"It's a different guy."

"Yes. That's obvious. But it's her all right." Alice indicated the photo. "This is the only one you could find?"

"That's it. And I went through all the others again, once I found this. To make sure I hadn't overlooked her. Since she looked different, I mean."

"She doesn't look different."

"She does to me. Anyway, this is all there was."

"It's very old."

It was indeed. And in rather poor condition. It had actually been creased twice. Across the bottom, and diagonally across the top-right corner. The corner crease had flopped around enough to have worn thin enough for the corner to be in danger of falling off. The picture was in such poor repair that Ratface, the porn-shop owner, could hardly believe I wanted to buy it. Or that I only wanted one. "Three for a dollar," he whined. "I mean, come *on.*" To shut him up I'd finally given him a dollar just for the one print.

Alice put the picture down. "So," she said, "what now?"

"I don't know. I gotta try to trace it. I don't really know how. There's nothing on the picture to indicate where it was processed. Which means the photographer probably did it himself."

"That's not what I meant," Alice said.

"Oh? What do you mean?"

"The cops. Are you gonna show it to the cops?"

Shit. What was I gonna do about the cops indeed? I mean, I didn't want to give this to Thurman. No *way* I wanted to give this to Thurman.

I said as much.

Alice said, "You don't have to give it to Thurman. You can give it to Frost."

"Who'll give it to Thurman. Same difference. The question is, do I turn it in at all?"

"Don't you have to?"

"Yeah, I do."

"So?"

I exhaled. "All right, look. I found this picture. It's the woman we've been looking for, but it's not the guy. So it's not one of the blackmail photos. So is it really evidence?"

Alice looked at me. "Don't be a jerk. This woman is a murder suspect. The cops are going nuts trying to find her.

That's why we were down there doing the drawings. Now you got a photo of her and you wonder if it's evidence?"

"All right, I *know* it's evidence. And I know I gotta hand it in. The point is, is there anything I need to investigate before I do?"

"Stanley. I don't want you to go to jail."

"I'm not gonna go to jail. I'm gonna turn the picture in like a good boy." I jerked my thumb at the window. It was already getting dark. "But not now. It's late. It's nighttime. These guys wouldn't be there. I'm not gonna go rushing down to the police station now. On the other hand, tomorrow's Saturday. Will these guys even be there?"

"Stanley."

"Alice, I am definitely turning this picture in Monday morning. No argument there. But am I legally required to bust my ass going down there over the weekend when the guys I wanna see may not even be there?"

"Bullshit," Alice said. "You know what they'll say? They'll say, legally you should have gone downtown straight from the porn shop."

"With what?" I said. "I wasn't even sure it was the same woman till I talked with you."

Alice frowned. She shook her head. Then she looked up at me. "You're different," she said. "Since the drunk tank. It's not just getting even. It's like you're a different person. The guy they threw in there would never have thought of withholding this from the cops."

"Maybe not," I said. "But the point is, I don't feel like giving this to 'em. I'll give it to 'em Monday morning. At the latest." I shrugged. "Maybe not. Maybe I'll give it to 'em tomorrow. But first I got it and I want to see what I can do with it."

"Like what?"

I grimaced. "That's the problem. It's the weekend. Places will be closed. I was thinking I could contact skin-mag companies, get the names of their photographers. Show the picture around. See if anybody recognizes the work."

"Please," Alice said. "As if the style were distinctive."

"All right, but maybe I'd find a photographer who remembers taking the pix."

"And maybe you'll win the lottery," Alice said.

"You got any better ideas?'

"Well, what about the guy?"

"I couldn't find any pictures of the guy."

"Not *that* guy." Alice pointed at the picture. "*This* guy."

"Him?" I said. "He had nothing to do with it."

"Yeah, but he knew her. At least from the photo shoot. If you found him, he might remember who she was."

"How am I gonna find him?"

"Was he in any other pictures?"

"Shit, Alice. I didn't look."

"There you are."

"And what if he was? What good would that do me?"

"Aren't some of these pictures stamped with the photographer's name?"

I groaned. "Shit, I didn't look."

"Well, there you are," Alice said. "You find one of those, and the photographer fingers the guy who fingers the broad."

"Broad?"

"I got carried away."

"Fingers?"

"Don't change the subject. Wouldn't that work?"

"It might."

"And even if it didn't, wouldn't that be a good way to get the names of some photographers?"

I stood up, held up my hand. "Stop. You win. I'm on my way."

42.

Ratface gave me the most marvelous deadpan when I walked in. I could tell the prospect of making another dollar off me didn't exactly thrill him. I paid no attention, just headed for the photos in the back. When he saw that, he shook his head and I believe actually rolled his eyes. I can't say that I blamed him, really. After all, I had taken close to half an hour to spend my first dollar.

It just wasn't Ratface's day—he didn't even make his buck. 'Cause the guy I was looking for didn't happen to be in any of the pictures. That was one of those ideas that sounds real good when you hear it, and then turns out to be a total washout.

The photographer-name-on-the-back-of-the-photograph bit wasn't so hot either. Believe it or not, not that many photographers seemed eager to claim their work. In all the photographs I looked at—and there must have been hundreds—I found a total of three names.

A number of the photos had been stamped Harrison Garrison Studio. A smaller number were stamped Art Smith. And a couple of them, so help me, were stamped F-Stop Fitzgerald.

I took the information home and Alice and I went to work. Unfortunately, none of the three names was listed in the *Yellow Pages* under Photographers-Passport, Photographers-Portrait, Photographic Color Prints & Transparencies, or Photographic Equipment & Supplies.

The white pages were a different story. There was no Harrison Garrison, but there were three H. Garrisons listed. There were seven Art Smiths, eight A. Smiths, and four other two-letter combinations, such as A. J. Smith.

Believe it or not, there were no F-Stop Fitzgeralds.

Unpromising as it looked, I began calling. Considering it was nine-thirty on a Friday evening, I didn't do that bad. Two of the three H. Garrisons were home and denied being Harrison Garrison. The third did not answer. Three of the Art Smiths were home and denied being photographers. The wife of a fourth Art Smith was home and denied that her husband was a photographer. Two A. Smiths, A. J. Smith, and A. P. Smith all denied being photographers, though one of them actually admitted to being named Art.

Fruitless as the phone calls were, I was perfectly happy to make them. Because they were an excellent excuse for not taking the picture down to the police station.

At any rate, by eleven-thirty that evening, Alice and I had amassed a huge amount of information.

All of it totally worthless.

43.

Saturday morning was gorgeous, and by nine-thirty Alice, Tommie, and I were all in the car tooling up Route 17 to Tuxedo, New York, and the Renaissance Festival, which is something we do almost every year. The festival is a wonderful thing for a New Yorker. People dress up in medieval costumes, and kids run around with swords and shields and bows and arrows, and you keep bumping into actors from the company who are roaming around the grounds playing characters from Robin Hood, and just for one day it's as if Manhattan didn't exist and you were back in Merry Olde England, when the times were simpler, purer, and somehow much more grand.

After all the pressure I'd been under, it was real nice to stop my mind for a while, go with the medieval flow, and not really think about anything.

Plus, hanging out in the woods all day made it impossible for me to be downtown at the police station.

By the time we got there, the place was mobbed. We parked in Parking Lot Four, and piled onto a large yellow school bus that took us to the main gate, where we waited in line, purchased tickets, and stepped through the turnstile into the past.

We whiled the day away with bits and pieces of the Robin Hood legend, sandwiched among other highlights of the festival, such as the Living Chess Board, where actors on a giant chess board actually fight each other after each move, and the mud wrestlers—actors who improvise comedy skits in a mudhole, which, needless to say, involves plenty of slapstick, including splashing in, falling in, and actually eating mud ("And you *paid* to see it!").

At the end of the afternoon the whole thing culminated in the joust, fought by actors from the Robin Hood pageant. This involved a great deal of choreographed acrobatics, and touched off an argument between Tommie and Alice. Tommie likes watching steroidal wrestlers on TV, and Alice tells him it's stupid because the fights are fixed. Tommie wanted to know why that was worse than this. And if Alice didn't think so, he offered her any odds she wanted to name to bet against Robin Hood.

I kept out of it. I didn't give a damn. I was in upstate New York rather than the police station, and I just wanted to be left alone.

Finally the joust was over—guess who won?—and the pageant came to a close. We anticipated well and were in the first group through the gate and onto the school bus. It was already packed, which was good in that it kept us closer to the front, and bad in that we had to stand. But for such a short ride, it seemed a small inconvenience. We stood, waited impatiently for the bus driver to close the door. He finally did, just as one more couple pushed on.

They were young, and the man was broad and beefy. He was wearing a string T-shirt, under which muscles rippled, and he grabbed the door and held it wedged open while he tried to squeeze his girlfriend on. The driver actually waved him back, but the man said something to him I couldn't hear and stepped up onto the bus, pushing his girlfriend ahead of him.

Hell.

It had been a long if pleasant day, we had an hour-and-a-half to two-hour drive ahead of us, depending on traffic, I was not enjoying standing like a sardine in a crowded bus, and I just wanted to get the hell out of there and get home. But this guy had us immobilized.

I said nothing, but someone else on the bus said, "Come on, wait for the next one." But macho man just made a gesture and half pushed, half lifted the woman onto the bus. As he did, she looked up and I saw her face.

It was her!

I told myself it couldn't be true. I was just desperate, that was all. That was what had pushed me over the edge, was making me see what I *wanted* to see. What I *wanted* to think. That *had* to be the answer. It was certainly a lot easier to believe than that the woman who was holding up our bus from leaving the Renaissance Festival in Tuxedo, New York, was none other than the woman Alice and I had been looking all over for, the woman I had just paid Ratface a dollar for a picture of, the woman who was the prime suspect in the murder case I was investigating. I mean, come on, give me a break. If I read that in a book, I'd throw the fucking thing across the room. I mean, you really expect me to buy that?

I couldn't help it.

It was her.

I grabbed Alice by the arm. "Look!" I whispered, and pointed.

Alice looked. Then looked back at me and frowned.

"It's her!" I whispered.

Alice didn't have to ask who *her* was. Her eyes widened, and she looked again.

She looked back, smiled.

"No, it isn't."

44.

All right, so I felt pretty stupid. But it was actually mistaking the woman on the bus for the woman in the pictures that put me on the right track. Well, I wouldn't go as far as all that. But what it did, really, was show me how desperate I was to find an excuse for not turning in the picture. Or rather to find the woman in the picture, rendering the picture itself moot. That was why I was grasping at straws, recognizing people on the shuttle bus at the Renaissance Festival, for god's sake.

But what the humiliation actually did was shame me into thinking the thing out all the way home—all right, asshole, you don't wanna turn in the picture, you got an hour-and-a-half car ride to come up with a good enough reason.

Only, I have to tell you, I couldn't really keep my mind on it. Not on that gorgeous fall day in the country. Not after clowns and magicians and jugglers and Robin Hood and Living Chess Boards and mud eaters and swordsmen and damsels and knights and wenches and all that delicious childhood fantasy make-believe. It rattled around in my head, intoxicated me. The innocent escapism of youth. It took me back to simpler days, when triple homicides were no concern of mine, but fifty bad guys could be dispatched in the normal course of an afternoon without even making me late for dinner.

Anyway, all those notions fought in my head.

Play acting.

Porno acting.

Legitimate acting.

I shook my head to clear it. Gotta concentrate. Gotta straighten this out.

It was coming back over the George Washington Bridge that it finally hit me.

45.

Alice looked up at me in surprise. "*Back Stage*?"

It was later that same night. We'd gotten home, put Tommie to bed, and I'd gone out for the *New York Times*. The Sunday *Times* comes out Saturday night in the city. I'm not big on buying it then, because the sports section won't have Saturday's scores. But tonight I didn't care. I'd actually gone out for something else.

"That's right," I said. "*Back Stage.*"

"What for?"

"I'm going to auditions."

Alice looked at me. I'd recently done a part in summer stock, but aside from that, I hadn't acted in over ten years. Or gone to an audition.

"Are you kidding?" she said.

"Not at all."

"What's the gag?"

"It's about the picture."

"What about it?"

"I thought it over, and the way I see it, we've been going about it all wrong."

"Oh?"

"The dirty magazines, the photographers. F-Stop Fitzgerald, for Christ's sake. It's not going to get us anywhere."

"Why not?"

"The picture's old. You can see that."

"Right. Which makes it harder to trace."

"That's the least of it. I'm thinking about Jack Fargo."

"What about him?"

"How scared he was when I mentioned porn."

Alice had been sitting on the bed watching TV. Now she flicked it off with the remote control. She cocked her head, gave me a look.

"Stanley, don't make me drag this out of you. What's your idea?"

"Okay, look," I said. "Jack Fargo got upset about porn. The original idea was that upset him because he'd once done it but was legit now. His connection to the case would be that he knew the people in the pictures."

"Then he turned out to be gay."

I waved it away. "Never mind that. That's a tangent. The point is, porn star then, legit now.

"The same goes for the people in the pictures. That's why they'd be vulnerable to blackmail. If they weren't legit, there's no point."

"Of course."

"So the dirty picture has to be the wrong track. I'm wasting my time looking for a porn star. I should be looking for an actress."

"Makes sense," Alice said.

I jerked my thumb at the *Back Stage*. "So I'm going to auditions."

Alice nodded. "Me too."

46.

We made the rounds together, went to the auditions.

We didn't actually audition. Alice isn't an actress. I used to be an actor, but I hadn't auditioned in years, I was never any good at it, and there was no reason to thoroughly humiliate myself. Fortunately, it wasn't necessary. In most cases, we didn't actually have to *be* at the audition—just find out where it was and watch the people going in and out. It was only in cases where the audition was being held on, say, the fourteenth floor of some large office building, with three banks of elevators and four entrances, that we really had to go.

But it didn't matter. No one ever challenged us. I had some old pictures and résumés in my briefcase, and the worst that ever happened was, a couple of times, I had to hand them out. On both occasions, I managed to duck out before anyone could call on me to audition.

Making the rounds did not require me suspending my services to Rosenberg and Stone. There simply aren't that many open auditions in New York. There were never more than two a day, and some days there weren't any, so I managed to sandwich them in among my cases. I'd show up at the appointed place and time, and Alice would meet me there.

I needed Alice, of course, because of her memory for faces. As she pointed out, the woman could walk right by me with a different hairstyle and I wouldn't even know it. I couldn't argue with that, so I had to let her come along. I was reluctant to do so because it negated the reason I was doing this in the first place. No, not finding the woman. That was the reason I *gave* for doing this. My real reason, my real motivation, was to hang on to the photo and not give it to the cops. I figured I would need the photo to compare it with the women I saw at the auditions. With Alice along, that was no longer necessary. But Alice didn't raise the point. It was almost like an unspoken agreement—her not objecting to me keeping the photo, in exchange for my not objecting to her coming to auditions.

At any rate, that's how it worked out. Which was fine with me.

Except we weren't getting anywhere. As I said, there aren't that many open casting calls. And the ones we went to were not productive. The first week yielded a big fat zero.

It wasn't till the second week that I began recognizing people. Not the people in the pictures—then the job would have been over. I mean actors. See, I used to be a member of the theater community, albeit a while back, so it was only natural after a while I would bump into someone I knew.

As I say, that didn't happen till the second week. By then we'd gotten so used to nothing happening, it was a big surprise.

The first time it happened was at an open call for singers and dancers for chorus work. The talents displayed by the woman in the picture did not necessarily include singing and dancing, but she certainly seemed limber enough, so there was no reason to pass it up. The audition was being held at a vacant theater on West Forty-fourth Street, which meant Alice and I didn't have to go in. It was a nice day, so we were hanging out on the sidewalk and leaning up against my car, which you cannot park in midtown Manhattan under penalty of death, and which, if we turned our back and walked a mere ten paces from, would have been instantly ticketed, towed, and would wind up costing me over a hundred bucks and the whole afternoon to get back. Which simply would not have done, since I had just driven in from a hot trip-and-fall in Brooklyn and was scheduled that afternoon for a hit-and-run in Queens.

Anyway, Alice and I were standing there clocking the actresses in and out when I heard a voice say, "Mr. Hastings."

I turned around to find an attractive-looking blonde standing there. Flustered as that made me, and poor as I am at faces, I still recognized Jill Jenson, one of the actresses from *Love Strikes Out*, a showcase production I'd gotten involved in when one of the actors had gotten murdered.

That was a bit of a complication. I certainly didn't want any members of the acting community to know why I was there. So I was just on the point of telling her Alice and I were there to audition when I realized she didn't know me as an actor. She knew me as a detective. In fact, if my memory served me well, she might even know me as a *police* detective, since I'd certainly given the actors in that production that impression, and I couldn't recall if I'd ever disillusioned her.

I was not about to now. So I switched gears in mid-falsehood and came out with a plausible half truth—I was looking for clues in the murder of Jack Fargo, and did she happen to know him?

She said she didn't, but she'd ask around. I asked her please not to, because it was a case where I was trying to keep a low profile.

After that, I kept a *much* lower profile. Alice and I actually sat *in* the car, scrunched down, watching the people going in and out.

And it's a good thing I did, because not ten minutes after Jill went in, who should show up but the curly-blond-haired roommate of Cliff McFadgen's girlfriend.

That caught me up short. I wondered if I only recognized her because I'd just recognized Jill, which put me in the mood to recognize people. Which made me wonder how many of Cliff McFadgen's girlfriend's roommates, or maybe even Cliff McFadgen's girlfriend herself, might have been at any of those other auditions and I hadn't even noticed?

At any rate, after that I paid a *lot* better attention.

Which is why, two days later, I spotted Bradley Connely before he spotted me.

It was outside a loft on Prince Street, not two blocks from the loft where I'd found the body of his wife. It was an audition for an off-Broadway show. Alice and I were sitting in the car in front of the building watching the people go in, when I suddenly grabbed her by the arm.

"That's him," I said.

"That's who?"

"The husband. What's his name."

"Bradley Connely?"

"Right."

"You're terrible with names, you know it?"

"Yeah, I know it. Keep your head down."

"Why? He doesn't know me."

"He knows *me.*"

"What's that got to do with it?"

"Shh."

"He can't hear us, for Christ's sake."

While all that was going on, Bradley Connely, paying no attention to us whatever, went up the front steps and inside.

"So that's the husband," Alice said.

"Yeah? So?"

"So nothing. It's just after hearing so much, it's strange to put a face to these people."

"Does he look like you expected?"

"I don't know what I expected."

"Well, one thing in his favor."

"What's that?"

"He was alone."

He was alone when he came out too. Which, strange as it might seem, counted as a point in his favor. The mystery woman wasn't with him. Not that it would have mattered if some woman *had* been with him. But still.

Other high points in our vigil? There weren't many. In the

course of the next week I recognized a total of three actors. One I'd done summer stock with. One was another of Cliff McFadgen's girlfriend's roommates, the wallflower named Bernice.

The third was Bradley Connely again. And to be honest, this time I *didn't* recognize him—he had his long blond hair pulled back in a ponytail and tucked under his collar—and if Alice hadn't pointed him out, I wouldn't have had a clue. This was rather embarrassing, since she'd only seen him once in passing and I'd sat and talked with the guy. But it sort of underlined her importance in this little venture.

After that, nothing happened till the middle of the next week. I mean nothing. I got so I felt like *What's the matter with these actors? Why aren't they out here auditioning, don't they want to get any work?*

It was now the middle of the third week, and Alice and I were seriously thinking about giving up. From my point of view, the only thing *keeping* me from giving up was then I would have no excuse whatsoever for hanging on to the photo. However, actually finding the woman had proved such a fruitless task that, instead of doing that, I was now devoting most of my time trying to come up with *another* good excuse for hanging on to the photo. So far I hadn't managed to do it.

Anyway, it was three o'clock on a Wednesday afternoon and Alice and I were checking out an audition for an off-Broadway production of a play called *The Apron Strings*. For this audition, Alice and I were actually sitting in the audience. Events had conspired to make us do so. The theater was on the second floor of an office building, so waiting on the street was out. And when we got upstairs, it turned out waiting in the lobby was out too, because a woman at a desk there was accepting pictures and résumés. She wasn't patrolling the door to the theater, however, so we were able to walk right in, without even surrendering a picture and résumé. So at least, as I sat there in the auditorium, I was happy in the knowledge I wouldn't be called upon to audition.

I was pretty unhappy about everything else. As I say, after two and a half weeks, finding the woman seemed to be a lost cause. And nothing else was happening in terms of the investigation. I certainly wasn't doing anything, except going to auditions and working for Richard. That left things squarely up to Sergeant Thurman. I had spoken to Sergeant MacAullif on the phone at least once a week, and according to him there had been absolutely no progress. As far as he was concerned, the only bright note was there had been no further murders.

Anyway, Alice and I were sitting there watching people audition. We were sitting apart so, on the off chance someone I knew came in, I wouldn't have to introduce her. Alice is not an actress and wasn't keen on having to play one.

The audition itself was somewhat interesting in that, rather than making the actors deliver prepared monologues, the director was having them read scenes from the play. That was nice, because it meant I could get a look at more than one actress at a time.

In this particular scene there were three, a mother and her two grown daughters. The plot seemed to revolve around the younger daughter's impending marriage, of which the mother obviously disapproved, probably because she didn't want her little girl to leave home—apron strings, get it? From what I could see, the play was just a distaff rehash of *The Silver Cord*, but what the hell, it was letting me look at a lot of actresses.

The three on stage now were a dumpy, middle-aged woman, a tall, willowy blonde, and a little brunette with pigtails. The pigtails seemed a bit much—both women playing the daughters looked to be in their mid to late twenties, and the braided hair struck me as a desperate attempt to look young enough for the part.

I was having these thoughts because I had already written the women off as qualifying for our missing porn star. The blonde was too tall and thin, and frankly her breasts weren't big enough. And even discounting the pigtails, the brunette flunked out on her nose. Granted, actresses have nose jobs, but never in reverse. The woman in the porno pix had a little ski-jump. Pigtails had a hook.

I was sitting there watching the scene when suddenly I felt

a hand on my shoulder. I turned around, expecting either to see some actor I knew or to be asked to leave.

But it was Alice.

"It's her!" Alice whispered.

I turned, looked at the back of the theater. "Where?"

"There," Alice said. She pointed to the stage.

I looked up at the stage. Blinked. "It can't be," I said. "She's too tall and no tits."

"Not her. Her!" Alice said.

"Pigtails? She's got a hook nose."

"No," Alice said. *"Her!"*

I blinked again. Gawked.

There were only three women onstage.

Blondie.

Pigtails.

And the dumpy, middle-aged mother.

47.

I felt like a damn fool driving out to New Jersey the next day to interview her. Just like I'd felt like a damn fool when Alice and I followed her home from the audition to see where she lived in the first place. The answer—Teaneck, New Jersey—did not inspire me with confidence. Nor did the fact the woman drove a Ford station wagon and lived in a two-story frame house with a tricycle on the front lawn, a swing set in the side yard, and a clothesline out back.

I looked at Alice.

"Shut up," she said. "It's her."

So here I was, twenty-four hours later, driving up to the same house.

I had spent that twenty-four hours trying to get out of it. Because I knew doing it was going to make me feel like a damn fool. I mean, if it were anything else. But pornography? No, I really didn't want to be there. And I must tell you, as I drove out, I hoped when I got there her station wagon would be gone.

It wasn't, however. It was parked right out in front of the garage. It was a two-car garage, the doors were open, and I could see there was another car inside. It occurred to me, maybe her husband's home, maybe I should wait for a better time. It also occurred to me that if I didn't do it now, I wasn't going to want to come back.

However, what it came down to basically was that facing this woman wasn't as unattractive a prospect as facing Alice if I didn't.

I went up the front steps and rang the bell.

Despite the car in the driveway, I was hoping against hope she wasn't home. No such luck. After a few moments I heard the tired-sounding shuffle of feet, then the click of the latch, and the door swung open.

It was her, all right. I mean it was the woman I'd seen audition in New York. But the woman in the pictures?

"Yes?" she said.

"Mrs. Gardner?" I said. It was the name on the mailbox.

"Yes," she said again.

I hesitated. From within came the sound of a television, tuned to a children's program, and over it the unmistakable voices of kids watching.

I took a breath. "It's about the picture."

She frowned. "Picture?"

"Yes."

"What picture?"

I had it in my briefcase in a manila envelope. I pulled the envelope out now, undid the clasp, opened it, pulled the picture out. It was facing me, so she still couldn't see it.

"What is it?" she said.

I heard the sound of children's voices again. I felt sick. In the photo the woman was holding her vagina open with one hand and holding a man's penis in her mouth with the other.

"Do you have any idea what I'm talking about?" I said.

"No, I don't. Is there a point to this?"

"That depends."

"On what?"

"On whether you recognize this."

I turned the picture around.

Her face drained of color. She opened her mouth, closed it again. Her lip trembled. Then stiffened. And her eyes got hard.

She looked up at me. "What is this?" she said. "Blackmail?"

It was my turn to be stunned. But what else? Of course she saw it that way.

"I take it you recognize the picture?" I said gently.

"How dare you," she said. "How dare you do this."

"I'm sorry," I said. "But we need to talk."

"Damn it," she said. "Not here."

From within the house came another voice. Deep, masculine. "Honey? Who is it?"

The woman's eyes widened. I could see the panic in them. She shoved the picture back at me.

"Go! Please go!" she said. "I'll meet you. I promise. In an hour."

"Where?"

"Who is it, honey?" came the voice again.

Closer this time.

"Insurance salesman," she called. Then, to me, said urgently in a low voice, "Riverside Mall. In front of Conran's."

"Huh?"

"Riverside Mall in front of Conran's," she repeated. "Ask anyone. Now put it away!"

I shoved the picture into the manila envelope and tucked the envelope back in my briefcase just as her husband came into the foyer.

He was a cop.

48.

"Where did you get that?" she said.

We were seated in a small restaurant in the Riverside Mall, which I had found with no trouble at all. It's a large mall out on Route 4. I'd actually been to it with Alice a few times, I just didn't know the name of it. The first person I asked guided me there.

She showed up in an hour. As promised. Looking as hassled as you might expect.

Even if her husband *hadn't* been a cop.

We'd had to go somewhere, so I'd suggested a restaurant. She said she couldn't eat a thing, but allowed me to force coffee on her. So there we sat, having coffee in the mall, just like any other couple taking a break in the midst of afternoon shopping.

"Is it you?" I asked.

She gave me a hard look. "How can you ask me that? Why would you be here if you have to ask me that?"

"When was it taken?"

"What the hell do you care? Tell me how much you want."

"I don't want money," I said.

She drew back slightly. "I don't do that anymore."

I put up my hand. "No. Please. You don't understand."

She snuffled once, and I could see a tear form in the corner of her eye.

"I sure as hell don't," she said. "Damn it. Why did you have to come here?"

I looked at her. "Frankly, I don't know."

She raised her eyes. "What the hell does that mean?"

"I'm sorry," I said. "But are you really as innocent as all that?"

"Sure," she said. "When you've got that picture."

"That's not what I mean."

"Then what *do* you mean, for Christ's sake? What's this all about?"

"It's the other pictures, actually."

"The other pictures?"

"Yes. The blackmail pictures."

"Then this is blackmail?"

"Not at all."

She started to cry. Stopped herself angrily. "No, damn it," she said. "I won't let you do this. I've got a husband. Two children. You cannot do this to me. Now talk, damn it. What do you mean, blackmail pictures?"

"There were other pictures," I said. "Pictures of you. Of this type, but with a different man. Taller, with darker hair than the man in this picture. Would you know who that was?"

"No."

"But you don't deny being the woman in the pictures?"

"Why?" she said. "Why? This was nearly twenty years ago."

"Twenty?"

"Something like that. I was young, I needed money. I was desperate. Why would you want to smear me now?"

"I don't want to smear you, but you're going to have to answer some questions."

"Why?"

"Because of the other pictures."

"What about them? Why are they so important?"

"I don't know *why* they're so important. I only know, because of them, three people are dead."

She knocked over her coffee. And she hadn't drunk enough of it but what it made a hell of a mess. I had to call the waitress, get a towel, mop it up.

The waitress was the cheery type, all smiles. Without being asked she brought another cup.

And then she was gone and it was just the two of us again, sitting there over our coffee cups.

"Tell me," she said. "Tell me the whole thing. You say people are dead?"

I told her. Not the whole thing, but enough. I left out my part in it, for instance. Just gave her the bare bones of the blackmail scheme and the murder.

From the expression on her face while she listened, I might have been telling her the United States had opened a colony on the moon and she and her family had been chosen to be transported there.

When I was finished, she actually drank some of the coffee.

"That makes no sense at all," she said. "Why would anyone pay thousands of dollars for a twenty-year-old picture of me?"

"Only one reason I could think of," I said.

"What's that?"

"Your husband's a cop."

She reacted as if she'd been slapped. Then composed herself and looked at me hard. "Yes," she said. "And he doesn't know. And I don't *want* him to know. Now, that would be a reason for me to pay money to someone not to tell him. But no one's asked me for money. No one came to me at all. Except you. Up until this afternoon, as far as I knew, everything was just fine. And then you bring me this." She shook her head. "I can't see how my husband being a cop could have anything to do with it."

"Unless," I ventured gently, "someone wanted to exert some pressure on him."

Her eyes got hard again. "No," she said. "Absolutely not. Not Andy. If that had happened, I would know. I could tell. He'd be different. And he isn't. And, besides, how does that fit in with your story? The blackmail demands. The people paying money. And the murders. It doesn't fit at all."

I said nothing. It had just occurred to me, whatever the blackmail scheme had originally been, her husband, upright policeman Andy, killing all the participants and grabbing all the photos of his wife, fit in just fine.

"All right, look," I said. "You admit posing for the pictures?"

"Please," she said.

"No, no," I said. "The point is, do you remember the names of any of the men you posed with?"

"No," she said. "I barely knew them. I never saw them again."

"Were there many?"

"No, there weren't. It was three, maybe four times. I got a boyfriend, moved in with him. Got a job."

"You were an actress?"

She smiled slightly. Wistfully. "Yes. I was an actress. Still am."

"I know. And you've never seen those pictures again? From the time you made them?"

"I never even saw them *then*."

"You've never seen them?"

"This was the first one. My god, what a shock."

"And you know nothing of any blackmail scheme?"

"No."

"And you never heard of Patricia Connely, Cliff McFadgen, or Jack Fargo?"

She shook her head. "Not at all."

I took a breath, exhaled. "Okay," I said. "Mrs. Gardner, I'm really sorry I bothered you. And I hate to bother you some more, but I'm afraid there's one more thing I'm going to have to ask you to do."

"Oh? What's that?"

"Talk to my wife."

49.

Sergeant MacAullif looked somewhat less than pleased.

"You withheld this?" he said ominously.

"I may have neglected to mention it."

"Three fucking weeks you withheld this?"

"Well, two and a half, anyway."

"Two and a half, three, whatever. The point is, you withheld the fucking picture?"

"Actually, I believe it's a cocksucking picture."

MacAullif leveled his finger at me. "Don't get cute. You know how important this is?"

"It's not one of the blackmail photos."

"It's the woman."

"Yes. Who apparently had absolutely nothing to do with it."

"Bullshit."

"My wife thinks so too."

MacAullif opened his mouth.

I said, "Watch it."

He closed it again. MacAullif met my wife once. It was only for a few moments, but that didn't matter. There is a code, and wives are off limits.

"That's really very nice," MacAullif said. "I'm really pleased to hear it. But, taking nothing away from your wife's powers of detection, or yours, do you suppose there's the slightest chance a veteran police interrogator might do a little better?"

"Frankly, I don't think so."

"You arrogant fuck."

"There's nothing arrogant about it. I don't think the woman knows anything."

"You know how much I value that opinion?"

"I have some idea."

"I'll bet you do. You son of a bitch. You come in here, tell me you want to talk off the record, and then you tell me this."

"Well, I couldn't tell you *on* the record. Then we'd both be in deep shit."

"Where do you think we are now? You just confessed to withholding evidence. If I don't turn you in, I'm an accessory."

"And what if you do?"

"I'm a schmuck. You get a charge that won't stick." MacAullif banged his fist on the desk. His face was beet red. "You gonna tell me who this woman is?"

"Absolutely not. If I told you that, you'd have to do something, wouldn't you?"

"I have to do something now."

"Nonsense. Like you say, you got nothing to go on. You could never make it stick. We're talking hypothetically off the record."

"*You're* talkin' hypothetically off the record. I'm sitting here listening. And I don't like what I hear."

"Wanna stop griping and look at what we got?"

"I don't wanna do shit. I want you out of here, I never saw you, this never happened."

"Yeah, but it did. And if we don't talk about it, it's gonna eat you up all day."

MacAullif shook his head. "Fuck."

"I didn't give you the punch line, either."

"Punch line?"

"Yeah. There's a punch line. And you haven't heard it yet."

I let that sit there. Fuck him. If he wanted to hear it, he was gonna have to ask.

MacAullif glowered at me. Because of the position I'd just put him in. If he asked, he'd have a hard time griping. It was almost worth not asking.

Almost.

"All right," he growled. "What's the fucking punch line?"

"Speaking strictly hypothetically . . ." I said.

"Fuck you. Get on with it."

"Sorry," I said. "But hypothetically speaking, suppose this woman's husband was a cop?"

MacAullif's eyes widened. He blinked. "Connected to the case?"

"No."

"You sure?"

"Yeah, I'm sure."

"How can you be so sure?"

"Suppose he was from out of state?"

"Is he?"

"We're talking hypothetically here. If you stopped to think about it, you'd know that was best."

"Damn," MacAullif said. "If her husband's a cop, that opens up a lot of possibilities."

"Hypothetically, of course," I said.

"Fuck hypothetically. We're talkin' here. You got a cop, his wife used to be a porn star. Long time ago. Now she's not. Now she's a wife and mother." He broke off, looked at me. "Does he know?"

I shook my head. "No."

"No shit. What an interesting can of worms *that* opens up."

"Maybe, maybe not."

"What do you mean by that?"

"According to the woman, her husband *still* doesn't know. According to her, no one's given him a tumble. If the guy has any idea at all, he hasn't let on."

"Cops are pretty strong. They can hide a lot."

"She says no. I believe her."

"You'd believe in the fuckin' Tooth Fairy."

I shrugged. "For what it's worth. And if her husband *really* doesn't know, then maybe him being a cop has nothing to do with it."

"You mean it's just coincidence?"

"Right. You don't believe in coincidence. Well, it's *not* coincidence. He just *happens* to be a cop. Coincidental to nothing. It's just what he *is*. He could be a plumber."

"But he happens to be a cop?"

"You don't like that?"

"Do you?"

"Not much. But it's what I'm stuck with."

MacAullif squinted at me. "You're sayin' the woman in the pictures isn't important, and her husband isn't important?"

"That's the problem. That's the way it looks."

"Which leaves you with what?"

"I have no idea."

"Great."

"That's why I'm here, basically. I thought you might."

"Thanks a heap. Come here, make me an accessory to a crime. Feed me with a heap of garbage don't make sense, and ask me to interpret it for you."

"Could you?"

"Fuck you."

"Well, that's a frank answer."

"You got a lot of balls."

"That's what Thurman said."

"Is that why you're acting this way? Because of the drunk-tank bit? You'll remember *I* didn't throw you in there."

"I know that."

"So how come I'm the one catching the shit?"

"You think I should be talking to Thurman?"

"Bring him this, you're lookin' at twenty years to life."

"For withholding evidence?"

"No, but you piss him off enough, he'll get you for murder."

"He's got nothing on me."

"Fuck it. He'll frame you."

"I thought Thurman was straight."

"Yeah, but he thinks you're guilty. So anything that nails you is fair."

"He doesn't think I'm guilty of murder."

"Let's not quibble. Guilty is guilty. And jail is jail. The charge is rather immaterial."

"Hmm," I said. "It would seem my only defense would be to figure out who did this. Too bad you don't want to help."

"You're pissing me off."

"You're pissed off already. I might as well get something out of it."

"I got nothing for you."

I nodded. "Maybe not now. But maybe you get something that, based on what I told you, adds up."

"How the fuck is it gonna add up? You didn't give me any names. All you did was play what-if."

"Names don't matter. I'm convinced of that."

"Then how the hell am I gonna hear something that adds up?"

"It doesn't have to tie into a person. Just the general scheme of things. That fits in with the facts as we know them."

"But we *don't* know them. All we got is a porno photo you won't admit has anything to do with the case, and the woman in the photo and her cop husband, who you say don't mean shit. And what the hell does that do for us?"

"I don't know. But assume that's true. Then how does the case add up? That's all I'm asking, really. You're usually real good at putting a spin on the facts so they make sense. All I'm saying is, whether you want to trust my judgment or not, let's *assume* the woman in the pictures and her cop husband don't mean shit. Then how does the evidence look to you? What sort of slant does that put on it?"

"It fucks it up the ass."

"Could you be more explicit?"

"If the woman doesn't mean anything, the key has to be

the man. In the original blackmail photos. He has to be the target, the focus, the one setting this in motion. What fucks things up is, by rights, one of the people in the pictures should be the target, and the other should be the instigator. Or at least the tool of the blackmailers. See what I mean? The person *supplying* the pictures. Giving the blackmailer the leverage. You say the woman's out, that leaves the photographer. As the most likely source. But when you're talkin' twenty years . . ." MacAullif shook his head. "It's hard to imagine a porno photographer hanging on to something that long."

"If he was planning blackmail?"

"For twenty years? How would he know? It's just dumb luck if one of the people he shot twenty years ago gets famous enough to be blackmailed. There's no way for him to know which one it's gonna be, so you gotta figure this guy hung on to *all* the pictures he ever took, on the off chance someday some of them might get valuable." MacAullif shrugged. "Well, it's a possibility. I think you should try to find the photographer."

"The woman doesn't remember the photographer. She doesn't have a clue. My wife questioned her at some length on the subject. A lot better than me, actually. Put her at her ease, got her to remember back. And she doesn't remember who shot the film. It wasn't important to her. She was young, scared, more concerned with what she was doing. The whole thing's a blur. One she's tried to blot out of her mind. Fat, thin, old, young, she hasn't got a clue."

"Great," MacAullif said. "And the man in the pictures—the real ones, I mean—what does she remember about him?"

I shook my head. "Nothing. Nothing at all. She didn't even recognize the man in the picture I showed her. Wouldn't have remembered him if she hadn't seen it, couldn't remember the others. In that regard she was absolutely no help."

"If she's telling the truth."

"Yeah, but I think she is."

MacAullif grimaced. "Okay. So you gotta figure the man's the key. Most likely blackmail victim, most likely killer."

"Except for one thing."

"What's that?"

"The pictures are twenty years old. How the hell does this happen with the pictures that old?"

"It doesn't matter *how* it happened. The point is, it did. If the woman ain't the answer, the man's gotta be."

"What if he's not?"

"Then the whole thing makes no sense."

"I know that. That's what I keep coming back to. That's where I need your help. So take it one step further. Say the guy isn't the answer. What then?"

"Then the pictures are worthless," MacAullif said. "Which we know isn't true. Because someone tried to pay a lot of money for 'em. At least once. The second time they gave you funny money." He frowned. "Now there's a concept. You got a packet full of newsprint to buy a packet full of worthless blackmail photos. That would fit. The photos are phony, just like the money. But that's the *only* way it would fit, and it fucks up everything else. We *know* the photos mean something. Why? Because everyone who touches them dies. Which brings us back to square one. Who wanted those pictures enough to kill for 'em? Or rather, who wanted to *suppress* those pictures enough to kill for 'em. Or who *cared* enough about those pictures one way or another to want to kill for 'em. It all comes down to that." MacAullif picked up a cigar and leveled it at me. "Now, you," he said. "What you gonna do with that picture?"

"What picture?"

"Don't fuck with me." He pointed to where it was lying on his desk. "*That* picture. The hypothetical, fucking, cocksucking picture you brought me and said 'what-if.' What are you gonna do with it?"

"Nothing. It has nothing to do with the case."

"That's the woman the cops are lookin' for."

I shrugged. "If you say so. But how would *you* know? We were talking hypothetically. So maybe I brought you another dirty picture just as a prop. Maybe this isn't the woman at all. And even if it was, do you think I'd turn it in? If I *had* found the woman in the pictures, do you think I'd ruin her life by handing her over to Thurman?"

"Bullshit," MacAullif said. "High and mighty motives. You'd withhold it from Thurman 'cause you're pissed off at the son of a bitch. For purely selfish, personal reasons."

"I'm sorry you think so poorly of me."

I stood up, picked up the picture.

"Where you going?"

"I'm going to talk to my lawyer."

"Good idea. You *need* a lawyer."

"It's not just that."

"Oh?"

I shoved the photograph back in the manila envelope, stuck it in my briefcase.

"If I didn't show him this picture, he'd never forgive me."

50.

"Interesting," Richard said.

I gave him a look. As a comment on the photograph, that seemed somewhat inadequate.

I'd told him the whole story before I showed it to him. Every twist. Every nuance. Even every speculation. In light of all that, I could have hoped for something more than "interesting."

"Is that all you have to say?"

"I don't know what there is to add. You seem to have covered the subject quite thoroughly."

"To absolutely no avail. I've got a whole bunch of data that adds up to absolutely nothing. I was hoping you might suggest a new slant."

"Well," Richard said, "from a legal point of view, if this woman is the same woman you saw in the blackmail photos, then this is a material piece of evidence, and you are guilty of withholding it from the police."

"But it *isn't* evidence," I said. "Since it *isn't* one of the original blackmail photos."

"If it's the same woman, it's evidence," Richard said. "There's no getting away from that."

"I don't believe this," I said. "You're my lawyer. I thought a lawyer always found a way to interpret the evidence in his client's favor."

"Oh, naturally," Richard said. "But the facts are the facts."

"Are you telling me I have to turn the picture in?"

Richard looked at me in surprise. "Don't be a damn fool," he said. "Of course you're not going to turn the picture in."

"So I'm guilty of withholding evidence."

"In a manner of speaking," Richard said. "But that's just between you and me. Who gives a shit about that? But from a legal standpoint, I'm sure you're in the clear."

"What do you mean by that?"

"If you would let me continue," Richard said. "I was merely exploring possibilities. Now, as I said, if this woman in the picture is the same woman who was in the blackmail photos, then you're guilty of withholding evidence."

"So?"

"So say she isn't. Take the position she's *not* the woman in the blackmail photos."

"But she is."

"How can you be sure of that?" Richard said. "I mean really sure. Surely there must be room for doubt."

"I talked to the woman myself. She admits it's a photo of her."

"Did *she* see the blackmail photos?"

"Of course not. I don't have them."

"Who has them?"

"Whoever stole them."

"Really? What are the chances of getting them back?"

"I have no idea."

"So," Richard said. "You didn't have one of the blackmail photos to compare this with."

"No, of course not."

"So when you say it's the same woman, you're relying solely on your own memory."

"Yes, of course."

"The woman you spoke to never saw the blackmail photos, so she can't identify them. She can't swear that she's the woman in them."

"I guess not. No, of course not."

"Did she *look* like the woman in the blackmail photos? If you bumped into her on the street, would you have said, 'Hey, that's the woman in the blackmail photos!'?"

"No, of course not. She didn't look anything like her."

Richard spread his hands wide. "Well, there you are. She can't identify herself as the woman in the blackmail photos. And you can't recognize her as the woman in the blackmail photos. So there's no reason to assume she is. At the present time, I would have to take the position that she's not. If she isn't, this picture you have is totally irrelevant, and there's no reason to turn it in to the police."

"Are you advising me *not* to turn it in to the police?"

"Absolutely. As your attorney, I advise you to hang on to that picture. To turn it in now would be very misleading. The facts being what they are. This is a situation which would seem to bear investigation. But you don't want to do anything rash."

"Of course not. Thank you."

"For what?"

"Taking the responsibility. Advising me not to turn in the picture."

Richard shrugged. "Oh, yes. Oh, well, that's just between you and me. I could always deny giving you that advice."

My mouth dropped open. "Richard!"

"Not to fear," he said. "I won't do that. I just don't want you getting too complacent."

"I wouldn't worry about it," I said. "Anyway, I thank you for the advice. Aside from that, do you have any clue as to what all of this means?"

Richard considered. "No, I don't," he said. "And that's significant."

I gave him a pained look. "That's one of those annoyingly enigmatical statements. What do you mean by that?"

"Enigmatical?" Richard said.

"You don't know what *enigmatical* means?"

"No, I'm just amazed you can pronounce it. I'm also not sure it's a word."

"Richard."

"All I'm saying," Richard said, "is that all the facts you've given me don't add up. Not at all. I can't make head nor tail of them. And that is significant, because in some way or another they should. This happened, after all. Three people are dead. And there's got to be a reason for it. And nothing I've heard sheds any light on that reason."

"That's not very helpful."

"Maybe not, but that's how I see it. When you're putting facts together, ideally you want to make them add up. If they don't add up, the best you can do is try to come up with a theory for why they don't."

"You have one?"

"Not at all. After all, I'm digesting most of these facts for the first time. I'm merely suggesting a line of inquiry."

"Fine. Of whom should I inquire?"

"That was a figure of speech."

"Great."

"Hey, don't be such a grouch. After all, I said you could hang on to the photo."

"I know."

"All right, so you're not any closer to solving the crime. But look on the bright side."

"Which bright side?"

Richard shrugged. "No one's been killed for weeks."

51.

Funny how seemingly irrelevant things will add up and eventually make sense.

Richard's statement that no one had been killed for weeks didn't really strike me at the time. It wasn't till later, when I was out of his office and driving up to the Bronx to do a sign-up, that the implications of that actually occurred to me.

Right. No one *had* been killed in weeks. Not since Jack Fargo.

What did that mean?

One interpretation would be that I must be on the wrong track. When I'd gotten the lead to Fargo, he'd immediately been killed. Since then, no leads I'd gotten had resulted in anyone's death. Hence, they must be worthless.

Including Mrs. Gardner, the middle-aged porn star from New Jersey. She was still alive, and therefore unimportant.

Except.

It had been weeks since the killings when I'd found her. Say Jack Fargo got killed because I led the killer to him. Was it reasonable to assume Mrs. Gardner *hadn't* been killed because by the time I found her the killer considered himself safe and was no longer paying any attention to my investigations? Or more simply, if the killer knew I'd uncovered Mrs. Gardner, would she be dead?

That opened up avenues of speculation. With that as a premise, would it be possible to devise a trap? Let the killer know I'd found Mrs. Gardner, and see if he'd try to eliminate her. Of course, not knowing who the killer was, I'd have to let *everyone* know I'd found Mrs. Gardner.

Including her cop husband.

I wasn't prepared to do that. At least not yet.

And assuming I set a trap, who would be there to spring it? Not MacAullif. He wouldn't go near it. That left Thurman. I didn't want to *help* Thurman, I wanted to *get* Thurman.

Me and Richard? Me and Alice? How about Richard and Alice, and I stay out of it?

By the time I'd arrived at my first sign-up I'd more or less washed out the idea of setting a trap.

I'd also come to the conclusion that I didn't know what the fuck was going on, and desperately needed more facts.

The problem was, finding Mrs. Gardner should have cracked the case. Instead, it had turned out to be a dead end. Leaving me no real leads to investigate. Unless you wanted to count F-Stop Fitzgerald. But aside from the mystery man in the blackmail photographs, who for all my effort I was not one whit closer to discovering, was there any lead in this case, however slim, that I hadn't traced yet?

I thought about it the rest of the day as I drove along doing sign-ups and photo assignments. I thought about it hard.

By the time I was heading home, I had only managed to come up with two things.

52.

The young man looked at me suspiciously. "You're not a reporter?"

"No, I'm not."

"Swear to god?"

"I'm not a reporter. I'm a private detective. You don't have to believe me, but it happens to be true."

"If you *were* a reporter, that's just what you'd say."

"Maybe," I said. "But if I *were* a reporter, I'd already have my story, and it wouldn't matter if you confirmed, denied, or sat there and said nothing. I'd print what I've got."

He frowned and bit his lip.

I felt sorry for him.

His name was Mark Cirrus.

He had been Jack Fargo's boyfriend.

We were sitting in his apartment in Chelsea. It was a studio apartment, not unlike Jack Fargo's. Or Cliff McFadgen's, for that matter.

Mark Cirrus frowned again and took a breath. He was a good-looking young man, with a clean-cut, country-boy face and sandy hair. It was hard to imagine him with the pudgy, middle-aged Jack Fargo.

"How did you find me?" he said.

He was obviously stalling for time, but for my purposes it was as good a point of departure as any.

"It has to do with the murder of Cliff McFadgen."

He frowned. "What?"

"Did you know the murders of Jack Fargo and Cliff McFadgen were connected?"

"No. Not connected. They were lumped together in the same news story. Along with that woman. Because they were all actors. Who got killed. But connected?" He shook his head. "I doubt it. The guy was shot. And Jack . . ."

His face contorted. He broke off, couldn't go on.

"I know," I said. "I know this is hard, and I apologize for being here. You asked me how I found you. I started to tell you. There *is* a chance the murders are connected. When I was interviewing actresses in the McFadgen murder, I naturally asked them if they knew anything about Fargo. One of them mentioned he was gay. That was a while back, when it happened. But it occurred to me, in going over the police files, that no one had ever come forth. So I went back, jogged the actress's memory to come up with a name. She couldn't, but she asked around and a girlfriend came up with you."

He frowned. "Damn."

"You *were* Jack Fargo's longtime companion?"

He made a face. "I hate that expression. That's how they refer to someone whose lover died of AIDS."

"I'm sorry. But the fact is, you and Fargo were involved."

"You're *sure* you're not a reporter?"

"If I were, and I'd taken this long to find you, I'd be fired. Look, let's ignore these personal questions. They're preliminary anyway, and I don't give a damn. I'm only concerned with solving this crime. If you knew Fargo at all—and I don't care how—maybe you can help me. I take it you'd like to see his killer caught."

He said nothing, just gave me a look.

"Okay," I said. "Help clear up some things for me."

"What things?"

"First off, were you aware of any connection between Jack Fargo and Cliff McFadgen?"

"They were in a showcase together. That's the only connection. Otherwise I wouldn't even know his name."

"Did you see it?"

"Of course."

"Then you knew Cliff McFadgen."

"I didn't *know* him. I saw him in that play."

"And he and Jack weren't close?"

"Absolutely not!" Mark Cirrus said. He flushed slightly, embarrassed by the overreaction. "I'm sorry," he said. "I don't think Jack ever mentioned him. Except that he was pushy in rehearsal."

Exactly what he'd told me. I didn't mention it. I didn't want this young man to know I'd seen Fargo just before he died. Perhaps even contributed to his death.

"What about Patricia Connely?" I said.

"What about her?"

"Did you know her?"

"No, I didn't. I'd never even heard the name."

"What about Bradley Connely?"

"Same thing."

"You never heard of him?"

"That's right."

"I see," I said. I paused, took a breath. "This is somewhat delicate."

He looked at me defiantly. "Yes?"

"Jack Fargo was somewhat older than you."

His face got hard. "Yeah? So what?"

I put up my hands. "I'm sorry. That was preliminary. I'm just wondering how long you'd actually known him."

"Is it important?"

"It might be."

"I'd known him two years. Can you tell me why that matters?"

"If you'd only known him two years, it probably doesn't. I'm wondering if you are aware if, in the past, Jack Fargo had had any experience with pornography?"

Mark Cirrus came out of his chair. "Damn you!"

I stood up too. I wasn't sure what his intentions were, but I wasn't about to sit there and get slugged.

"Please," I said.

He pointed at me. "No. Don't *please* me. What's the matter with you people? You hear *gay*, you think pervert. If you're gay, you must be into pornography, right?"

"That's not true," I said. "But the heterosexual angles in this case seem to lead to pornography. So if the homosexual ones did too, it would be a connection."

"There's no connection."

"You're very quick to judge. What if I were to tell you the Cliff McFadgen murder was connected to a blackmail attempt involving pornographic pictures?"

Mark Cirrus's eyes widened. "You're crazy," he said. "I read all the newspapers. There's been no mention whatever."

"Exactly," I said. "Because the cops aren't giving it out. They always withhold something only the killer would know. But there were blackmail photos, and they happen to have disappeared."

Mark Cirrus looked at me as if his world were collapsing. "You mean photos of . . . Jack?"

I put up my hands. "No, no. Not at all. Still, there's the question of whether he *knew* the people in the blackmail photos."

He thought that over, rubbed his head.

I felt sorry for him. I'd planned to get him on the defensive, ask him why he hadn't come forward, why he wasn't in the police file. But that would be pointless and cruel. With the guy so concerned I might be from the press, it didn't take a genius to figure out why he hadn't stepped forward. Most likely he had parents back in Iowa somewhere, who didn't know he was gay.

And his grief for Jack Fargo seemed genuine to me.

I guess I'm just too soft to be a private detective. It was like the Mrs. Gardner thing all over again. I didn't want to be the one to blow the whistle.

He looked up at me. “Who were they? The people in the pictures?”

I shook my head. “The police don't seem to know.”

He frowned, looked at me. “Then I don't understand.”

I nodded. “Join the crowd.”

53.

"That's very interesting," Bradley Connely said.

It was kind of him to say so. What I'd just told him *wasn't* very interesting. In fact, it was dull as hell. I hadn't mentioned the porno photo, for instance. Or Jack Fargo's boyfriend. All I'd done was given him a rather bland rehash of everything we'd known a month ago.

I'd done it because I'd needed a reasonable pretext to get into his building. Calling on him had seemed as good as any. Of course, I didn't have anything I wanted to say to him. Hence the bullshit.

Which he found interesting. Or at least said he did.

I found *that* interesting. Actually, it was the situation I found interesting. Because Bradley Connely was being much more gracious to me than one would have thought necessary. At the same time, I could tell he wasn't really paying any attention to what I was saying, he just wanted to get me the hell out of there. Not that he gave any evidence of it—as I say, he was perfectly gracious. So perhaps I was just projecting it.

I had good reason to. Because I was there chasing down the other loose end, the other lead I still hadn't traced yet.

Bradley Connely's girlfriend.

And what made me feel I was on the right track, that I was *not* just projecting it, and that Bradley Connely really did have something to hide, was the fact that at one point during our conversation I could have sworn I heard a sound come from the direction of his bedroom. It wasn't a voice, it wasn't a footstep, it wasn't a click, snap, thud, cry, or anything else identifiable. It was in fact so insignificant I might have even missed it.

Except Bradley Connely reacted.

Nothing big. Nothing major. Just for one split second, his eyes flicked in that direction. But that was enough to sell me on the idea. She's in the bedroom. The woman I want to find is in there right now.

If I were a different type of person, I suppose I could have stood up, said, "Excuse me, could I use your bathroom?" and before he could stop me gone crashing through the bedroom door. But that's not exactly my style. No, for my part I was perfectly content to sit there, talking aimlessly about the case and confirming my opinion that Bradley Connely wasn't about to tell me to go to hell, because he happened to have something to hide.

What he was hiding was probably just a hot babe in the bedroom, but even so. It was by now over a month since his wife's death, and even if I'd caught him *banging* a hot babe in the bedroom, there's no law against that. Since he was dressed when I rang the bell, she was probably dressed when I rang the bell, so why he had to hide her was beyond me. At any rate, it sure was interesting. Gave my theory an added kick.

When I felt I'd tortured him long enough, I thanked him for his time, shook his hand, went outside, and pretended to ring for the elevator. Instead, I slipped into the stairwell.

The first thing I did was make sure the damn door didn't lock. After all, this was the sixteenth floor, and if I were to get locked in the stairwell and find I couldn't get out without going down to the lobby, I was gonna be pissed. But there was no danger of that—the stairwell doors did not lock. Score one for the good guys.

They also had a window. Small, diamond-shaped, just at eye level. Score two for the good guys.

And from that window I could see Bradley Connely's apartment door. Score three for the good guys.

And she can't stay in there forever, so the good guys are gonna win.

Unless he had a kitchen door. That was an unsettling thought. There was a back door to someone's apartment right behind me. And it wasn't Bradley Connely's, of course, since his apartment was across the hall. So there had to be another stairwell over there, another back hall for the apartments on the other side. So, what if Bradley Connely's wise to what I'm up to, and she goes out the kitchen door and right down the stairs?

Well, then I'd be fucked, but there wasn't a hell of a lot I could do about it. If I went to the other stairwell where I could watch the kitchen door, then I wouldn't be able to watch the front door. Maybe I could hear it open, but what could I do then, pop out in the hallway? That would be a smooth move, particularly if it wasn't the girl at all, but was Bradley Connely himself. If it were him *and* the girl it would certainly be an interesting confrontation, but if it were him alone, I'd have blown my cover to absolutely no avail.

I stewed about that for a while, and the end result was I did absolutely nothing. Fuck it. If he's slick enough to send her down the back stairs, he deserves to keep his secret.

Of course, if he did that, his secret would sure be worth knowing. I killed myself with that thought. The saving grace was, as time wore on, as it got to be a half hour and then an hour after I'd taken up my position, I could console myself with the thought that if I moved across the hall now it would do no good, because if she was going down the back stairs, she was probably already gone.

Of course, the unsettling corollary to that thought was, if she was already gone, my present surveillance was also worthless, and I could wind up standing here all night.

It was not a happy thought. And as time wore on, the diamond-shaped glass window that had appeared such a blessing became a horrible curse, since I had to stand there and look through it. It only took me an hour or so to figure out that if the door *hadn't* had a diamond-shaped window, I would have had to keep watch by opening the door a crack. And it didn't take too long after that before I realized I could *pretend* the door didn't have a diamond-shaped window and act accordingly. And sure enough, with the door pushed open, I could sit on the floor of the back hallway and keep watch on Bradley Connely's apartment just fine.

Maybe it was working out that tough logistics problem that gave me a feeling of accomplishment, or maybe it was just that I'd been batting zero for so long that it seemed like my number was sure to come up, but it was right about then that I started to get excited. That I began to start thinking, maybe this would be it. The final piece of the puzzle I needed to crack the case. She's in there and any moment now she's gonna walk out and I was gonna see her. And once I knew who she was, everything else would suddenly become crystal clear.

For that to be true, I had to know her. If she wasn't a known quantity, there couldn't be a revelation. For this woman to be the piece of the puzzle to crack the case—which I truly believed her to be—she would have to be a member of the cast of characters.

Mrs. Gardner would fit the bill. Oh boy, would she fit the bill. Respectable housewife and mother. Married to a cop. Caught up in a torrid affair with married actor Bradley Connely. Haunted by pictures from her past.

Yeah, if it was her, I'd cracked the case. The details could be sorted out later. But in terms of the broad brush strokes, I'd have everything I needed. Yeah, if it was her it would be perfect.

Only I didn't want it to be her.

Next on the list was Cliff McFadgen's girlfriend. Or any of her roommates, for that matter. If it was any of them, could a solution be far behind? I played with the possibilities. Though all were certainly possible, my favorite had to be the wallflower, Bernice. After all, she saw the money.

True, she told me about it, but that could be an elaborate double bluff. Wasn't that the sort of icy-cool logical move a repressed woman like that would love? Laughing at me while gloating in her own secret knowledge. Yeah, all in all, Bernice would do quite nicely too.

As I sat there speculating, trying to figure it out, I thought back to that afternoon when I'd first known Bradley Connely had another woman. When the fax had come through and I'd seen him try to hide the purse. I wondered if there was anything about that afternoon that was significant, anything that might give me a clue.

The purse had been hanging over the back of a chair. An office chair pulled up in front of the computer. The cover was off the computer, lying next to it on the printer. The cover that Bradley Connely had picked up and draped casually—too casually—over the purse.

Was there anything about the purse itself? No. It was a plain saddlebag sort of thing, leather, with a shoulder strap. Nothing ornate or fancy. Just a simple leather purse and—

It suddenly struck me there was nothing particularly frilly or feminine about it.

So what if? . . .

Jesus Christ, what if? . . .

What if when Bradley Connely's apartment door finally opened, *Mark Cirrus* came walking out?

Hell, that would do it. It suddenly occurred to me, that would explain everything. The murder of Patricia Connely. The murder of Jack Fargo. Not the murder of Cliff McFadgen, but that would follow naturally if he were a blackmailer. And there was every indication he was.

That had to be it.

Just as I thought that, the apartment door swung open and out came Bradley Connely's lover.

It was a woman I'd never seen before.

54.

Yeah, I followed her home and found out who she was, but I have to tell you, my heart wasn't in it. The woman—one Sharon Renzler, if the name on her mailbox were to be believed—lived in a brownstone on West Eighty-first Street. She was an attractive if not glamorous woman of around thirty, of tasteful but conservative dress, and as far as I could see was the very model of propriety. In fact, the only thing I could think to fault her on was her undue lack of caution in listing *Sharon Renzler* rather than *S. Renzler* by the doorbell. Aside from that, she was a perfectly nice, respectable woman, and if widower Bradley Connely, whose wife was by now more than a month dead, wanted to date her, who was I to say him nay?

I have to confess, I was not in a particularly good mood when I got home. Especially since it was nearly eight o'clock by the time I got there, and Tommie was eating at a friend's house, and Alice hadn't cooked. We ordered Chinese and, when it came, went in the bedroom to watch TV while we ate it.

Psycho was on channel eleven. That's one of those movies you know you've seen a million times, but somehow are still worth watching.

While Alice and I ate snow peas with water chestnuts and chicken with orange flavor, Janet Leigh took the money she was supposed to deposit in the bank and drove off in her car. Poor woman. So upset with what she'd done, and what a fate lay in store for her.

It occurred to me, in all the times I'd seen *Psycho*, I still hadn't remembered that part—about the bank and the money and her taking it. Watching it the first time, it all seemed so important. But if you were familiar with the movie you knew that—

Good god.

I sat there stunned, blinking at the screen.

55.

"MacGuffin."

MacAullif frowned and squinted up at me. "What?"

"MacGuffin. Do you know what a MacGuffin is?"

"Sounds like a McDonald's breakfast."

"That's McMuffin. This is MacGuffin. You know what that is?"

"Obviously I don't," MacAullif said irritably. "You want to gloat over that, or do you actually have a point?"

"A pencil has a point. I have an inspiration."

"Holy shit!" MacAullif said. His eyes widened. "Hey, who writes your fuckin' dialogue? That was fantastic. You make that up on the spur of the moment, or you been savin' it up for the right occasion?"

"Are you through clowning around?"

"Hey, like *I* started this. You come in babbling about McMuffins—"

"MacGuffins."

"I heard you the first time. I assume you're gonna tell me what the fuck that is or you wouldn't have brought it up."

"Good thinking. Well, my wife was watching the movie *Psycho* last night—you know the movie *Psycho*?"

"This another trick question?"

"Aw, fuck, MacAullif."

"Yeah, I know the movie. So what?"

"Well, at the beginning of the movie Janet Leigh's got all this money she was supposed to deposit in the bank. Remember?"

MacAullif frowned. "No. What money?"

"Exactly," I said. "If you know the movie, all you think about is the motel, the shower, Tony Perkins. But the beginning of the movie is all about the money she took—the money from the real-estate deal that her boss gave her to put in the bank. The reason you don't remember is because the money isn't *really* important in the movie. In the beginning it *looks* like the money is important, but it isn't. It's a MacGuffin."

MacAullif exhaled, looked at me in exasperation. "You'll pardon me if that doesn't help me a lot."

"It's a movie term, associated largely with Alfred Hitchcock, used to describe something in a movie that appears to be important but actually isn't. Like the money in *Psycho.* Or the uranium in the wine bottles in *Notorious*."

"Uranium?"

"Another Hitchcock film. Cary Grant and Ingrid Bergman. *Notorious.*"

"I've seen it."

"You remember the uranium in the wine bottles?"

"No."

"Another MacGuffin."

"Gee, that's interesting," MacAullif said. "And *what* is a MacGuffin again?"

"It's a plot device. It's something a director puts in a movie to help the plot along. Something that *appears* to be important, but actually isn't really."

MacAullif frowned. "You mean a red herring?"

My face fell. "Son of a bitch."

"What's the matter?"

"Shit. Do I mean a red herring? I hope not. That's so commonplace compared to a MacGuffin."

"Hey. Schmuck."

"Sorry. Okay, here's the deal. I know this sounds like garbage, but it's really the clue that cracked the case."

"Cracked the case? Are you telling me you solved this thing?"

"More or less."

"Don't fuck with me."

"I think I know who did it. I can't prove a damn thing. But I figured out the key clue."

"What's that?"

"The blackmail photos. No one could get a line on 'em. You, me, Thurman, Baby-Face Frost were all getting nowhere. Yeah, so I found a woman and maybe she was in 'em, but it's another dead end. Everything about 'em's a dead end. And now I know why."

"Why?"

"MacGuffin. The blackmail pictures are a MacGuffin. Like the money in *Psycho* or the uranium in *Notorious*."

MacAullif waved his hands. "Wait a minute, wait a minute. Time out. Flag on the play. You just got through telling me what a MacGuffin was. Maybe I'm just a dumb cop, but didn't you say it was something the director puts in the film to get the plot going, but it's misleading 'cause it don't really mean anything?"

"Absolutely. Very good definition. I think that's even better than what I said."

"Fuck you."

"I was serious."

"Who gives a shit? The point is, it's something the director puts in the film, right?"

"Right."

"Well, that's real nice if you're making a fuckin' movie," MacAullif said. "I hate to break it to you, but this is not a movie. This is real life."

"Yeah. So?"

"So?" MacAullif said. "There's no director."

"Yes, there is."

56.

"We are going to reconstruct the crime."

I was standing on the stage of a rehearsal hall in SoHo, not ten blocks away from the loft where I had found Patricia Connely dead. I had not chosen it for that reason. I had chosen it for the fact that I was able to get it cheap. In fact, free. I'd called around, and Jill Jensen, the actress I'd run into at the audition, happened to be in a showcase and managed to talk the director into letting me use the theater on the night they were dark.

I looked out over the audience. Present were:

Bradley Connely.
Mark Cirrus.
Cliff McFadgen's girlfriend, Martha Penrutti.
The wallflower, Bernice, along with Martha Penrutti's other roommates.

Richard Rosenberg.
Alice.
Sergeant MacAullif.
And Baby-Face Frost.

Conspicuous by their absence were:

Bradley Connely's girlfriend.
Mrs. Gardner and her cop husband.
Sergeant Thurman.
And F-Stop Fitzgerald.
Just kidding.

I stood center stage, addressed the audience. "Why are we doing this? We're doing this because all else failed. And when all else fails, you try something different. This is a popular notion in detective novels, reconstructing the crime, though I doubt if it actually happens much. Still, that is what we are about to do. We are not only going to *reconstruct* the crime, we are going to *reenact* the crime. To do that I will need help."

I looked around the audience, as if picking them at random. "Mark Cirrus and you, Bernice. Would you come up here please?"

Everyone watched while Jack Fargo's lover and Cliff McFadgen's girlfriend's shy roommate got up from their seats and made their way up onto the stage. When they stood flanking me I put my hands on their shoulders and said to the audience, "Please bear with me for a moment." Then I turned my actors around, piloted them upstage into the far corner, and proceeded to converse with them in low tones.

I left them there, went back downstage, and addressed the audience. "We have here three separate crimes. The murder of Patricia Connely, the murder of Cliff McFadgen, and the murder of Jack Fargo. However, these crimes *are* related, as I intend to demonstrate through this acting exercise. For shorthand's sake, please understand that when I'm talking about the crime, I'm talking about all three."

I paused, looked out over the audience. "And when I'm talking about the *killer*, once again I am talking about all three. Because it is my contention that not only are the crimes related, but the same person killed all three people."

I put up my hands. "I realize this is somewhat complicated. Particularly since some of you didn't even know there were three crimes to begin with, much less that they might be related. So in order for you to appreciate this exercise, let me briefly bring you up to speed.

"First off, let me introduce myself. My name is Stanley Hastings and I'm a private detective. Shortly before the murders began, I was approached by a woman who gave the name Marlena Smith. She told me she was being blackmailed by a man named Barry, and hired me to pay him off. Which I did. On the following night, I was hired to make another blackmail payment. On that night, the woman who hired me to make the payment and the blackmailer Barry were both murdered. That woman was Patricia Connely. The blackmailer Barry was actually Cliff McFadgen."

I held up my hands again. "This much we know is true. What we don't know is why. Why any of this happened. Which is what we hope to show through this acting exercise." I turned, gestured to my actors. "Mark. Bernice. If you will?"

My two actors had been huddled together, whispering. When they looked up at me I gestured downstage, then gave way for them. I moved to the edge of the proscenium and stood there, watching.

Mark Cirrus took charge. He took Bernice by the arm and led her downstage.

"All right, look," he said. "Here's the picture. You're being blackmailed by a guy named Barry. That's me. I got some pictures and you wanna buy 'em. You have to buy 'em. Or else. So you're hiring a private detective to make the blackmail payoff. You're gonna give him the money, he's gonna pick up the blackmail pictures and bring 'em back to you."

"What if he asks me why?" Bernice said.

"That's none of his damn business. He doesn't need to know. If he won't play on that basis, the hell with him, you get someone else."

Mark Cirrus reached into his jacket pocket, pulled out the fat envelope I'd given him. "You give him this."

"What's that?"

"Money for the payoff. He's to take it and pay for the pictures. Only he's not to open the envelope. Or the one he gets. The one with the pictures."

"Why not?"

"You don't need to know that."

"What if he asks?"

"Same answer. It's none of his damn business. You're hiring him to do a job. Okay?"

"Okay."

"No, it's *not* okay!" came an angry voice from the audience.

It was Bradley Connely. He stood up, pointed his finger at Bernice. "She's playing the part of my wife, and my wife wouldn't have done that."

"Done what, Bradley?" I said, crossing to center stage.

He waved his hand. "Any of that. You've got her conspiring with this blackmailer. She wouldn't have done that."

"You think she was actually being blackmailed?"

"No, I don't."

"Well, it has to be one or the other."

"Why?" Connely demanded.

"Because she told me she was."

"Well, we've only got your word for that," Connely said.

That caught me up short. That was a new thought. One I was sure glad Sergeant Thurman wasn't in the room to hear.

"Right," I said. "But this is my demonstration." I smiled. "For the purposes of it, we are going to go on the supposition that I am telling the truth."

Before Connely could say anything, I went on, "Anyway, I thank you for your input. And while you're up, that's good, because I could use another actor." I turned to Bernice. "Thank you, Bernice, but that's all for the time being. And could I have that, please?"

Bernice handed me the fat envelope and left the stage.

"Mark, stay up here, I need you some more." I turned back to Connely. "Bradley, I need another actor. For the scene at the motel. To play the part of the investigator."

"Oh, come on," Connely said. *"You're* the investigator. Why don't you play the part?"

"I can't," I said. "I'm the director. Help me out. Please."

"I don't want to have anything to do with it."

"Why not?"

"I told you. Because you're not telling it right."

"Then I should think you'd want to help straighten things out." When he hesitated, I persisted. "Come on, Bradley. I know this is painful for you. But you want your wife's killer caught, don't you?"

What could he say? While he was trying to think of something, I took him by the arm, led him up onstage.

"Thank you." I turned to the audience. "Now then, once again I need your indulgence."

I piloted Bradley Connely and Mark Cirrus upstage.

In the huddle I said, "Okay, we're going to do the scene in the motel. Mark, you're still the blackmailer. Your name's Barry. You got these pictures and the investigator wants to buy 'em. Oh yeah, just a minute."

I darted offstage, picked up a manila envelope, came back and handed it to Mark. "Okay, here's your prop. The blackmail photos." I handed the fat envelope to Bradley. "And here's your blackmail money. You stick it in your jacket, you pull it out at the proper time."

Bradley Connely looked terribly hassled. "What proper time?" he said. "Just what am I doing here?"

I bit my lip to keep from smiling. For a moment I was sure he was going to say, "What's my motivation?" Before he could, I said, "Play off Mark. He's the blackmailer, so he's the one in control. I know you think you don't know what to do, but it should be easy because you'll be responding instead of taking the initiative. Bradley, you have the blackmail money, you've been instructed to come and buy these photos from a guy named Barry, you're here to buy them, and you want the guy to hand them over."

I turned to Mark Cirrus. "Mark, you're a blackmailer, you've got the photos, you *intend* to hand them over, but you're getting off on being in charge, so you give the guy a bad time."

I clapped my hands together. "Okay," I said. "Just try it."

I went back downstage, held up my hands, said to the audience, "Now, this may be a little rough, but just bear with me because we're working these things out. This is the second scene, the private investigator goes to buy the blackmail photos. Mark. Bradley. If you will."

Mark Cirrus took Bradley Connely by the shoulder and led him downstage.

Bradley Connely, looking terribly uncomfortable, glanced around, then looked over at me. "I really don't know what to do," he said.

"Think of it as an acting exercise," I said. "Look. This is a motel room. Okay? So pretend the door is there. Walk up and pretend to knock on the door. He'll answer it."

"I really don't see the point."

"Of course not. Because we're just getting started. Just try it, and I think you'll begin to see how it all ties in."

I indicated a spot on the stage. "Okay, say the door's here, downstage left. Bradley, walk up and knock on the door."

He gave me a long look, but shuffled over stage left and got into position.

I resumed my place offstage right.

"Okay," I said, "let's give it a try."

Bradley Connely very reluctantly walked up and pantomimed knocking on the door, the standard acting pantomime where you pretend to bang with your fist at the same time you stamp your foot.

Mark Cirrus strode over, pantomimed opening a door.

"Yeah?" he said.

There was a pause while nothing happened.

"Ask him if he's Barry," I prompted.

Bradley Connely gave me a look, then turned and said, "Are you Barry?"

"If you say so, champ," Mark Cirrus said. He gestured. "Come on in."

Reluctantly, Bradley Connely walked in center stage.

Mark Cirrus followed him. "Well," he said. "You bring the money?"

Bradley Connely reached into his jacket pocket, pulled out the envelope. "Right here," he said.

His performance was so lifeless I'm sure no one was at all

surprised when I walked onstage saying, "No, no, no, this won't do."

I think they *were* surprised when I proceeded to take Mark Cirrus to task, instead of Bradley Connely.

Because that's exactly what I did. Ignoring Bradley Connely completely, I walked right by him, threw my arm around Mark Cirrus's shoulder, and said, "Mark, *baby*. Come *on*. You're a *blackmailer*. You gotta have *fun* with this. You gotta *enjoy* it. Now, come *on*, get into it and let's *torture* this guy."

I wheeled him around, demonstrated. "First off, pat him down for a *weapon*. Get him on the *defensive*."

I held up my finger for emphasis. "And remember," I said. "He's been told *not* to open the envelope. So the minute he gives it to you, you *rip it open* and dump the money out on the bed. I got hundred-dollar bills on the outside, it will look like a huge wad of cash. Then there's the photos. He's been told not to look at 'em, so you *rip it open* and you show 'em to him. Each and every one. Rub his *nose* in it."

I looked at Mark Cirrus, shook my head. "Come on, Mark. Put some *life* in it. Are you an actor or not? I mean, what am I paying you for?"

Mark Cirrus took the criticism well.

The man standing next to him didn't.

During my harangue, Bradley Connely turned a whiter shade of pale.

"This is absurd," he sputtered. "I can't be a part of it. It's too hard. It's too cruel. It's not right. It's . . ."

With that, Bradley Connely hopped down from the stage, ran up the aisle, out the back door.

And straight into the arms of Sergeant Thurman.

57.

Confused?

You won't be, after this week's episode of *Soap*.

Remember that show? Funny show. And somewhat fitting that I should think of it now. After all, it was on a soap commercial that I recognized Cliff McFadgen as the blackmailer Barry. And after all, the whole grand and glorious blackmailing scheme was really just another soap opera.

But enough of that. Time for the explanation.

The postmortem was conducted by me and Baby-Face Frost. But not in the conference room where I'd given my deposition—this time it was in his office. And this time we were alone. No police officer. No stenographer. Just me and Baby-Face, shooting the breeze and sorting things out.

"Okay," Frost said. "We got flight, that's an indication of guilt. If he doesn't confess, what else have we got?"

"Right now, not much," I said. "Just a theory. But you

start checking that theory out, you're bound to find some corroborating evidence. A witness. A fingerprint. Maybe even an incriminating phone call."

"Come again?"

"What if he called Cliff McFadgen from home?"

"I doubt it."

"So do I. All I'm saying is, if you know your theory's true, you should be able to find things to support it."

"Run through your theory again."

"From the top?"

"Sell it to me the way I'll have to sell it to a jury."

"I'm not selling anything. I'm just telling you what I think."

Frost nodded. "Good. Good. Humble and credible. I like it. Go on."

"This was a very simple crime. In fact, one of the simplest of crimes. Bradley Connely killed his wife. And why? For the simplest of motives. Another woman. Why couldn't he just divorce his wife? Because she was rich and he was poor." I shrugged. "So there you have it. Two primal motives, lust and greed. What could be simpler?" I held up my finger. "Or more obvious. That was the problem. The crime was so simple, even a cop as obtuse as Sergeant Thurman could have figured it out. So Bradley Connely had to disguise it and make it look like something else. That's why he invented the whole blackmail scheme.

"How did it work? Easy. First he hunted up an actor with whom he had no connection whatsoever. That couldn't have been too hard. Probably just hung out at Actors Equity one afternoon, pretending to read the bulletin board until he spotted a likely candidate. Then followed him outside and struck up a conversation—'Didn't I see you coming out of Actors Equity? Are you an actor? Would you like to play a part?'"

I smiled. "See, that was key all along. What Bernice said."

"Bernice?"

"Yeah. Cliff McFadgen's girlfriend's roommate. The one who acted the part of Patricia Connely in my little skit."

"What about her?"

"When I questioned the girls, she told me about seeing Cliff flashing a wad of money. And when he realized she'd seen him, what does he do? He tells her he's got an acting job he doesn't want anyone to know about. Well, that could have been bullshit, just the sort of thing he'd tell her to cover up his role in the blackmail. Which is the first thing I thought when I heard it. But the actual explanation is, what he was telling her was the absolute truth. He'd been paid money to act a part. The part of a blackmailer."

"And Patricia Connely?" Frost said.

I shrugged. "Here I'm only guessing. There's two ways it could have gone. One, she was originally in on the play. That is, her husband sold her on the idea he was going to have her and Cliff McFadgen act out this blackmail scheme. *Why* he would have wanted that done—I mean what explanation he could have given her—I have no idea. I can't even come up with a logical reason, and I doubt if he could either, and that's why I think it didn't happen that way.

"I think it happened the way I had Mark Cirrus and Bernice act it out onstage. In other words, Patricia Connely had no idea her husband was involved. Bradley Connely contacted Cliff McFadgen, hired him, and programmed him to hire her. To teach her her part, coach her on her lines."

"Why?" Frost said.

"Because it saves explanations. If Patricia Connely knew her husband was involved, she wouldn't do this without demanding an explanation. But she doesn't know. And if she demands an explanation of Cliff McFadgen, he doesn't have one. But he doesn't *need* one. His explanation is, 'A guy hired me to do this. He wants us to act these parts out. Why, I don't know. But he's paying us to do it.' Now, coming from her husband, there's no way that satisfies Patricia Connely. Coming from Cliff McFadgen, it would."

Frost frowned. "That's not evidence. It's just speculation."

"Of course it is. I told you, all I've got's a theory."

"You must have something to support it."

"I have logical inferences. Like the one I just gave you. Either Bradley Connely had some incredibly elaborate scheme his wife thought she was party to, or else she had no idea he was involved. The simpler explanation is that she had no idea that her husband was involved, that her only contact was Cliff McFadgen. Who of course had no idea who Bradley Connely was, or that Patricia Connely was his wife."

Frost frowned. "Does that work?"

"Perfectly reasonable," I said. "You gotta remember, Bradley Connely was an actor too. No problem for him to slip into another character to deal with Cliff McFadgen. And that long hair of his—all he's gotta do is tie it back and tuck it in his shirt collar to change his appearance enough that, even if McFadgen were to describe him to his wife, she'd never suspect it was him."

"I'm not sure I buy that," Frost said.

"Okay, but accept it as a premise. Then what happens next? Bradley Connely programs Cliff McFadgen who programs Patricia Connely. Patricia Connely comes and calls on me. Gives me the name Marlena Smith, tells the story of being blackmailed and asks me to buy the pictures back. And gives me the envelope that's supposed to contain the money to make the purchase.

"Because it's like I said onstage. The envelope's supposed to be filled with hundred-dollar bills. But it's actually a pack of ones with a hundred on each side. Just a stage prop, to convince me I'm actually part of a blackmail scheme.

"So I take the money, go out to the motel. There's Cliff McFadgen, having the time of his life. Getting to play this wonderfully juicy role, an arrogant blackmailer, and getting paid for it too. And he follows his instructions to the letter. Dumps the money on the bed and makes sure that I see it, then tears open the envelope and shows me the dirty pictures. Pictures supplied to him by Bradley Connely.

"Which is why they led nowhere. The blackmail pictures, I mean. Because they weren't blackmail photos at all. They were a prop, just like the money. Just a bunch of dirty pictures Bradley Connely picked up in a porn shop somewhere.

"Anyway, I take them back and give them to Patricia Connely. Who proceeds to play the scene of being very upset that the envelope has been cut open. Which is of course just an act—she *knew* it would be cut open, that was part of the script.

"What she *doesn't* do is take them out of the envelope and look at them. At the time I wondered why. Now I know. It was just bad acting on her part. Like she blew her motivation. The pictures were a prop, and she forgot her character should be interested in that prop. That was a key clue right there. I mean, if those were *real* blackmail pictures, there's *no way* she doesn't look at them.

"Anyway, she leaves in a huff. Setting the stage for Act Two.

"And what is Act Two? Buy the pictures again. She contacts me, gives me the envelope, sends me on my way."

I held up my finger for emphasis. "But this time I don't go straight to the motel. Cliff McFadgen sends me running around all over town. The George Washington Bridge. Out to Queens. Then finally to the motel. Why the runaround? I've been to the motel before. What is the purpose of having me trotting around? From a practical point of view—in terms of the blackmail, I mean—absolutely nothing. But the *actual* reason for having me running around is to give Patricia Connely time to get to the loft in SoHo where I would eventually wind up, and to give Bradley Connely time to get there first and kill her.

"She gets into the loft with a key supplied to her by Cliff McFadgen. A key he hung on to from when he did the showcase production there. The loft was still vacant and the lock hadn't been changed, so McFadgen suggested it when Connely needed a place for the scene.

"So she's there waiting for the private investigator to show up—waiting to play a scene with me. Only, when the door opens it isn't me, it's her husband. And he kills her."

I looked up at Frost. "I'm sure he killed her first, by the way. That's how the timing works out. He killed her while I'm playing phone tag with Cliff McFadgen. From there he went straight to Cliff's. Whether he got there before or after the last phone call, I don't know. It wouldn't matter. Cliff McFadgen knew him. He was the employer, the money man, the gravy train. Cliff McFadgen would welcome him with open arms.

"Bradley Connely rings the bell, goes in. Asks Cliff McFadgen if he's made the last phone call, sending me to the motel. If he has, fine, Connely takes out a gun and shoots him. If he hasn't, he waits with him there till he makes the call. As soon as the call is done, bang-bang.

"And what is the result? Instead of a simple husband/wife murder, and him the guy with the big motive who stands out like a sore thumb, instead we have two people killed as the result of a blackmail scheme.

"And look at the beauty of the thing. We have two people who never knew each other, whom no one could connect together. Except for yours truly. The poor dipshit P.I. who's been led on the scene like a lamb to the slaughter to tie the two deaths together and expose the blackmail scheme."

"What if you hadn't done that?" Frost said.

"What do you mean?"

"You started in by clamming up. I'm sure you'll recall. You spent a night in the drunk tank as a result of it."

"I seem to remember that."

"So, what if you decide not to cooperate?"

"Well, then I would imagine I go from being the prime witness to being the prime suspect in the case. I would imagine also, if that happened, you would have gotten an anonymous tip, telling you all about the blackmail on the one hand, and the fact I was holding out on it on the other. As it happened, and as I think you'll agree was most likely to happen, I came clean. So you knew all about the blackmail from the word *go,* and there was no need."

"What about Jack Fargo?"

I shook my head. "I feel really bad about that. Not that it was my doing. Bradley Connely chose him, not me. But I still feel partly responsible."

"Why?"

"I called on Bradley Connely that day and showed him the program from the showcase Cliff McFadgen was in. I didn't point Jack Fargo out, or anything of the kind. What I *did* do was advance a theory of the case, one I'd been working on."

"What theory?"

"The idea that Cliff McFadgen and his wife were in cahoots. That rather than him blackmailing her, they were actually working together as part of a more elaborate scheme. I didn't know what that scheme was. In fact, what I *thought* it was, was the two of them grooming me to fleece some third party, perhaps the woman in the blackmail photos. Anyway, that's the theory I advanced to him—that the two of them were working together. I'm afraid that's what killed Jack Fargo."

"I don't follow."

"Indirectly, I mean. See, that theory was right on. It hit too close to home. Cliff McFadgen and Patricia Connely *were* working together. Not the way I doped it out, but still they were. As part of Bradley Connely's scheme. When he saw me headed in the right direction, he panicked. He wanted to do something to draw attention away from that theory and back to the whole larger blackmail scheme.

"So what did he do? When I gave him the program, he picked the name Jack Fargo. Picked it at random. Actually, I'm sure he'd never heard of him. But that didn't matter. All he needed was to give me one clue, one lead I'd follow up.

"Which I did. I called on Jack Fargo. Asked him some questions. None of which revealed a damn thing. Except for the fact he got vaguely uneasy when I mentioned porno pix. I thought that implied guilty knowledge. That he was involved in the pornography end of the blackmail.

"I'm now convinced I was way off base. It was just that Fargo was gay and must have had something to do with gay porn when he was young.

"Anyway, Fargo knew nothing, had absolutely nothing to do with it. He was an innocent bystander who just happened to have had the misfortune to have once been in a showcase with Cliff McFadgen. No matter. That was enough of a connection.

"That and the fact I questioned him.

"When I left Bradley Connely's, I went straight to Jack Fargo's. Connely followed me. As soon as I left, he went in and killed him."

I spread my arms. "And there you have it. A crucial witness with key information is silenced before he can talk. Proof positive the perpetrators of this nefarious blackmail scheme are still at work."

I shook my head. "I have to admit, that was a flash of brilliance. A spontaneous, unrehearsed, off-the-cuff murder. Which is why the means was different. The first two he'd planned out. He had the guns. This one he hadn't planned, hadn't intended, so he had no murder weapon to use. Which is why he used whatever came to hand."

"Fine," Frost said. "I still got nothing. Except flight. And even that's shaky. The guy stormed out because he was upset about how you were portraying his wife."

"Bullshit. It was flight."

"Okay, *why* did he flee? Sell it to the jury."

"I don't know if I can, but I know I'm right. I *know* he fled because I *expected* him to flee. I played for it to happen."

"How?"

"First off, by playing the scene between Cliff McFadgen and his wife. That was a key element—the conspiracy theory. The same idea that made him uncomfortable enough to go out and kill Jack Fargo.

"Next, I finessed him into playing the private investigator in the motel scene. He doesn't want to do it, but he can't think of a way out of it, and suddenly he's up there onstage playing me.

"What drove him over the edge was when he realized *I* was playing *him.* I walked out onstage and started giving Mark Cirrus direction. That's when he suddenly realized what was happening. I wasn't just directing the scene, I was playing a part in it. He was playing me, and *I was playing him.* The *director.* I was coaching Mark Cirrus on how to play a blackmailer in the scene with him, just as he'd coached Cliff McFadgen on how to play a blackmailer in the scene with me."

I shrugged. "Realizing that had to be like getting hit by a thunderbolt. He suddenly *knew* that I *knew.* He felt naked, like I could see right through him. That's why he ran."

Sergeant Thurman stuck his head in the door.

"He's confessing."

"What?" Frost said.

"Yeah. Bradley Connely. I thought you'd want to know."

"Damn!" Frost said.

Thurman put up his hand. "No, no. It's according to Hoyle. He was Mirandized up the wazoo."

"What about his lawyer?"

"He's there. The guy's still talkin'."

"Why? What's the deal."

"We brought in the girlfriend. This Sharon Renzler. Connely's goin' noble. Sayin' it was all his doin' and she's got nothing to do with it."

A grin spread over Frost's chubby face as if his mama'd just given him a bottle. "Is that so?" he said. "What's his story?"

"He hired Cliff McFadgen to set up his wife." Thurman jerked his thumb. "You'd better get down there. The guy's so eager to talk, he spilled half of it before we could get a stenographer in place."

"Shit," Frost said.

He hurried out the door.

Thurman started out too. In the doorway he stopped, turned back.

"Damned if you weren't right," he said.

Then he was gone.

I stood there alone in the office of A.D.A. Baby-Face Frost, looking after him.

Yeah, Thurman.

Damned if I wasn't.

58.

Yeah, I know. You're not happy with the ending. Because I let Sergeant Thurman in on the play. And he beat me up and threw me in the drunk tank. And you wanted to see me stick it to him. Solve the crime without him, and then rub his nose in it.

Well, I felt that way too. But when it came right down to it, I just couldn't do it.

Because life isn't a storybook, and everything isn't black and white. The good guys, the bad guys. It's not that easy.

Sergeant Thurman may be a schmuck, but he doesn't know it. He doesn't walk around saying, "I'm a bad guy, I'm gonna go beat up private eyes and make their life miserable." He has his own code of ethics, and he does what he thinks is right. And he doesn't like crooks, and he gives them a hard time.

All right, he beat me up and threw me in the drunk tank.

But why did he do it? He did it because I was a witness to a murder and I wouldn't talk. Now that's no excuse, but still. When you come to think of it, why did I refuse? I refused because I had something to hide. What was that? My participation in the blackmail scheme.

Because that's what I was doing, wasn't I? Whether Richard said I had a right to or not—and he didn't really say I had a right to, he was hedging his bets—the fact is, I was involved in it.

Funny how things get to you. How they come back to haunt you. MacAullif, when he was laying out his theory of how things were, telling me *I* was the blackmailer. That was the first kick in the head.

Then there was Mrs. Gardner. What she said when I showed her the photograph. "What is this, blackmail?"

Those two things taken together tell me just what it was I was up to. Yes, I meant well. The valiant P.I., protecting his client, going out and fighting insurmountable odds. Helping the poor, defenseless woman who was being blackmailed.

But what was I *really* doing? Aiding and abetting. Being an accessory to a blackmail. Compounding a felony and conspiring to conceal a crime.

Yes, with perfectly laudable motives.

But still.

See? Everything's not black and white.

So, yes, I can resent Sergeant Thurman throwing me in the drunk tank. But when push came to shove, I realized I couldn't get any satisfaction out of revenge.

Alice didn't understand when I tried to explain it to her later that night. Because Alice takes a simple, direct approach and doesn't fuck herself up with convoluted thinking. Thurman wronged me and I should get him, what's to think about?

I gave her the whole equivocation, and she gave me a look that told me I was a total moron. She's good at that look. But I've gotten used to seeing it. So I countered by saying, if I weren't who I am, if I were a different person, the person she implies I should be by giving me that look, she probably wouldn't have married me in the first place.

That cuts no ice with Alice.
Simple and direct, she assures me that she would.
And I lose another argument.
Still, I like hearing that.